Kendra L. Saunders

Dating an Alien Popstar

ISBN:978-1-63422-175-7
Cover Design by: Marya Heiman
Typography by: Courtney Nuckels
Editing by: Cynthia Shepp

This book is dedicated to Karmen

SPACE TRAVEL HAD NEVER COME EASY FOR GRIFFIN, EVEN IN THE SMALL jumps from his planet to a neighboring moon, but nothing could have prepared him for the head-jarring, stomach-wrenching mess that was landing on Earth. Especially landing in Manhattan's Chinatown.

"Don't stand yet," a familiar voice said. Between the dizziness and nausea, it took all of three blinks before Griffin could clear his dazed head and focus his eyes on his best friend. "I mean it, Griff. Don't stand up until after you're sick."

"Sick? I won't be sick." Griffin sat up, raising his head in the haughtiest manner he could. Unfamiliar gravity and pollution were certainly not going to stop a prince of Kalesstria from behaving like a prince. He managed to regain his feet, and even to open his mouth to say something, but then his stomach betrayed him and he bent in half to lose what seemed to be the entire contents of his guts all over the strange, gray-colored ground.

"Told you," Dev said. "You really need to learn to listen to me one of these days."

Griffin waited out a second wave of sick, this one turning out to be nothing but sputtering and dry coughs, before straightening and shooting his friend a scowl. Dev's crossed arms perfectly matched the somewhat smug look on his face.

"We need to acquire new clothing, so we can blend in while we create our personas," Griffin said, though his legs were still weak and his body hurt from toes to hair roots. He hadn't felt this jostled since he'd walked through the wrong travel tunnel and ended up on an abandoned mining facility on a nearby planet called G16's moon.

Or, no, maybe he'd felt worse when he'd attempted to drink a whole bottle of mood enhancer in one sitting. *Maybe.*

"Are you certain you can even walk yet?"

"I'm walking now, aren't I?" Griffin said, stumbling forward. He checked and double-checked that he was still wearing a chain around his neck, and more importantly, the warm, gently pulsing home stone that hung from it. He tucked it under his collar to keep it hidden and, hopefully, safe. He'd chosen the stone himself, had it placed into a setting, and wore it whenever he traveled away from Kalesstria, as much for the energy it provided as for reminding him of home.

"You're walking like a newborn balak."

Balaks were quite possibly the least coordinated animals on their home planet, and the babies even more so. Griffin shoved his friend, and then raised his eyes and looked around at his new surroundings. For years, he'd dreamed of walking on this planet, of touching the trees, wearing the colorful clothes, and eating the strange food. Although he'd always held out hope that he might convince his father and the Travel Alliance to allow him to come here, it had seemed unlikely.

"We're here," he said quietly, as much to himself as to Dev. "We did it. We're here!"

Dev stepped up beside Griffin, patting him on the back.

"Clothes. Clothes first," Griffin said, waving one impatient hand in the direction of his standard uniform—all black, clean lines, and dull, gold buttons. "No one dresses like this here." Griffin turned toward his friend, leaning in until their heads were almost touching. "Where's the human money?"

Dev produced a wad of light green paper. "This is the local money, I've been told. Dunno what the fuss is all about, though. It's just a lot of trees they've torn up."

Griffin snatched the money away, sorting through it. "These are one-hundred dollar bills, so they're worth a lot. I know almost all of their denominations of paper money, you know."

"Oh, glory." Dev rolled his eyes.

"You're always going on about learning things before trips. Guess I have one over on you for once, huh?" Griffin snickered and hid the money in his jacket pocket. "We'll buy something to wear for now until we can find a human companion."

"Or we could save time and just find a human companion first, Griff."

"No! We'll change into human clothes and then seek out a helper."

Dev sighed, but he didn't argue this time.

"Now," Griffin said, taking a deep breath of Manhattan's strange, heavy air. "Let's go find some clothes."

Chapter 1

I'M STANDING IN LINE AT STARBUCKS, YAWNING FROM THE KIND OF sleepiness that makes your eyes water right through your smudge-resistant black eyeliner, all the while listening to two girls in front of me complain about their love lives. Or, rather, one of the girls moans to the other that she's been single for, get ready for this... four months!

Four whole months, and God, isn't that awful?

Her friend places one bony hand on her shoulder—complete with talon nails that look like weapons—and makes pitying noises and offers words of encouragement. Together, they probably weigh about the same as one of those giant teddy bears you win at fairs, and both are spray-tanned to the color of a burnt orange crayon. They are probably in their early twenties.

I console myself with the fact that, despite being three weeks on the wrong side of twenty-nine, and so eternally single that I've started getting advertisements in the mail for solo vacations, I'm wearing a very rare vintage Bjork T-shirt, I'm living in the best city on earth, and I will soon be meeting all sorts of wonderful, attractive, and interesting men. With jobs! Men who won't be anything like the terrible man I dated five years ago and never quite properly recovered from.

And more importantly, I'm now living in the epicenter of legendary concert venues.

A few minutes after acquiring an expensive, but much-needed, delicious latte in the largest size I can afford, I assimilate back out into the afternoon masses of Manhattan. I try to ignore the buzzing in my pocket that signals my mom's daily one PM texts.

My mom could win an Olympic medal in worrying. She's always prepared for worst-case scenarios, preaches about stranger danger, and enjoys watching disaster films for 'research.' She still hasn't quite recovered from my decision four months ago to quit my boring office job, take all of my money out of savings, and follow my favorite band around America on their LEMONADE FROM LEMONS tour. I'm pretty sure, according to my aunt, that Mom throws around the phrase "psychotic break" when she talks about that period in my life.

My subsequent, and penniless, move to NYC caused her to renew her anxiety medication prescription and buy six books about living in the city. Of all the things she's underlined, circled, and shared with me, including instructions for what to do if you're mugged and how to escape your apartment if the building catches fire, I think the only thing she hasn't covered is alien abduction and accidental pregnancy. The latter, especially, is something even she doesn't worry about, considering that my last real date was… well, five years ago.

I walk toward my day job on Prince St. in SoHo, thinking

of how exactly I'll handle my day and night jobs tomorrow, considering my schedules overlap by ten minutes. I'm a waitress at my evening job, and I'm fairly certain my boss is Satan's cousin. He spends most of our interactions calling me rude names or staring at my butt, rather than actually listening to anything I have to say. He also loves to schedule me at times when I've told him I'm not physically capable of working. It's a hobby of his.

Despite the evil boss and scheduling conflicts, I like my day job at a clothing store and have my eyes on a music shop in the West Village. I've sent my resume to the owner twice, stopped by and said hello a number of times, and special-ordered a few rare items to show off my musical prowess. So far, I haven't been offered the job, and I've spent more than I can afford on rare vinyl, but it'll be worth it in the end. There's no greater dream than to work in a real record store in New York City. I'd get to wear my favorite vintage music tees and rock-star-off-duty jeans every day. Spend my nights out at concert venues, catching obscure new bands and secret shows from established acts.

I'll get it. I just need to be persistent. Maybe tomorrow morning I can pop by there first thing, before work, and remind them of how perfect I'd be for the job. After all, my friend, Kammie, who has lived in the city for a lot longer than I have and even has her own little recording studio, says that persistence is the most important thing in this city—

A man with shaggy, blond hair reaches out and catches my arm.

In New York City, you bump into people, elbow them, step on them, and sometimes even punch them without meaning to. It's just how it is. But usually, no one full on grabs your arm, unless you've wandered into Brownsville. My first thought, thanks to Mom, is that I'm about to be mugged and murdered and my body will end up somewhere in Central Park, discovered weeks later because desperate pigeons have been munching on it. My second thought is that I'm not even wearing a good outfit today, and everyone who's found dead in Central Park has a chance of ending up on the news.

The guy smiles at me, a big, toothy smile, and then I'm suddenly surrounded on all sides by a ring of intimidating men in suits, full out like something from the movies. They part, briefly, for a brown-haired man wearing an oversized, fluffy purple sweater and black skinny jeans. And sunglasses. I've never seen an outfit like this outside of fashion magazines from the '90s and strange Japanese movies, especially not on a man. Even one as strangely handsome as this one.

"Ah, you're right, she's better than the other two we considered," the shaggy-haired one says in a drawling English accent. He smiles at me, but his fuzzy companion just scowls.

"Ask her where David Bowie is."

"My name is Devon London," the shaggy-haired one says. Between the ridiculous name and his glowing, golden-kissed skin, he strikes me as a playboy billionaire on holiday. "And this is Griffin Valentino. We'd like to know where David Bowie gets his coffee."

"David Bowie?"

"Yes, David Bowie. Where does he get his coffee?"

"I... I'm not sure, actually," I finally say.

"This is Manhattan, is it not?" Griffin demands, pursing his pouty lips and picking at the fuzzy sleeves of his purple sweater with the precision of a full-tilt diva.

I glance between them, my tone hesitant. "Yes."

"Then why is it so difficult for us to find out where David Bowie gets his coffee?"

After a lot of careful consideration, I stammer, "I'm not sure. New York is big, and I-I've never seen David Bowie. I'm sorry."

Suddenly, I imagine a news anchor telling everyone I've been murdered by two obsessed stalkers of David Bowie. It isn't really the way I want to make headlines.

Griffin snaps his fingers, and Devon turns around to face him. "Why doesn't she know where David Bowie is? Is it really that difficult? This planet's tiny."

"We'll find him. Don't worry," Devon says with a heavy sigh.

At this point, I feel more confused than afraid, like when you dive too deep into YouTube and end up on a fourteen-minute video about the Illuminati hiring Prince as a secret assassin for the Jehovah's Witnesses.

"Why do you want to find David Bowie so bad?" I ask. Devon and Griffin turn to stare at me. Or, rather, I think Griffin stares at me. His sunglasses envelop his small, pointy face a bit too fully to confirm anything other than the existence of his killer bone structure. It would take most people half an hour and a professional makeup artist with a degree in contouring to create cheekbones that impressive. "I mean, everyone's looked for David Bowie once or twice in their life, but they don't actually expect to find him."

"David Bowie claims to be from another planet," Griffin says, marching forward until we're almost toe to toe. He stands only a few inches taller than I do, maybe just over five-and-a-half feet, but his presence feels impressive. "I've done my research and as far as I can determine, he's from your planet. Born and raised and all that. I want to find him and question him." Griffin shrugs. "Also, I'd like him to sign my Ziggy Stardust record. So where is he?"

"I have no idea!"

"She's no help at all," Griffin says, his face twitching a bit. He thumps Devon on the chest with one hand. "He's one of the most famous beings on this planet! How hard should it be for someone to tell us where he is? You certainly have a knack for digging up the dullest of creatures, Dev."

Devon's eyes narrow. "Now watch it. You're the one who chose her."

"Yeah, watch it!" I say. "I'm not dull, and both of you are crazy. I'd like to leave now."

If I can just break through the circle of scary people, I can make a clean getaway. Maybe, I think.

"You can't, Wanda," Griffin says.

"Wanda?"

Griffin's angular face twists up into a satisfied expression. "Your name is Wanda, is it not?"

"No, and I don't think anyone else's name is Wanda either." The smile slides off Griffin's face. "Your name is… Danielle."

"No."

"It's Veronica."

"No."

"Damn it! Wait. Your name *is* Wanda, isn't it?"

"My name is not Wanda. My name is Daisy Kirkwood, and I need to go to work."

"No, Daisy, we need you for a few important tasks," Devon says, stepping between Griffin and me. "Don't worry about the David Bowie thing; we'll sort that out later, somehow. For now, you're going to help Griffin put together the rest of his wardrobe. We bought a few things earlier." Devon motions at Griffin's outfit. "I'm not sure we're on the right track, as you can see."

As much as I should make a run for it, some part of me

can't help feeling a bit curious. "Wardrobe?"

"We're visiting your planet and have some work to do," Devon says in a very reasonable tone, as if he's explaining something to a small child. "We figure the best way to do so is to achieve a bit of public attention and adoration."

They're crazy. Truly crazy. I just hope they're not the cannibal kind of, 'take you into a dark alley and eat you' crazy. "And how were you planning to do that?"

"I'm going to become a British pop icon, obviously," Griffin says. "They're the most powerful people on this planet."

"And I'm supposed to believe you're really aliens?"

"We're not aliens!" Griffin says. "We live elsewhere from here. You're the aliens, if you want to get technical about it. Your planet is tiny, polluted, and hasn't even been around that long. We've existed for loads longer. We're the superior beings." He hesitates then and looks almost apologetic. "Well, you have better clothes, I suppose."

Devon nods, crossing his arms over his chest. "So that's that, Daisy Kirkwood. You're going to be our human assistant for a while. Congratulations. Griffin's about to become the most famous person on your planet."

The entourage of scary dudes in suits begins to move around us like a donut of tailored intimidation, pressing us forward, and I have no choice but to follow Griffin and Devon. From behind, they look a bit like eccentric birds, especially since Griffin repeatedly bounces on his heels and points at things, letting out exclamations of surprise, and his brown hair sticks up at the back of his head. Devon laughs at his antics, and everyone seems to entirely forget my existence.

This is so not cool.

Even as I plot manners of escape, our group halts and I run full into Griffin, all but toppling him over. He wheels around. "Don't step on these shoes!" he says, with the exact frantic tone of someone who's standing on the edge of a cliff. "They're Ferragamo!"

I glance down at the sparkly, gold shoes on his feet. "Sorry," I finally say. "Anyway, we need to talk about what's going on here."

"You're going to help me dress like a pop star."

"No, I mean, you think you're an alien, and a British alien at that, Doctor Who style. There's no such thing as aliens."

"Listen, Wanda, I've already told you that I'm not alien. You're the alien. Now, should I stop at Christian Siriano's place or is he any good?"

"My name isn't Wanda!"

"I want lots of gold, lots of sparkle, and some trench coats. Maybe Burberry. Maybe Siriano."

This is too much for me. "You're an alien, but you know who Siriano is? What, do you keep up to date with *Project Runway* on your planet?"

"As a famous English pop star, I need to know as much about fashion as possible. Balenciaga would be good. Where can I get some of that? I want lots of Versace, too. That's a requirement for my career."

Devon nods, though with an element of distraction. His eyes keep wandering about, to the sky, to the bodyguards, to me, and back to Griffin.

"Just how do you expect to be a famous English pop star when no one's ever heard of you?" I demand. "I'm obsessed with music. I listen to it all day! I've been to a ton of concerts. And you know what? I've never heard of you."

Griffin's lips twitch just a little and then he bursts into laughter, which only makes Devon laugh, too. "No one's ever heard of me? They will in about an hour, darling. Now,

Christian Siriano, yes or no?"

My face flames with embarrassment, anxiety, and that little bit of gritty New York City pollution I still haven't adjusted to. "If you're an alien, prove it," I say. "If you can prove it, I'll help you pick out any clothes you want. In fact, I'll help you become famous."

I fully expect him to turn down my offer, or at least mull it over, but Griffin just shrugs.

"Done," he says, snapping his fingers.

A song, remarkably catchy even from the first listen, washes over me from the open door of a nearby shop. I've never heard it before but it feels familiar, like a favorite song from the past, and then I hear the same song pouring from a shop a few doors down. And then another. The song envelops us from all sides. When I finally look at Griffin again, he's smirking behind his oversized sunglasses.

"Good, isn't it? But not good enough yet." He pushes a few of the tall, scary guys aside and steps out into the pedestrian traffic on the sidewalk. When he catches the arm of a middle-aged woman wearing ugly glasses and sweatpants under a puffy jacket, they stare at each other for all of three seconds before the woman's face lights up.

"You're him!" she says. "You made this song!"

"I did. Do you like it?"

"It's been my favorite song for..." She pauses, squinting. "Errr... for... for... for... well, for a long time, I think! A long time."

At this point, Griffin's casting satisfied little glances in my direction. "Would you like my autograph?" he asks, and the woman nearly pees herself in her hurry to dig a pen and paper from her overflowing book bag. Only seconds later, she's joined by other gawkers and fans, all of them clamoring to get

Griffin's attention, autograph, and photograph.

After a few seconds of getting fawned over, Griffin waves his hands. "Go away now, all of you," he says, and they slowly walk away, each of them with a dazed expression on their face. Griffin walks back to me and places his hands on his bony hips. "Now. You're going to help me find some Balenciaga."

I've been kidnapped by aliens.

I'VE NEVER SHOPPED 5TH AVENUE WITH AN ALIEN. FOR SOME REASON, if I'd ever actually imagined such a thing before, I probably would have pictured it differently... maybe people pointing and screaming or Donald Sutherland tugging at his hair and yelling about pod people.

But shopping with Griffin and Devon is a bit more like shopping with a spoiled toddler and his famous handler. Both of them march directly into a shop, crowd of scary bodyguards in tow, and the store's staff nearly tramples themselves to help us.

"What are you looking for?" one of the saleswomen demands, all but throwing herself on top of Griffin. He seems immune to gorgeous twenty-somethings in expensive clothes. Instead, he's completely transfixed by the fashion aspect of the store. He lets out a few gasps as his fingers trail over fabric and buttons, leaving Devon to speak to the staff.

Dating an Alien Popstar

"Thank you very much for your offer of help," Devon says, "but we have a stylist right here. Miss Kirkwood."

One of the male employees eyes me and shakes his head in the most judgmental manner I've ever seen. "We are professionals," he says. "And I really don't think 'sales-bin chic' is in this season. It went out somewhere around the time her clothes were made, which I'm guessing was before I was born."

"Excuse me?" I say, my face flaming with embarrassment. "I happen to call my style 'off-duty rock star,' and I think it's pretty great."

"Off duty? I think you mean retired rock star. Maybe even deceased rock star."

"Well, at least I'm original." I point at his suit, but I can't think of any good insults.

"Wanda will do just fine!" Griffin yells from across the sales floor, accosting a shirt with the enthusiasm of a starving man receiving a meal for the first time in days.

"Oh my GOD. Your name is Wanda?" the male employee asks, cringing. "Did your parents give you up for adoption…?"

As I try to leave the store, a couple of the scary guys step in the way of the door. I have to give up on that plan for now.

"Wanda! Get over here and help me!"

Wait—is he stripping down in public?

Much to my horror, Griffin peels off the purple, fuzzy sweater, revealing a slender and taut body underneath. Tugging off his skinny jeans next, he tosses them aside. Just when I think he's going for the underwear and might get arrested for public nudity, he snatches a pair of pants off a hanger and tugs them on, along with an ugly, mustard-colored shirt from a nearby display.

"Good choice, sir," one of the employees says, and they all chime in with their encouragement.

"It's very David Bowie," another employee says. "So avant-garde to wear women's clothes."

Griffin, who has just pranced to a mirror to stare at himself, stops spinning and looks at his crowd of admirers and then at Devon and me. "Yes or no?" he demands. "Is it very David Bowie?"

I sigh and walk toward him. "Let me choose a few things for you to try on," I say. "And in the fitting rooms, please, not out here. It goes against our customs to parade around in nothing but underwear."

"What about Victoria's Secret?"

Now I'm staring at him. "What do you mean—what about it?"

"When your kind wears that brand, you don't wear anything else. Isn't that true? I saw the pictures everywhere." Griffin takes off the expensive clothes and leaves them in a crumpled pile on the floor. "So I'll do the same, thank you very much."

Great. Well, with any luck, he'll take it too far and get arrested. The NYC police can take over dealing with the aliens. That's probably well within their skill set, considering some of the Elmo-costumed weirdos they deal with in Times Square.

I sort through clothes, thinking of what I'd most like to see my favorite rock stars in, and procure accordingly. On a whim, I grab a frilly, slate-colored shirt that will look good with Griffin's eyes. He didn't seem to object much to wearing women's clothes, after all.

When I return to Griffin, he's talking with Devon in a low whisper. The words are only slightly unfamiliar, which makes them eerie, like something you'd hear during a confusing nightmare.

"Here," I say, holding the outfits out in offering. "These two go together, these two, and these two. Try them on." Hopefully, the clothes will distract them enough that they'll stop talking in their creepy language.

Some of the employees have given up and retreated to help other customers, but I frequently catch people staring at Griffin and Devon as if they want to approach and say something.

Griffin ultimately buys everything I've chosen for him, as well as the ugly, mustard-colored shirt he tried on earlier, and a pair of shoes. At no point during this whole thing has he ever taken off his sunglasses. Even as he pops the tags off a pair of shiny, black pants and slips into them—along with his original purple sweater—he leaves the sunglasses on.

"Your taste isn't bad, Wanda," Griffin says to me as we exit the store. "But it is a bit boring at times. I'm an English pop star. I'm supposed to be better looking than anyone else on the planet. I must drip sex appeal."

"My name isn't Wanda, and your taste is awful," I mutter, but he doesn't hear me, because he's already gone back to conversing with Devon in their weird language. We continue our journey down 5th Avenue surrounded by the scary guys, stopping in a few more stores with similar results.

By the time the sun sets, we're armed with enough shopping bags to sink a battleship. Griffin's still spunky and interested in visiting more stores, but Devon puts his foot down.

"We're going to get some food now. I'm hungry," Devon says, catching Griffin by the collar as he tries to walk into another store. "You've got quite enough clothes for now, Griff."

"But what will I *wear* to dinner? Do I have anything that's good for dinner? Are we going to Mr. Chow?"

I've lived in New York City for only three weeks, but even I know that normal people don't just *go* to Mr. Chow. Mr. Chow is for Cameron Diaz and One Direction.

Devon considers. "Let's go back to the hotel, and then I suppose we can go to Mr. Chow."

"Good. Now, Wanda, what should I wear?"

"If you call me Daisy, I might help you."

"The deal was that if I proved myself to you, you were going to help me. So, what am I wearing? We'll have a good table, of course."

"Why—because you'll use your alien powers to get it? I'm not impressed."

"Hotel, Griffin, and then you'll have two minutes to choose your outfit. I'm starving," Devon says, an undercurrent of firmness in his voice that I haven't heard before. It seems to do the trick on Griffin. He pouts as we halt beside a huge, black vehicle.

Devon motions for me to climb into it after Griffin's settled himself deep within, and although I hesitate, I slide in, too. It looks like one of those cars that celebrities ride around in, and in a way, I suppose it is. Devon sits beside me. A line of the scary guys perch across from us, none of them speaking. After the car's in motion, I can't help but say something.

"Who are those guys...?"

"Oh, just a bit of security. The Emperor President doesn't want his son scampering around the universe without protection. It can get dangerous, you know," Devon says in a very reasonable tone. "Thank goodness, things should be safer on this planet than back home."

Emperor President?

I glance over at Griffin, who has fished a device from his pocket that looks like a phone except it's completely round. His fingers fly over the screen, as if he's texting someone.

Dating an Alien Popstar

"So he's a prince or something?" I ask.

"Griffin? Of course!"

We leave it at this because, apparently, Devon can't believe I wouldn't know that, and I have no idea how I could have known such a thing. All I see is a weird little man in an awful purple sweater. And those sunglasses, which he still hasn't removed.

Their hotel is quite swanky, complete with a huge lobby that contains enough chandeliers to deck out the Titanic. We're ushered into an elevator and escorted up to what might as well be the wing of a castle for all the rooms and fancy furnishings it has. I've only seen rooms like this in movies and magazine articles about my favorite rock stars.

"Wow," I say. "Do you have a bunch of cursed candelabra and clock servants, too? Singing plates? Champagne?"

Griffin marches over to me. "You have singing plates here? I haven't seen any singing plates. Where are they? Why don't I have them?"

"No. I'm just making a Disney movie reference."

"Disney! Oh, I've heard of him." Griffin shrugs and walks away, having clearly lost interest in me.

Devon disappears into one of the rooms very briefly and returns wearing a jacket over his spiffy white dress shirt and black slacks. He looks quite streamlined compared to Griffin, who is still a purple fluff ball on two legs, sorting feverishly through his bags and boxes for something to wear.

"Griffin, we need to leave," Dev says.

"Yeah, yeah, but I've not found a bloody thing to wear. I'm not going to walk into Mr. Chow looking like some kind of wanker."

"Daisy, might you help him? Otherwise, we'll be here all night. I'm hungry," Devon says, placing a hand on my arm and pushing me toward Griffin.

Come to think of it, I'm hungry as well. Starving to be honest. My stomach has been growling for quite some time, but I've ignored it in favor of taking in all the weirdness happening around me. I push Griffin aside, crouch down, and dig around a bit until I can find something suitable for a dinner at a famous restaurant, namely a pair of slim-fit black pants, that slate-colored shirt, and black jacket with little epaulets on the shoulders.

"That's not enough color!" Griffin says, pointing at the clothes I'm holding.

"Do you want to eat at Mr. Chow or not? You won't look like you belong if you don't wear this. Trust me, I'm a… a human," I say with as much confidence as I can muster. "Besides, this will look really good on you. The jacket made your shoulders look nice."

He huffs a bit but accepts the clothes and changes into them right in front of me, unceremoniously throwing his other clothes aside, most of them at my feet. When he's finished redressing, he looks quite good, other than still wearing those silly sunglasses.

Without thinking, I step forward and pull the sunglasses away from his face. One of his hands moves, at lightning speed, clamping over my wrist, but he only prevents me from tossing the glasses aside. I've already taken them off his face and seen what he's been hiding all this time.

His blue eyes glow bright with something that's immediately, inescapably, not human.

"It's not my fault," Griffin mutters for the tenth time during our drive to Mr. Chow. He's sulking in the seat to the left of me. Devon's on my right, continuously sighing and sending Griffin displeased glances. "She's the one who ripped my glasses off."

"You could have put your lenses on, you know," Devon says. "I put mine on."

"I don't like them!"

"Well, too bad. You've given her a fright."

Griffin pinches my arm so hard that it hurts, so I slap his hand. "She's fine, see?"

"Griffin. Stop acting like such an arse."

Finally, as if everything else just fell away for an instant, I turn my head and look at Devon. "How did you get those accents?" I demand. "How? *How*? How are you so authentically English?"

Griffin sighs. "I told you. English pop star!"

"Yes, but how? You're from another planet, yet you have perfect accents."

"Oh, we could talk however we wanted," Devon says. "For instance…" He switches to fluent French, so far as my limited knowledge can ascertain. Griffin snickers in his seat and says something in French, and then they're chattering back and forth, Griffin making sweeping hand gestures all the while.

"Well, can you sound American?" I ask, and Devon hesitates.

"What region?"

"Here, I guess. New York."

Griffin launches into what sounds like a monologue from a movie, complete with realistic Brooklyn accent, though it descends into hysterical laughter by the end. Devon laughs a little, too, but I think he's more amused by Griffin than anything else.

"Want me to sound Texan?" Griffin asks, at this point laughing so hard he's gasping for breath and tears are spilling from his weirdly blue eyes. He says something in his language, or what I assume is his language, and Devon answers him. One of the scary guys says something as well. Suddenly, everyone in the car seems to be taking part in a discussion I can't understand.

"Stop it!" I shout. "All of you. Stop it. There's only so much alien I can take at once, okay? And right now, your eyes are my limit."

"Put in your lenses, Griff," Devon says, sitting back in his seat and running a hand through his wavy, golden hair as his smile falls away. He yawns. "Are we almost there? I'm so hungry."

Griffin, after coughing a lot and struggling to regain his composure, sniffles a few times and snaps his fingers. "Where's my lenses?" he demands, his tone returning to the annoyingly superior one he'd used when I first met him.

One of his bodyguards produces something that looks like a contact lens container. Griffin opens it, removing one tiny contact lens at a time and popping them over his eyes. When he turns to look at me again, his eyes are normal. Or, as normal as they can be, considering they still glow a bit. "Better, Wanda?"

I just close my eyes for the rest of the ride and refuse to say anything, even when Griffin asks me if Chanel is really all it's hyped up to be.

When we arrive at Mr. Chow, we're treated like royalty. I've never stood outside of the place, never mind gone inside, but it's a bit more crowded than I imagined. On our way to the table, I notice a few celebrities, although I don't remember their names until Griffin hisses them over his shoulder at me. Judging by the huge grin on his face, this is quite exciting.

I just wish someone cool could be here, if I have to be. You know, like Arcade Fire. Or Bjork.

Griffin sits beside me at our little table, and Devon sits across from us, casting a somewhat non-convincing smile at the bodyguard who perches on the chair beside him.

"Why do you always get to sit next to the girl?" Devon asks quietly, but Griffin's busy craning his neck to look around the restaurant.

"I think Angelina Jolie is over there," he whispers to me. "Where are her children?"

"Did you spend a month watching TMZ or something?" I whisper back. "How do you know all of this stuff?"

Griffin looks at me again, this time with wide-eyed suspicion. "E! News, your world's most famous news source, of course. What is TMZ? Is that the rival I sometimes hear about? Is it propaganda?"

Our waiter arrives and Devon places his order first, though Griffin's nearly bursting for his turn. He orders with the excitement of a child who's never been out to dinner, talking right over Devon when he tries to say something.

"Order whatever you want," Devon says to me as soon as Griffin's finished speaking. "It's on us, Daisy."

I place my order, the cheapest thing I can find on the menu, but Devon speaks up and adds something else to our order. However, his eyes remain on Griffin, watchful, as if he's waiting for something to happen.

"I want to see Macy's," Griffin says, to no one in particular. "It's your world's biggest store. I want to take a holopic there, out front. And inside, of course."

"You need to eat first," Devon says, and then clears his throat. "We all need to eat. I'm famished."

Griffin waves one hand. "Devon's always hungry, always making us stop and eat."

"Well, that's smart. Eating is good," I say with a little shrug.

Devon leans forward, folding his hands on the table and meeting my gaze. "We require nourishment a bit more often than you do. Not as much at once, but more often. Your digestive systems seem to be primed for longer delays."

"Ha, and his isn't primed for anything!" Griffin says, grinning. "See, mine usually holds out longer. And then, once, some time ago, I fell because I didn't eat, and Dev thought someone assassinated me! So he's paranoid the same thing will happen to him if he doesn't eat."

Any trace of a smile on Devon's face has disappeared, but he just shakes his head and looks away. I don't have to ask if Devon's eating schedule coincides with keeping his friend and prince out of danger, because it's obvious to every single person at the table besides Griffin.

When our food arrives, Griffin digs right in, which seems to relax Devon, and all of us eat in silence for a while until Griffin loudly, and quite enthusiastically, proclaims something in his language, gesturing at his plate. A few people eating at nearby tables turn to stare at us. Without thinking, I clamp my hand down over one of Griffin's.

"You're doing it again!" I say, and he actually blushes a little, shifting about in his chair with a clear air of discomfort.

"Do you want to hear my song?"

"What?"

"I said, do you want to hear my song again?" Griffin demands, louder this time. He snaps his fingers, staring pointedly at the roof above our heads. And just like that, his song fills the restaurant, bouncing off the walls and circling around us.

One of our table neighbors points at us and whispers something. No one actually dares approach us, but I notice several people snapping photos with their phones in a less-than-subtle manner. Griffin soaks this up with a huge smile, and even stands at one point so a woman can get a better photo.

"Thank you, thank you!" Griffin says, still standing. "Continue with your meals, wonderful people. You may buy my song at your leisure and talk with your friends about how much you love it. But for now, please enjoy your meals! Don't let me stop you."

Devon rolls his eyes, but he's smiling as Griffin regains his seat. "Finish your food, Griffin, and then we should get back to the hotel. We have a busy day ahead of us tomorrow."

"Can I leave?" I ask, and Griffin and Devon both say no at the same time.

By the time we arrive back at the hotel, I'm exhausted. Somehow, it feels like I've been kidnapped by aliens for about two weeks, rather than less than twenty-four hours. I think briefly of my two jobs, of one cool and understanding boss and one very angry and red-faced boss; the latter has probably already fired me. I think of my tiny room in the apartment I share with four other girls and a blind Siamese cat. I think of my mother, who has never prepared me for an alien invasion.

If I call her, she's going to panic and probably end up in the emergency room with an endless panic attack and heart issues.

The bodyguards spread out around the giant hotel suite, two of them remaining in the room that seems to be Griffin's, and I cast a helpless glance around for Devon.

"Where am I staying?" I give in and ask.

"Dev's got the other room; you don't want to sleep with him. He snores," Griffin says, peeling off the jacket.

"So I'm staying where…?"

"With me, of course. I need someone here with me, and it might as well be you."

This isn't the time to break out the whole 'twenty-nine and eternally single' thing, but it also kind of is. The last time I slept next to a male was three years ago during a camping trip with some friends, and the guy was Creepy Jerry. I'd only slept next to him because he'd squeezed in between my friend and me in the middle of the night.

"I think I should stay somewhere else," I say, walking toward the bed while trying to calculate if I'll be able to avoid touching him on a mattress that size. Of course, that will all depend on if he promises to remain on one side. And if he actually keeps his promise.

To be fair, the bed looks incredibly comfortable. It will

probably feel like heaven. But that doesn't matter right now.

Griffin raises a dark eyebrow. "Are you afraid of me?"

"I didn't say I'm afraid!"

"But are you?"

"No!"

"Good." He kicks off his shoes. "This will be a nice period of bonding for us, Wanda."

"Why are you here?" I demand, sitting on the edge of the bed and crossing my arms over my chest. "You say you want to become the most powerful being on the planet with your music and all of that, but why?"

"It's none of your business."

"It's my planet, so it *is* my business. You're not planning to brainwash all of us, and then harvest our organs or something, are you? Keep our livers in jars in a spaceship somewhere? Burn the planet and then plant your weird medicinal drugs here?"

Griffin stalks closer to me with every word, until he's standing directly in front of me, the glowing light in his eyes showing through the lenses. "And if I am, do you think you're going to stop me?"

A shudder traces through me. I'm not sure if it's because of his words or because he's standing so close. "I'll have to stop you," I say in a very brave tone. Okay, actually, it's not brave at all. More like a wheezy whisper. But Bjork or Kim Gordon wouldn't just bow down to an alien invasion without at least *attempting* to protect their planet, and neither will I.

Before I can fully process what's happening, Griffin's pinned me down, holding my wrists against the bed under his hands. His body, though slight, feels substantial and warm against mine—simultaneously threatening and a bit of a turn on. "You don't know me very well at all, do you, Wanda?" he

28

whispers, and I want to correct him about my name, but I find it hard to say anything at all. "I would never come all the way to your planet just to enjoy the food and then destroy it. I'm not cruel!"

"I don't know anything about you, other than your bad taste in clothes," I say, but his weight pressed against my pelvis has my body pulsing and warm all over. Bad, bad, bad.

"Then look into me, why don't you? You could see anything you wanted, if you'd just look. I'd let you."

When I shake my head, he releases me, climbing right over top of me to take his place on the bed. I can feel the mattress shaking a bit, and I gather my wits enough to sit up and glance at him. He's maneuvered his way out of the rest of his clothes, leaving only the underwear.

Thank God. Especially since my close proximity reveals he's not doing too bad in that department. Even under a layer of fabric.

"Aren't you tired, Wanda?"

Yes, I'm tired beyond the point of belief, but I don't want to tell him that, especially while he's stretching lazily on the bed as if he owns the city. "No. I'm going to sit right here in this exact spot all night."

"No, you're not. Get up here and go to sleep. Don't you know you sleep better if you're not alone?"

"Thank you, *Cosmo*, I've heard that one a few times."

"*Cosmo*? Who's that?"

"A magazine designed for women who are actually doing something with their lives, like working real jobs and living with men."

"Oh. Sex." Griffin shifts around a bit on the bed. "Speaking of sex..."

"No. No, no, no, no. I'm going to sleep in the bathtub, I

think."

"Wanda!" Griffin says, his voice incredibly stern. "Don't be daft; you're not sleeping in a bathtub!"

"It won't be that uncomfortable, don't worry. It looked big enough to fit six or seven people—"

"If I want to have a bath, I don't want you in there sleeping!"

At this point, I consider opening the window and jumping out, but suicide is still a bit too premature. After all, Devon made it sound like once I'm done helping Griffin with his pop star nonsense, I can return to my normal routine. Back to my lovely bed in my... tiny room... to my two jobs... and... All right, so maybe it won't hurt to spend one night in a big, comfortable bed with another person, since I've been kidnapped by aliens. These are definitely extenuating circumstances!

Right? Right.

With a bit of hesitation, mostly out of stubbornness, I crawl across the length of the bed and settle my head on one of the pillows. Griffin flops over to his side so he can smile at me.

"See. Isn't that better?"

"You'll have to shut up if I'm going to sleep," I say, tugging at the covers so I can slip underneath. Immediately, I feel that magical sense you get when you're in a really great, warm bed and your body tingles from pleasure at how wonderful impending sleep will feel. I let out a little sigh without meaning to, and Griffin moves closer until he's straddling my hips.

"What was that sound?"

"What sound?"

"You just made a sound. What sort of sound was that?"

I should push him off, of course, but I can't find the motivation to do it quite yet. "That was the sound of someone who's spent all day running around 5th Avenue with an energetic alien who wanted to buy too many clothes."

"Oh." He pauses. "You didn't make that sound because of me?"

I shake my head and think for a few seconds that he might try to kiss me or something, but he returns to his side of the bed.

"Someone turn off the lights!" Griffin says, and I remember all at once that we aren't alone, thanks to the two scary bodyguard guys in the corner. One of them switches off the lights and plunges us into complete darkness.

"Goodnight." I shift around, moving a bit further from Griffin. Hopefully, he'll stay on his side of the bed so I can enjoy my side without fear of entangling legs, or something else equally troublesome, given the still-warm-and-tingly sensations racing through the lower half of my body.

"Tomorrow, we'll get you some new clothes," Griffin says quietly, just as I close my eyes and attempt to drift off to sleep.

"What's wrong with my clothes?" I demand, fully prepared to smother him with a pillow if he says anything bad about my personal style, especially after what that condescending jerk at the store had said earlier.

"You can't wear the same thing two days in a row unless you're Karl Lagerfeld, which you are clearly not. Besides, you've been really generous to show us around." He pauses for so long that I think he might have fallen asleep. "And you said you don't have a real job."

I'm about to tell him that I actually have two jobs, and both are horribly real, but I decide against it. "Fine, I guess. It's the least you can do since you kidnapped me."

I wait for his response, but I never get one. Instead, a few minutes later, I hear quiet breathing noises like a kitten that's fallen asleep on its back.

Chapter 4

When I wake up, I can smell something delicious and feel the warmth of unfamiliar blankets. At first, I smile, stretching, thinking I must have fallen asleep at a friend's house, but then all at once, I realize exactly where I am and bolt upright in bed.

Griffin's beside me, cross-legged, reading from an issue of *Cosmo* while munching down a juicy piece of bacon. He turns his head and smiles at me, brown hair sticking up here and there in patches. He looks incredibly comfortable, casual, and familiar, except for those strange eyes.

"They brought us breakfast," he says. "Help yourself."

"Ugh, I thought you were a dream!"

Griffin finishes his piece of bacon and closes the magazine. "Do you know that most human men lie about wanting to get married so they can trick a girl into sleeping with them?"

"I'm sure they do."

Griffin clicks his tongue. "You slept with me last night,

and I didn't lie to you about anything."

"I didn't sleep with you. We did sleep beside each other, but that's not what they're talking about in that magazine. It means something different when people say it, you know... *that* way."

"Curious." Griffin leaps off the bed, leaving the room only long enough to retrieve two bags from Macy's. "Here you are. They should fit."

With a bit of hesitation, I peer into the bags and find dresses inside... several dresses, one red, one yellow, and one pink with black piping. I remove them, one by one, and stare at them. They are cute—really cute. The yellow one has a Kim Gordon vibe, too.

"Well?" Griffin says. "Do you like them?"

I turn over the price tag and spot a four-digit number. "They're great, but I think this one cost more than I earn in a year. Are you sure you want to spend this much...?"

"We acquired a good deal of your money before we arrived," Griffin says with a casual wave of his hand. "Today we meet our new fans, so you'll want to look good. There will be a lot of holopics."

"Holopics?"

"What do you call them? Photographs? There will be a lot of those." Griffin pats at his messy hair, grinning. "I've been told there are paparazzi waiting outside already."

"Why?"

"For me, of course!" Griffin stalks off then, into the bathroom, and I hear the water turn on. Thankfully, he doesn't request my presence or command me to join him in the bath, so I'm left to my own devices in the room, alone except for one of the bodyguards.

"You must have an exciting job," I say, laughing a little.

Wait, why did I laugh? I feel and sound nervous. And my hands are doing that nervous thing they usually do during job interviews or really long dinner parties at home with my mom and her sisters. "Following him around all the time, I mean. He's so peculiar."

"Dangerous is a better description," the bodyguard says, speaking for the first time. His voice is raspy and a little frightening—certainly less human than Griffin or Devon's. "The Emperor President's son is very… should I say, unpopular."

"With who?"

"Everyone."

Devon throws open the doors to his room, waltzing in wearing a gray robe tied tight around his waist. Now he really does look like a billionaire on holiday, complete with glowing, bronzed skin and a huge smile. He's holding a glass of orange juice in one hand. "Ah, good morning! What a beautiful day."

Beautiful? One glance at the window reveals it's a bit overcast and will likely rain at any moment. "Morning."

"I hope it'll rain today," Devon says. He takes a long sip from his orange juice. "This is wonderful. Very tasty. I much prefer it to that strange Coke stuff you have. But it's not as good as coffee."

"You want it to rain? In Manhattan?"

"Well, rain is wonderful."

"Not in Manhattan. Not when you're walking. Not when you're probably going to run into a really cute guy on your way to the subway, your hair's ruined, he's miraculously going to appear and see you, and you're a mess and you have to spend three stops hoping to sink into the floor, only to spill your latte all over yourself while trying to walk by him to get off the train."

Suddenly, I realize I'm actually standing in a swanky hotel suite with a bunch of aliens who kidnapped me, not reliving an embarrassing moment from my fifth day in the city.

"Well, I happen to like rain," Devon says. "It very rarely rains where we're from. We have to process a lot of our own water after what happened in the last war."

Now I *really* realize I'm in a swanky hotel suite with a bunch of aliens. "I'm sorry," I say after a long pause. "About the war."

"It finished up quite some time before I was born, so it's alright. We're figuring it all out as best we can. Our population is almost half what it was before the war, which is quite impressive, considering it had dwindled to thirty percent for a while. Of course, a lot of our population is a bit young, still."

When I think of wars, I think of the grainy, disembodied sort of things I've seen on the television since I was a little girl. Wars in deserts, in small villages, in places I'll never visit in my life, and in my history books. I've never seen anything outside of a television screen or a newspaper article that even slightly resembles a real war. It's the dumb luck of being born in America, but suddenly, I feel more than a little guilty.

"I'm sorry."

"It's not your fault." Devon shrugs. "Sometimes, it takes ruining everything you love to realize how much you loved it in the first place." He casts a wistful look at his orange juice, as if he too has disappeared elsewhere in his mind and memories, but then he smiles at me. "We're working on it, though. All of us."

"What was the, uh, the war about?"

"Oh, the usual. Resources. Fear. I'm a peace lover myself, but I can see how some people might justify their violence when fear's involved. Especially fear on such a massive scale. It's sad, because before all that, we'd progressed to a point of scientific excellence, a real beacon of thought and discovery in our galaxy."

"Is your planet sick now?" The theme music from Bill Nye the Science Guy fills my head, uninvited.

"Sick? Well, I suppose it's a bit worse than that, really. But we've made a lot of progress, all of us. Lots of advancements in new science and technology. And once we nearly destroyed everything in the name of making it better, we realized we needed to try a different approach. There's still those who believe in violence and seek to hurt anyone they disagree with, but their numbers are decreasing, I think. Griff's father's got a very strong grip on things." He pauses. "Some would say too strong, but he's got a real load to deal with, doesn't he?"

Without thinking, I raise an eyebrow and must look quite incredulous, because Devon laughs.

"Are you surprised?"

"No! Wait, what do you mean? Surprised about what?" I ask.

"That Griffin's the way he is, when his father's like that."

"Well, I don't know him very well, so who am I to judge?" I clear my throat. "But he is kind of spastic."

As if on cue, Griffin marches out of the bathroom, mostly dressed. He has on the black skinny jeans from before, along with that ugly, yellow shirt and half a sweater, which he seems to have tried to put on upside down. It's now hanging strangely around his neck, pooled at his shoulders.

"What're you two in here whispering on about?" he demands.

I can't help laughing at his predicament, even as I'm untangling him from the mess he's made. "You're not wearing the yellow shirt. And you're not wearing this sweater. Stand right there and don't move," I say as I remove the shirt from him. Maybe if I hide it under the bed, he'll forget about it.

"Today, I meet my fans," Griffin says. "So you need to dress me accordingly. You're my stylist."

I roll my eyes, but I don't say anything. After a bit of searching, I locate a white shirt and the black leather jacket I'd snagged for him during our unending shopping trip the day before. He complains and grumbles as I help him into it, but once he's dressed and run off to look in a mirror, he returns with a smirk on his face.

"I look incredible! Good job, Wanda. Why don't you go get ready now, so we can leave? I have loads of adoring fans waiting outside."

After gathering up the pink dress, I hurry to the bathroom and pause in the doorway. "Don't come in here for any reason," I say, pointing at Griffin. "Even if you have a fashion meltdown, you are not even to touch this doorknob."

"You don't want me to see you without your clothes?"

A blush creeps up my face. "No, I don't want you to, and that's my right and my choice. Not all of us are comfortable running around in our underwear."

Griffin sniffs. "Why? You're quite beautiful, Wanda. I'd think you'd want to show off at every opportunity. But don't worry; I'll respect your wishes." With that, he turns back to Devon and speaks in their weird alien language, lots of hand gestures included to punctuate his meaning.

I slam the bathroom door shut to hide a surprised smile that's trying to take over my face. I'm supposed to be mad at Griffin for kidnapping me, not feeling strangely proud he's just proclaimed, in that annoyingly superior tone, that I'm beautiful. That's just silly.

Now, this bathroom is big enough to need a tour guide, so I locate the shower and just leap in before I get too overwhelmed. Inside, I find about ten bottles; all of them have been left open, and most of them are oozing shampoo, conditioner, or body wash onto the floor of the shower. "Griffin," I mutter, glancing through them for something helpful. *Ah, shampoo. That'll work. And conditioner! Good.*

I've always been an expert at fast showers, thanks to the insistence of my parents and, more recently, the lack of sustainable hot water in my apartment, so I'm in and out of the shower rather quickly.

The towels are softer and more luxurious than I'm used to, and the array of products and tools waiting on the bathroom counter are a little shocking—a flat iron, two blow dryers, and one of those plug-in spinning brushes are among the selection. *Huh.*

After tugging and brushing my very curly, dark blonde hair into something resembling order, I indulge in a few drops of this, a few squirts of that, a bit of this, and a tad of that. Really, if one is offered a free Sephora counter, shouldn't one accept?

A screech from the other side of the bathroom door reminds me that I've been kidnapped by aliens, and I rush through the last steps of tugging on my new pink dress. It fits almost perfectly around my full hips and doesn't even gap at the top, like many dresses do. *Thanks, Mom, for the lack of substantial cleavage.* It swirls out around my knees as I walk to the bathroom door and prepare for whatever will be happening on the other side of the wall.

"What was that noise?" I ask, noting that everyone's in roughly the same place they'd been before I walked into the bathroom.

"Oh, Griff just found out he's been asked for an interview," Devon says with a little shrug. "Someone rang the hotel to inquire after him about this one and possibly another one tomorrow night. He's a bit excited."

Griffin screeches again, at a pitch I'm certain isn't even relatively possible for a human to make, and plants a huge kiss on Devon's cheek. "This is brilliant." Griffin waves me over. "They want me to come to the studio later this afternoon for an interview. Think they'll give me a swag bag? I want a swag bag. Maybe one with some fancy hand moisturizers."

"Maybe. But you should probably stop making that noise before you break a window."

Griffin just laughs, and Devon disappears to change his clothes. I locate my shoes and before I know what's happening, we've all been herded out of the room and into an elevator by the security team. Griffin's rocking on his heels even before the doors open, insisting on bursting out first. His security team nervously keeps to either side of him, watchful and vigilant in a manner they weren't the night before.

Odd.

Chapter 5

Outside the hotel, we're greeted by a noisy crowd of people with cameras and phones. Griffin grabs my hand and tugs me closer to him as a bunch of paparazzi swoop in for pictures. The noise is deafening and the lights are painful to my eyes, but Griffin squeezes me against his side and poses away like a long-time Hollywood starlet, complete with a practiced duck-face smile.

"Hello, everyone!" he says. "I know you all love me very, very much. I love you, too. If you want me to sign something for you, you may form a line. I'll get to you just as soon as I can. If you want to name your baby after me, that's alright, too. And if anyone wants to have a baby with me, you'll have to send in your name and information to Devon here. He's my manager. He'll sort through all those requests and forward them to me."

Oh my God.

"Who is this?" someone asks, and I realize, with a great

deal of horror, that the man is pointing at me. It's like middle school all over again, standing next to a really hot eleventh grader at a Christmas party and hearing his girlfriend say '*who is that?*' while half the middle/high school stands by to hear the dismal answer of '*I have no idea, probably one of my seventh grade fangirls,*' and then proceeds to heartily laugh in unison. Basically, this is Stephen King material.

I attempt to pull away from Griffin and escape, but he just dances his fingertips down my side until his hand cups my hip and he says, in a clear and loud voice, "This is Wanda Kirkwood. She's the most desirable woman on this planet."

The mood shifts around me, the confused stares turn to smiles, and for a few seconds, I don't even care that my name is actually Daisy. Well, until everyone starts screaming, 'Wanda, Wanda!' at me.

But I guess I can deal with people calling me Wanda.

"Is she your girlfriend?" someone else asks.

Griffin nods and smiles. "Of course she's a girl friend! And I'm wearing Dior, if you want to take note of that, but I'm open to other designers sending me clothes."

A lively group of fans rush toward Griffin, hands outstretched, offering him pens and papers and shoulders and arms and chests to sign. He releases his hold on me and happily signs whatever anyone asks him to, his left hand a blur of motion as he works his way through the seemingly endless crowd that's growing with every passing second.

"Isn't he wonderful?" one girl gushes at me. "I love his song! I love his accent! He's *British!*" She lets out a little happy gasp. I pat her gently on the back, hoping she won't faint.

"Am I part of any scandals yet?" I hear Griffin ask one of the fans as he signs the top of her ample breasts with a black marker. "Has anyone claimed to be my son? Or accused me of tax evasion? Ooooh, has anyone stepped forth and said they're actually my biological father, and I need to go to a rehabilitation center for a secret cocaine addiction?" He pauses. "What is cocaine?"

One fan slings her arm around Griffin's neck and kisses him square on the lips, but one of the bodyguards steps in and pulls the girl off with a bit more force than is strictly necessary.

"Alright, alright!" Griffin says. "I really must go now. Off to do important pop star sorts of things. Remember to buy my song and listen to it and share it with your friends and tell whoever makes that wonderful television play, Doctor Who, that I'd like to be on the show! Cheers!" He presses both hands to his lips and blows kisses to all of them before turning back to me and offering his arm. His face is flushed with excitement, and I can't help smiling a little at just how ecstatic he is.

As we walk away, he slips his arm around me again, casting a glance here and there over his shoulder at all the people still snapping pictures.

"You smell very desirable," Griffin says, so suddenly that I don't even know at first that he's talking to me. He leans in close, sniffs my neck, and then lowers his face over my chest, taking a deep breath. "I like that. I like that very much."

"Uh, thanks."

"*Cosmo* said you can tell a lot about a potential mate by their smell. I like your smell."

Why did I ever tell him about *Cosmo*…?

"I feel a powerful attraction to your smell. I guess that means we should mate," he says just before releasing me and surging toward the black car waiting for us. He climbs inside and shouts for Devon, chattering on and on about how excited he is to go to his first interview.

Traffic is awful as always, so we spend what feels like a

thousand years in the car, so long that I almost drift off into a boredom coma, despite all the noise radiating from Griffin and Devon.

Well, mostly Griffin.

As we crawl along, I stare out the tinted windows at all the people rushing here and there, coffee cups in hand, and wonder why I'm not still out there.

Why me? Why did they choose me, of all people? I'm five-foot-four, five-five if anyone asks, so I'm not exactly one to stand out in a crowd. I can't afford anything fancier than an occasional large drink at Starbucks, so I don't have any money or influence. And the highest level of fame I've achieved up to this point was first place in a state-level tug-of-war contest the day after my twenty-second birthday.

I glance over at Griffin and Devon and find them with their heads leaned together, laughing and whispering in their language, like the best and oldest of friends.

Why me?

The whole interview thing seems a lot less glamorous than I imagined it. We're offered coffee in white, Styrofoam cups and saltine crackers in tiny, plastic packs of two. Griffin's fussed over to a ridiculous extent, but all of this takes place in a dressing room that looks as if it was sent forward in time from 1987, complete with a pair of neon-yellow leggings strewn over the back of a chair.

Devon insists that Griffin eats some of the crackers, and then he lingers at my side as the lights and cameras are set up and Griffin's introduced to the interviewer.

Griffin's fully prepared for every question, barely waiting until the interviewer finishes speaking before he jumps into his answer.

"I love music! I love my fans! I want to thank the Academy!" he says at one point, which makes me laugh and seems to confuse Devon. But Griffin turns rather earnest when the interviewer asks about his hopes and plans for his career. "Well, of course, I, like everyone else, would love to become a member of a few secret organizations of powerful individuals who control the very fabrics of society. Go to loads of great parties. Be Karl Lagerfeld's muse for a fashion show. Meet David Bowie. Appear in an episode or two of Doctor Who."

"Wow! Nothing big, then," the interviewer says, and everyone chuckles politely except for Griffin, who is completely earnest, and me, since I'm somewhere between shocked and impressed. In a world of people who hide everything, Griffin's certainly changing the dialogue with his blunt aspirations.

Of course, the bit about secret organizations makes me curious with that whole aforementioned 'taking over our planet and harvesting our livers' thing. I'll have to ask him to expound on that later.

"We love your song," the interviewer says. "Can't wait for another one!"

Griffin grins. "Of course you can't. It's the best song of all time."

"Noel Gallagher might disagree with you about that, but I'm pretty much in agreement."

"Who's Noel Gallagher?"

Everyone laughs again, me included. Actually, I'm laughing harder than anyone in the room, because I know Griffin's not joking, and I know Noel Gallagher is probably having a fit somewhere without even knowing why.

"You're hilarious!" the interviewer says.

"Yes, I really am. I've got a wonderful sense of humor,

though it's not quite as impressive as my taste in fashion," Griffin says. "Wanda Kirkwood is my stylist, and she's very good, but I always have final say."

"And she's your girlfriend, I hear."

"Yeah, she's great! We slept together last night, bonded. I didn't even have to lie and pretend I want to marry her."

My laughter dies away as I imagine my mother's face.

The interviewer seems quite excited about this revelation. "Oh yeah? And how was that?"

"Great! I'm lucky to have her. She takes very, very good care of me."

The interviewer lets out a lecherous laugh, and I start planning what exactly I'll say to my mother next time I see her. Somehow, I can't see her feeling too comfortable with the idea of me being some pop star's casual fling.

Griffin finishes his interview by announcing to his fans that he wants to meet every single one of them. He leaps out of his chair, running over to ask Devon and me how he's done.

"Why did you tell everyone you slept with me last night?" I demand, pinching the sleeve of his shirt between my fingers and leaning close so he can't escape.

"Because I did sleep with you last night. And I want everyone else to appreciate you as much as I do, Wanda."

"But we talked about how 'slept together' doesn't mean what you think it means, remember? It means sex."

"Does it?" Griffin smirks. "Well, then everyone thinks you're the woman the most important and powerful man in the world wants to shag." He stalks away from me then, head held high and swagger turned up to ten.

I'm going to strangle him with a Hermes scarf.

The interviewer eyeballs me as he walks by, which just strengthens my resolve to get Griffin back later, but for now, there's little I can do besides allow the group of bodyguards to herd us along. Judging by their expressions, they feel nervous about something.

"You should come out tonight to Wolf Head," the interviewer says to Griffin in an undertone. "Great place; you'll have a lot of fun. It's very exclusive. I'll mention your name, so it won't be a problem getting in."

"Wolf Head? I haven't heard of it."

I grab Griffin's arm as we leave the studio and yank him closer, leaning in until our heads are nearly touching. "We have to go to Wolf Head."

Griffin glances sidelong at me. "Oh?"

"You're taking me there."

"While I like the idea of attending a real dance club, I'm not sure it's a good use of my time."

"No, no, this isn't a question, Griffin. They have killer DJs, and some nights, they have live music from really good bands." I've wanted to go to Wolf Head since way before I moved to the city, thanks to years of following the sorts of bands who play in a place like that. One of my best friends, Kammie, has been there and consistently raves about it. "Look, if you want to learn about music, you need to go there."

"Well, I suppose if you think it's important for building my reputation as a famous pop star…"

"It's important to everything. And I want to go, so you're going to take me." Holding my breath, I wait to see if he'll accept my command. Thankfully, after a very short moment of hesitation, he nods and tells Devon that we're going out tonight.

Even if it's not exactly in the way I had envisioned it, at least I'm about to check off a *major* box on my New York City wish list…

I'VE LOVED MUSIC EVER SINCE I CAN REMEMBER, AND THOUGH MY first small collection of musical purchases as a kid was pretty embarrassing, I now have an impressive record collection amassed in the basement at my parents' place and can make a killer playlist for any mood, including something really specific like 'Haven't Slept in Two Days and Need to Eat Chocolate,' or the more generalized 'Sleepy Sunday Mornings.'

Wolf Head is sort of an extension of the music fanatic in me, because it opened five years ago with a legendary acoustic concert by Little Sandwiches, one of my favorite obscure bands. Since then, the venue has hosted concerts by everyone from indie bands to legendary '80s rockers looking for a few extra bucks to spend on getting their skinny clothes tailored to something bigger and more comfortable. It's the sort of place where music lovers of all types—goths, rockers, indie hipsters, pop lovers—can come together to dance, mingle, and drink cool, expensive drinks, and look incredible while doing it. I've watched enough documentaries and concert DVDs from various bands playing at Wolf Head to feel like I know the layout even with my eyes closed.

Even Alexander Flan, when he was temporarily separated from Fourth Squid Movement, went there once. Or so legend says.

When we return to the hotel, I dig through all the clothes we bought Griffin and find that lovely black jacket with the epaulets. Thankfully, Griffin's shoulders are about the same size as mine and the jacket mostly fits. "I'm borrowing this!" I say, running into the bathroom with my purse for some emergency makeup application.

You don't just go to Wolf Head without preparing.

Griffin appears at my side as I lean over the sink, dotting blush onto my cheeks with my fingertips. I have no idea if he walked into the bathroom or if he teleported or something, but either way, I just glance at him in the reflection of the mirror and cock an eyebrow. "Yes?"

"Is that the Orgasm blusher color by Nars?"

"Uh, no. I can't afford Nars."

He continues to peer at me. "But you want to create the appearance of female pleasure?"

"It's… it's just something we wear. It puts color in our face."

"Why do you use blusher to do that? Wouldn't it be easier to just experience pleasure?"

I laugh without really meaning to. "Women could never achieve any sort of pleasure that would last as long or look as good as makeup. Welcome to my planet."

Griffin's eyes narrow. "On my planet, a proper mating ritual would leave both beings in a state of pleasure for days, no paint needed."

I'm fairly certain the bathroom lights flicker and that he's the one causing it, so I attempt to turn my focus back to the task at hand. It's not as easy as you might imagine.

As soon as I've applied an abundance of black eyeliner and mascara, I rough up my thick hair and blast it with the hairspray bottle provided by our hotel. It smells great and feels heavenly; it's certainly the kind of thing used by rich people. Splurging on hairspray for me usually means buying the six-dollar can.

"You don't go to Wolf Head looking like a bum," I say, and then catch Griffin still staring at me. *Hmmm.* "You know; you could use a little rock edge."

"Rock edge?"

"Yeah, we're gonna make you look like a proper pop star." I tug him close and inspect his eyes; that odd blue color would look quite enchanting with the right amount of eyeliner. "Hold still, okay? Close your eyes and trust me."

He squirms when I apply pressure with the pencil at the middle of his top lash-line, fighting me as if I'm going to hurt him.

"Hey! Stop it! I told you to trust me." I wait until he's still. "Now let's try this again." With a little work, I'm able to apply a steady line of kohl around his eyes, and then step back to admire my work. "Open your eyes; I'm done."

Griffin blinks a few times, his eyes focusing on me. Judging by his tense body language and how tight his lips are pressed together, he didn't particularly enjoy the experience, but I have a feeling he'll get over it when he sees the results.

"Go look in the mirror."

Whatever funk he's in disappears as soon as he's caught his reflection, replaced by a delighted smile. "I look bloody amazing, Wanda—like a proper pop star!"

I nod, quite proud of myself, but before he can leave the room, I say, "Why were you so nervous about me touching your eyes? Are your eyes sensitive?"

Griffin pauses just in front of the door, thinking for a few seconds. "No. They tried to blind me once, that's all."

"Wait, what? Who did?"

"The ones who killed my mother." With that, he's out the door and off to show Devon, loudly proclaiming what a great stylist I am and how Devon needs to wear some eyeliner, too, really, because that's how you get 'rock edge.'

A few minutes later, we're all herded out the door to get dinner before we head to the club, and no one mentions anything more about what Griffin revealed to me in the bathroom.

Some people wait in line forever to get into Wolf Head, and most people never get in at all. As we approach the bouncer, I notice a few B-name actors and reality TV stars in line. I can't help thinking Griffin will need his alien powers to get us in.

"Hello," Griffin says, stopping just in front of the bouncer and looking up at him with a haughty expression on his face. "I've arrived."

Impressively, this works, and we're allowed entrance.

The thing about New York City is that it holds a special pocket of meaning to any hundred or thousand people in a given moment. Whether you're talking about the famous buildings or the hidden Thai place that you love to hit up on Sunday afternoon with your friends, it's full of brick-and-mortar importance.

Wolf Head is one of those places.

Inside, we walk down a wide, curved set of red velvet stairs, descending into a play land of shadow, sparkle, and musical notes. The faux-fountain statue in the middle of Wolf Head's circular bar stretches to the roof and serves as an anchor in a room that could otherwise float away into golden and maroon whimsy, complete with sparkling gold bulbs hanging from black wires here and there, and cigarette girls wearing little more than high heels, fishnets, and sparkly, black bras. Wolf Head's male employees are marked by their oversized black top hats, bowties, and a wolf head symbol scrawled across the back of their suit jackets. High-backed baroque chairs and overstuffed couches dot the club in unexpected places, providing a lounging area for beautiful people who are tired of dancing, too drunk to stand, or in need of a horizontal surface to explore their new friends. Curtains strategically hide sections of the club to provide for more privacy for the richer or braver of the patrons.

Between the shadows and gold lights, I can just make out faces and sparkling clothes as we step out onto the crowded dance floor. It seems that tonight's entertainment leans to the goth side, judging by the dark, deconstructed clothes and the loud music pouring down over us. I glance at Griffin and Devon, both of them looking quite handsome in their eyeliner, and then at the ring of scary bodyguards. We fit in. Sort of.

"What's this music?" Griffin demands, moving close enough that I can hear him over the noise and feel his breath on my neck.

"I'm not sure."

"I thought you knew everything about music!"

I'm already swaying, which is a good sign, even if I'm not familiar with the song. "Look, that's why this place is so great. Everything's cutting edge and amazing!" I push away from Griffin and Devon. Thankfully, no one stops me. For the first time in a long time, even before I was kidnapped by the aliens, I feel completely, ridiculously, recklessly free. It's almost like my cross-country road trip to follow my favorite band on tour, and that's really saying something.

Dancing is the first thing on my mind, of course, because of the power of the pulsing music overhead, but I also can't help fishing my cell phone out and snapping a couple of pictures of the mismatched, sparkly gold light bulbs hanging from the ceiling, a couch with cobalt cushions and gnarly brown legs, and the fountain statue in the middle of the bar. I've seen countless pictures of that statue on the Internet over the years, but I can't help wanting my own.

One of the unfairly beautiful cigarette girls offers me a sample of the night's special drink, and I accept it with a grin I can't seem to control. I'm really here! I'm really at Wolf Head! I'm really drinking a sparkly drink from a tiny plastic cup that says *Wolf Head*.

As the cigarette girl walks away, I snap a picture of her.

I need these memories for when I go back to my semi-boring life with the overcrowded apartment, two jobs, and lack of time for fun.

After snapping a few too many pictures and dancing with no one in particular, I remember I should probably check on my alien companions. I dance my way slowly back through the crowd, keeping an eye out for a blond and brown head. Griffin and Devon are both on the short side, so finding them isn't the easiest task, but at last, I spot one of the bodyguards. Perfect. I'll use him as my North Star.

Sure enough, just before I reach the bodyguard, I spot Devon and Griffin dancing with each other. They've got a bit of an audience, which is remarkable given the wide variety of interesting and attractive people in the crowd, but they're dancing away as if they have no idea anyone's watching, comfortable with each other among a sea of strangers.

After a few seconds, Griffin spots me and crooks his forefinger in my direction to summon me. I intend to keep a respectful distance as I approach, but he all but shoves me between him and Devon and takes me by the hips, pressing the front of his body tight against mine. Suddenly, I've got these handsome aliens on either side of me, and I have to say, this is not the worst thing that's ever happened to me. At all.

Griffin, in particular, loses himself in the music, eyes closed and his head rocking back and forth with the fervent passion of a man well on his way to ecstasy. Watching him is entrancing and dangerous, but somehow, I think he's unaware of his magnetism. Devon's more reserved, allowing me a bit of room and smiling almost politely when I glance over my shoulder at him. He steps away after a while, leaving me with Griffin.

"Do you like it?" I say, and Griffin half opens his eyes, the peculiar blue color glowing back at me from between a kohl outline. I wonder if maybe he didn't hear me, so I dare to lean in close to ask him again, this time directly in his ear.

He nods and turns his face, brushing his lips across my cheek as he does so. A pleasant tingle dances down the back of my neck, over my lower spine, and up my fingertips. My arms settle around Griffin's neck. From this close, I can see a slight sheen of sweat forming over his skin, strangely inviting and deliciously intimate. It's been years since I danced this close to a guy, mostly because I'm usually too shy to ask strangers to dance when I go out with my girlfriends.

I don't realize until the third or fourth flash that someone's taking pictures of us.

"Uhhh… Griffin?" I say over the noise. "Someone's taking

pictures!"

"Of course they are!" he says, turning to smile and pose. Then he's off to talk to the photographer, leaning in close so he can hear what the man says, and leaving me with Devon.

"Do you like the music?" I ask Devon, who seems to be eyeballing a group of scantily clad female dancers near us.

"What? Oh, yes. It's quite good. Quite different from Griff's music, too. I like it very much!" he says, and his gaze trails off again.

"Why don't you go introduce yourself? You can dance with anyone you want here," I say. "That's pretty much the first rule of Manhattan, you know."

"Is it?"

I nod and laugh at Devon's expression. "And you can buy me a drink. That's also a rule in Manhattan."

"What, over at the bar?"

"Yeah, just go order me a vodka and cranberry."

Devon considers this for a few seconds, looking at Griffin and then back at me. "Alright, I'll be right back. Keep an eye on Griffin, though, okay?"

"Sure!" I say as Devon's walking toward the bar. "It's not like anything's going to happen to him here."

But wouldn't you know it, only about two minutes after Devon disappears, so does Griffin.

First things first, I try not to panic. He can't be that hard to find, right? After all, he couldn't have gone far. And besides, one of the bodyguards probably still knows where he is. A glance around the room reveals the bodyguards are stationed at a lot of conspicuous locations, but none of them are moving.

Devon asked me, specifically, to keep an eye on Griffin, whether he's in danger or not.

I try to think of where an alien prince would go in a club.

Bar? Stage? Wait, maybe the bathroom! I should try there first.

There's no line for the men's bathroom, and no bathroom attendant, either, so I look both ways and then barge right in. You see, with the right amount of adrenaline, a woman doesn't fear seeing any strange, wayward, hairy man parts or urinals or other such horrifying entities.

"Sugar? You're funny," a voice says from one of the stalls. "Here now, hold this and watch what I do."

I'm about to flee the restroom when I hear the unmistakable sound of Griffin's nervous laughter. "Your nose? Why? Is that cocaine?"

Oh no.

Chapter 7

"*Do not touch that, Griffin!*" I shout, all but kicking in the door of the bathroom stall. I find Griffin leaned against a wall, an incredulous expression on his face, and the photographer dude next to him, halfway through a line of coke.

"Wanda."

"Don't you even think about touching that!" I grab Griffin's hand and pull him out of the stall. "That could kill you, do you understand? Don't ever, ever, ever touch cocaine. That's bad news for anyone, but especially for you."

"Oh, so that is cocaine," he mutters. "Am I going to a rehabilitation center now…?"

"No, you're leaving this disgusting bathroom right now and coming with me to the bar." After a few seconds of hesitation, I snatch the scummy photographer guy's camera up from where he'd left it on the floor. "Real nice, trying to sell photos of Griffin for blackmail!" I say. "Real nice! But you failed this time! Ha!"

I claim a better grip on Griffin's hand, squeezing hard enough to get a few little huffs and puffs of protest, but I drag him along anyway, out of the bathroom. A man standing outside the bathroom eyes Griffin and me, attempting to give me a high five as I breeze by, but I ignore him.

After all this heroic behavior, I want a drink.

Devon seems to have made himself rather comfortable at the bar, chatting up a red-haired lady and sipping something that looks incredibly similar to a vodka with cranberry. Oh well, I'll give him his moment. I sense he doesn't usually get the opportunity for much flirting when Griffin's in the room. Any room.

"You're going to buy me a vodka and cranberry," I say to Griffin, and then wave for the bartender before he can argue with me. "Vodka and cranberry! Actually... make that two. They're on this guy."

The bartender squints at Griffin, as if trying to place how he knows him, and then he goes strangely stiff. He offers us a huge smile. "No problem, Mr. Valentino, these are on the house," he says, and then whips up two vodka and cranberries. Extra vodka.

Maybe I should have ordered more drinks.

I turn back to Griffin, handing him one of the cups. "You might want to go easy on that, until you see how you handle it. You're kind of petite."

"Petite?"

"You're not that much taller than me."

Griffin shoots me a venomous glance. "I'm tall! Or, well, at least above average!"

"On your planet?" I take a long sip of my drink. "So you look like this on your planet, too? Just like this?"

Griffin frowns. "Well, I dress a bit differently, if that's what you mean."

"No, I mean..." I lean forward so I can speak directly in his ear. "You're aliens, but you look just like us. Except for the weird eyes. Oh, and the quick digestive systems."

"I think you're the ones who look like us, but I suppose otherwise you're correct. We're superior to you in many other important regards, however."

I roll my eyes at his superior comment. "Most of us imagined aliens looking really different. My friend, Kammie, for instance. She's always talking about aliens and what they look like."

"You know, there are all sorts of beings on all sorts of planets around the universe, Wanda. We don't all look the same. Your people and my people happen to be descended from the same matter, but not everyone is. That's terribly racist of you." Griffin takes a sip of his drink and swishes it around a bit in his mouth. "Hmmm, this tastes good." He slurps down the rest of his drink in one big gulp.

Griffin orders another drink before I can stop him, and soon, we've both had a few drinks and he wants to dance. I let him drag me back to the floor, and we dance together for so long that I almost forget the circumstances that have brought us here. For a while, I'm just dancing with some hot English guy who has entirely too much energy and smudged eyeliner, and who doesn't know any normal dance moves at all. His hands wander all over me, and his heavy-lidded gaze roaming my body feels tingly and palpable, so it's okay.

After a while, maybe a long while, Devon joins us, smirky and satisfied, as if he's been up to no good. Griffin all but tackles Devon and kisses him on the side of the head before whispering something in his ear and hysterically laughing

They converse in secret, and then Griffin raises his hand into the air, about to snap his fingers.

"Heeeeeey, I think it's time we headed out!" I say, catching his wrist and yanking it back down to his side. "No tricks in here, okay? You don't want to call attention to yourself."

"Of course I do, Wanda, don't be daft! I'm a famous pop star!"

"I mean, you don't want to call attention to your magic tricks. Come on. Let's go get some air."

With more than a little griping and giggling in turn, I manage to bully Griffin through the crowd and to the door, with Devon trailing along behind us. The bodyguards surround us long before we reach the doorway, once again enclosing us. This time, I feel a bit less claustrophobic than before.

Outside, it's lightly drizzling, though even a three-week education in the weather of Manhattan warns me that drizzle will soon turn to the sort of rain that makes you sneeze the next morning.

Griffin shivers and one of the bodyguards leaps forward, holding his jacket over Griffin's head as a shield against the rain. Another follows suit with Devon.

"We should return to the hotel," one of the bodyguards says. "You aren't walking properly, Prince Griffin, and this precipitation is cold."

"Yeah, I suppose he's right," Devon says, though in a rather disappointed tone.

I catch Devon's sad smile, and I think of what he'd said earlier about rain. "The rain won't hurt you," I say. "Not if you're only in it for a few minutes." With the sort of courage you acquire from alcohol, I reach up and push the jacket away from over Devon's head. Mercifully, the bodyguard doesn't decide to murder me. "Go on," I say. "You might as well enjoy the rain while you can."

Devon tips his face upward, like someone in a movie, and his mouth melts into a big smile. "It's so cold! It's rain, Griffin! Real rain!"

I've never really thought about rain in positive terms; it's usually a nuisance, slowing progress when you're driving or walking, or ruining your hair. But watching Devon stand in the rain, face tilted up and eyes closed, I second-guess everything I've ever thought about it.

Maybe it is a little special that we have clean water falling from the sky, naturally recycled and replenished.

Griffin shoves away the jacket over his head and snaps his fingers, squinting his eyes, as if concentrating. The rain pours down around us much heavier than before. Devon lets out a little gasp, but his smile is one of pure delight. Everyone else seems to fall into a panic, rushing around to escape the rain or scrambling to rescue their hair, their clothes. Umbrellas snap open with a pop, pop, pop, pop like popcorn, and the line outside Wolf Head thins out.

But amid all the scrambling and hastening, Devon's simply entranced by the rain, holding his hand out and watching droplets of water splash against his skin, blinking rapidly when rain falls into his eyes, laughing as he passes his fingers through his wet hair. His leather jacket looks like it can't stand to shrink any smaller than it already has, but it's soaked through and Devon hasn't even noticed.

Taxis speed past us. Everything is a blur of rain, yellow and gray, and vodka-infused laughter as Devon finally takes note of Griffin's soppy appearance. I'm soaked clear through. My dress is clinging to my body, and my hair is hanging flat around my face. It's probably not a pretty sight, but I can't help laughing with Devon about Griffin, especially since his eyeliner has migrated under his eyes.

"Alright, he's shivering," Devon finally says. "Griffin's shivering!" His tone takes on that stern edge again, though still laced with just a bit of laughter. "Let's get him out of the rain."

The car returns soon after, and Devon bundles Griffin inside, his arm slung around him.

I stand on the sidewalk for a few seconds, watching the protective way they cling to each other. Good thing I intercepted them, really, because if someone else had... well, who knows what might have happened. They're strangers here, naïve to the power of our confusing world, and unfamiliar with slimy dudes in bathroom stalls with cocaine and cameras.

But they kidnapped me.

Looking around, I realize that all the bodyguards have already piled into the car, and I could probably make a run for it. You know, go home and try to explain to my roommates where I've been. Call my boss at the restaurant and beg to keep my job, call my boss at the clothing store, call my mother, and...

"Hurry up, Wanda!" Griffin says. "I'm bloody freezing!" He leans forward in his seat to look at me. "Also, I found a bottle of champagne in here. Do you know how to open it? I've always wanted to try champagne."

After a few seconds of rain-soaked hesitation, I climb into the car and slam the door shut behind myself.

You just don't say no to champagne with aliens.

Chapter 8

Or, maybe you do.

I wake up slowly, unsure of why it feels like the insides of my head are leaking out through my ears and why I'm wearing shoes in bed. A raging headache welcomes me to consciousness, and I sit up with a loud groan. The hotel is entirely too bright, and the inside of my mouth is so dry that I almost gag.

How much champagne did I have?

And where are Griffin and Devon?

Memories of the night before flicker in tiny flashes. We'd opened the champagne bottle in the car. Griffin was so cold when we returned to the hotel that Devon had wrapped him up in a bunch of blankets, which only made both of them laugh hysterically. I think I laughed hysterically, too. I told Griffin that the dresses he got me were very nice, but I needed fresh underwear to go with them. I think I actually talked about underwear with him. Oh God, yes, I did. I talked about *underwear* with him. And Griffin had done something with his hands that made the room go completely dark. Or maybe it made the whole hotel go dark. He'd apologized profusely, and the lights had switched back on.

At some point in the night, I'd decided I should climb onto the bed.

"Hello?" I call, but I find that my vocal chords are on strike. My throat hurts, too, but I barely notice over the pain in my head. After gathering a great deal of stamina, I croak out, "*Where is everyone?*"

No answer.

They've abandoned me! They've left me hung-over and helpless on the zillionth floor of a massive, swanky hotel, with nothing to my name other than whatever's in my purse and a couple of new dresses.

With the rest of the strength in my body, I stumble across the room. At this point, the first goal is to throw up, possibly multiple times, and then to drink as much water as I can. And then maybe I'll throw up again.

But then Griffin bursts into the room, with Devon at his heels, and all the bodyguards in tow. Griffin's chattering up a storm in his language, swinging several department store bags from his skinny wrists. He's dressed cheerfully in a T-shirt with the Union Jack logo printed across the chest, tight white jeans, and oversized yellow-framed sunglasses. Even with the sunglasses, I can tell by his body language that he's not about to throw up and die from alcohol over-consumption. He looks annoyingly good, in fact.

"Ah, Wanda!" he says. "How did you sleep?" Before I can answer, he approaches, holding out the bags. "I went to Victoria's Secret for you. I tried to buy a pair of wings, but they told me they're not for sale. Damn it, I really wanted to wear them!"

I wince at how loud his voice is.

"These should fit you. The shopkeepers were a bit cross and quite unhelpful. Apparently, none of them have heard my music yet. Oh well, they will soon." He unloads several sparkly bras and a handful of lacy underwear from the pink bag, holding them out to me in offering. "On the way there, I bought a real hot dog from one of the hot dog stands. Disgusting! But delicious. I want another one."

"You're not having another one," Devon says, walking toward his room.

Griffin has become utterly entranced by one of the sparkly bras. "I think this will decorate your breasts quite nicely. I hope you like it."

"Griffin."

"What will you wear with this? A long skirt? Is that the current style?"

"*Griffin*," I hiss. "*Shut up.* Please."

He raises his gaze from the expensive undergarments, stares at me for a few seconds, and then narrows his eyes. "Are you ill, Wanda?"

"Do you remember how much we drank last night? My head is killing me, my throat hurts, and my mouth feels like I ate a teddy bear!"

Griffin takes off his sunglasses and drops everything. Well, everything except for the Versace bag, which he places very delicately on the ground. He steps closer until I can feel his warm breath against my face. He snaps his fingers.

All at once, my headache vanishes, chased away by the general pulsing unhappiness in my body, and even the gross taste in my mouth. It's as if I never had any alcohol at all, and I got a really great night of sleep. And maybe took part in a killer make-out session.

For a long time, we just stand together.

"Is that better?" he whispers, tilting his face to the side so our lips are almost touching.

"Maybe."

"Maybe? Is there still something wrong?"

New memories of the night before leak in, bit by bit, including a flash of Griffin pulling the covers up over me. "What happened last night?" I ask, though a bit fearful to know the details. "We didn't do anything, uh, intimate, did we…?"

"Of course not!" He stares directly into my eyes. "It's nothing if not dishonorable to engage someone in an important activity when they're heavily intoxicated, Wanda."

I let out a heavy breath. "Well, you'd be surprised at how many guys on this planet wouldn't agree about that."

"Perhaps they could use a lesson in war and peace, then. Only the evil seek pleasure in taking advantage of weakness," he says, his voice particularly husky and thick and his eyes glowing a much darker blue than usual.

I feel warm all over, content to just stare at him. I want to close the scant space between our lips, want to drag more of those words out of his mouth with my tongue, but a noise from Devon's room startles both of us and breaks the spell we've put over each other.

Griffin walks away from me, throwing open the door to Devon's room. "I'm starving! Let's go get something delicious and dodgy. Maybe another hot dog!"

I wander into Devon's room, curious about this new territory. It's as clean as Griffin's is disorganized, with a few clothes hung neatly in the closet space and the bed wrinkle free.

"No more hot dogs, Griff. You vomited," Devon says from his station at the window, sipping from a coffee cup.

"I did not!"

"You were sick all over your shoes. You bought new shoes. No more hot dogs."

Griffin stalks over to Devon, taking his coffee cup away and drawing a long, long sip from it. "What's this? It's hot. Is this coffee?"

"Yes. I like it a lot."

Griffin jabs one finger into Devon's ribs and then looks at me. "He's had about ten of those since we arrived. He thought he'd hate it here, but we'd barely landed and he was already in love with your coffee. Ha! Aren't you glad you came now, Dev?"

Devon's lips twitch into a half smile. "Not as happy as you are, of course, you pompous little idiot. But I suppose it's not so bad."

"You love it."

"I don't love it. I still want to go home as soon as we can," Devon says, the last part so quiet I can barely hear it.

"I have my very first musical performance scheduled this evening," Griffin says, flinging himself on his back across the top of Devon's bed. He looks at me. "I'll be performing for your people for the first time ever. I must look smashing. I want everyone to melt at my feet. I want them crying and shouting my name and waving signs and throwing their clothes at me. That's the proper way to do it."

I roll my eyes, but I can't help laughing. "If I remember right, last night, you were the one throwing your clothes around. But who knows, maybe you were just trying to figure out how to take your jacket off."

Devon snickers, and Griffin shoots him a murderous look.

"Anyway, Wanda, you will help us prepare for that." Griffin

props himself up on his elbows. "How does your head feel now?"

"Much better than when I woke up."

Griffin's smile stretches across his face. "Ah-ha! I still have my touch. I have the strongest healing sensitivity of anyone in the capital city. It's so strong that they don't even have a name for my category. It puzzles them. They tested me six times to make sure they weren't wrong."

"He's not exaggerating for once," Devon says, taking another sip of his coffee.

With a little hesitation, I settle on the edge of Devon's bed. "So you guys have magic—"

"It's not magic!"

"Okay, okay, whatever. But do you each have specific kinds? Like Griffin, you have healing and magic for making music play in random stores, and Devon has... I dunno, cleaning magic that makes his room look amazing?"

Griffin casts a heavy glance at Devon, and the two of them stare at each other for a few long seconds.

"Errr, no, Daisy. I don't really have any of the sensitivities. My talent lies more in diplomacy and translation, I suppose," Devon says.

"Translating me to everyone else." Griffin shifts around a bit on the bed. "But he's also really smart about science and whatnot. He's working on these plants that might help the environment by sucking bad things out of the ground. And this other thing, too. I can't explain it; he'll have to. Dev's the smartest person I know."

"Well, considering all the issues you guys had in the past, it's good you two can do the stuff you do. Dev working on science stuff and you healing," I say. "Right? Plus, you can make people like you and give you free drinks and listen to your music."

They exchange another glance, and Devon speaks up. "For a leader who understands war as famously as Griff's dad does, healing isn't a popular option for an heir. Military strategist might have been more useful, in his father's opinion." Devon turns away and stares out the window. Without the sound of his voice, the room falls too silent.

For the first time, I see them as something very different than I have up until this point. They're a team, alone, brothers and best friends, but also outcasts in some twisted sense that goes far beyond being visitors from another planet.

"Can't you just snap your fingers and make everyone love you at home?"

Griffin laughs. "I can do that to your people because your minds aren't as sharp as ours."

"Wow, thanks, Griffin."

He smiles at me. "No offense intended."

"You make people here fall in love with you pretty easily," I say. "Wouldn't it be easier to stay here?"

Devon turns back from his station at the window. "Daisy, Griffin and I have a very specific mission on your planet, and then we return home. The longer we stay here, the more complications arise." He hesitates. "For us and also for everyone back home."

"What exactly... uh... is that mission? Besides becoming a famous pop star?"

Devon starts to say something, but Griffin cuts him off. "I need to make contact with the Origin Collective and prove to my father that your planet has some sort of worth or value and isn't just a lot of frivolous stupidity."

"Hey! We have... well, we have this sauce that's so hot that people have actually almost died from eating it," I say, hoping to get a laugh. Neither of them seems to find it amusing. "Really, though, we've done a lot of good things. We've made some great music, we've walked on the moon, and we... well, we haven't taken very good care of our oceans or natural resources, I guess, but we're working on solar power and better cars."

The more I think about it, the worse it all seems. We've actually been pretty irresponsible, haven't we?

"What happens if you can't prove it to your father?"

"I'll be executed," Griffin casually says.

I jump clear off the bed. "What!"

"I'm joking, Wanda. Don't be daft; my father wouldn't execute his only heir." Griffin sits up and stretches his arms over his head. "I'm hungry, Devon. Let's go get something to eat."

"What will happen to you if you can't prove to your dad that my planet has some kind of worth? You can't just leave me hanging like this."

"I'll have to marry someone I completely despise. She's evil."

"Why would your dad want you to marry her, then?"

"Oh, she's the daughter of—well, she's—she's perfect, you know? She's perfect. She's good at everything he wishes I were good at, he's blind to anything negative about her, and she's beautiful. I'm beginning to think he'll just make her the next Emperor President, instead of me."

"Empress, Griff," Devon says.

"Nah, Emperor. She'd choke anyone who called her otherwise."

Devon sighs and stares down at his coffee cup. "She's very unpleasant, you see. And she's got a lot of bad ideas that she thinks she'll carry out once she's married to Griffin."

"She told me as much! Last time we met, she told me that I ought to feel lucky to have been matched with her—else we'd all be in danger from my stupidity. Well, she'll lead us right back into a war. Everyone's already struggling as it is, between the regulations, the new recycling laws, the terrorists, and those bloody awful gray uniforms and..." All at once, Griffin stops, his pale face tingeing red. "Errr, Wanda, you should get ready. I need to eat and then prepare for my performance."

Griffin walks back to his room without another word, leaving me with Devon.

"You have to understand, they think you're very frivolous here," Devon says to me in a near whisper. "Griffin keeps telling his father about things you do... concerts, dancing, and colorful clothes, charity things for the poor. It's become a point of contention between them."

"Great. His dad sounds like a grump."

"Someone from your planet, the Origin Collective, sent a lot of messages out, offering peace and friendship to citizens of other worlds. They sent a lot of them directly to us, but the Emperor President believes they're only morbidly curious, or maybe acting out of selfish motives." Dev sighs. "Griffin offered to talk to them, but the Emperor President believes they'd only meet with us because of our heritage. Griffin made a wager with his father that he could secure a meeting with them without revealing his identity. Once we secure the meeting, however, and this is the bit Griff's father added, we have to discover something worthwhile or helpful for our planet. Otherwise, Griffin has to give up his obsession with Earth and do what he's told."

I think of last night, standing in the rain. Maybe I should have run away while I had the chance, escaped back to my ordinary life, worrying only about paying bills and attempting to talk to cute guys on the subway. Maybe I should have untangled myself from all of this strange, universe-wide political intrigue.

But maybe it's for the better that I didn't.

"Griff thinks bringing some color and fun to everything might improve the general outlook, but it's certainly not a popular opinion among those in power. I happen to agree with Griff. Some peace and happiness might go a long way. If he can learn how you do things here and bring it back, it might do some good. None of that can happen if he doesn't win the wager against his father, though."

I shake my head. "So I guess my planet does actually know about aliens." Oh God, a government cover-up. This is exactly the kind of thing Kammie is always talking about—the government covering up the existence of aliens, giant, man-eating rats in Manhattan, alligators in the sewer, tax breaks for poor people, or whatever.

Devon looks at me as if he wants to say something else, but he just pinches his mouth into a thin line and nods.

"Well, how're you going to find a secret society if you don't reveal you're aliens? They don't exactly hang out on the street corners waiting for people to talk to them."

"The Origin Collective will find Griffin if he's made himself important enough for them to take notice."

I consider this for a few seconds. "Alright. Listen. It was completely wrong of you guys to kidnap me," I say, giving him a pointed look. "But here's the deal… if you'll tell me right now that I'm free of all this kidnapping business, I will help you. On my own, I mean, voluntarily."

Griffin materializes at my side. "Whatever, you're free. Now come help me get ready for my performance. We have a lot of work to do!"

Chapter 9

WHEN YOU NEED TO HELP ALIENS ATTRACT A SECRET SOCIETY BY WAY of a flourishing music career, you have to start with the basics—finding out how to attract the secret society. And according to a quick Internet search, the best man for the job is a conspiracy theorist who Kammie loves, but he lives in Scotland and is famously reclusive. The best man in New York City to help with that sort of thing is one Kyran Gray.

A woman who says her name is Primrose answers for Kyran, setting up an appointment for us that afternoon on the front steps of the New York Public Library by Bryant Park. Griffin puts on his yellow sunglasses and his best mysterious, pouty pop star façade, and we head to the meeting with all of Griffin's very concerned bodyguards sticking quite close by.

Among the tourist-littered front steps of the library, I notice a bearded man wearing a smart gray trench coat and heeled black boots, carrying a big, leather man purse. His square face is set off by a wave of light brown hair shaped into a faux-hawk, and he generally has the appearance of a model who secretly eats cake. Before I can even point him out to Griffin, the man has made a beeline toward us, hand extended.

"You must be Daisy," he says to me. "I'm Kyran Gray, paranormal detective. I'm also Lady Grieve's second in command in the New England Chapter of North American Witches, as you may have noticed by the pins on my lapels."

Griffin steps toward Kyran, inspecting him from behind the oversized sunglasses. "You're a witch? I thought witches were females."

"Welcome to the future, time traveler," Kyran says. "Any other stupid questions before I decide if I'm going to offer you my services?"

"I'm not a time traveler. I've traveled through space and two small dimension doors, almost instantaneously. But you won't know how to do that for another four hundred years or so, at the rate of your governments' current space programs. If ever."

Kyran's big eyes widen just a little, and it takes him a few seconds before he speaks again. "Did Arson send you to screw with me?"

"I'm not interested in screwing you. I need to know important information about the Origin Collective."

"It was Arson, wasn't it?" Kyran demands. "That damn faerie. He's not satisfied with his millions of little zombie girl admirers and his leather pants. No, no, that's not enough." Kyran takes a step backward. "Tell him I didn't find this amusing, and he can go f—"

"No one sent us," I say, reaching out to put my hand on Kyran's arm. "Look, this is crazy, I know, but you have to give us a chance to explain. You came highly recommended as someone who can help us."

Kyran looks between Griffin and me as if considering. "Of course I'm highly recommended. I'm an expert in magic, history, and three types of combat."

"Then please listen to what we have to say." I take a deep breath. "My friends here are from another planet—"

"Oh please. Prove it."

Griffin snaps his fingers a little louder than strictly necessary and a burst of blue light appears at Kyran's feet, shaking the ground. Kyran yells a word I don't recognize and holds his trembling hands out over the blue light, causing the light to turn orange. Then, all at once, the light is gone.

"Alright, alright. *Whoa!* Alright. Either you're one of Viktor's relatives and you're lying to me or you're… well, what you say you are. And if you're the latter, then ha-ha, I guess I just discovered aliens, too. Wait until Primmy hears about this." Kyran straightens his jacket and the blue scarf knotted neatly at his throat, and then sniffs and says rather reluctantly, "You're wearing white Diesel jeans. That's a good choice."

Griffin perks up at that. "Thank you. I do look quite good in them." He motions at Kyran. "Yours aren't bad either."

"Rag & Bone. You can't go wrong with Rag & Bone." Kyran sighs heavily. "Come sit down and explain your dilemma to me. First consultations are free."

To Kyran's credit, he listens to our explanation without interrupting or looking too shocked, and he's patient even when Griffin interjects into almost every sentence Devon or I say. As we reach some point of conclusion—or rather, when I have nothing to say but "uhhhh…," Devon has finished his very polite and concise explanation, and Griffin has stopped talking and has instead crossed his arms over his chest in a snobby manner—Kyran sits back and considers everything.

"Okay, first of all, you're British."

"Yes, British pop stars."

"Do you have those accents at home, too? Are the English just a superior race? Because I wrote a paper on a similar subject once and got a ninety-three."

Griffin and Devon exchange a glance, and then Griffin says something in their weird alien language. Apparently, that's enough for Kyran, because he stares at them, wide-eyed, and then shakes his head and continues speaking.

"Secondly, it's wise of you to contact the Origin Collective, since they tend to shape the world in positive manners, rather than going around and bumping people off and pretending to do important things."

"Good. I was quite concerned when we arrived and I found out that your planet only recently discovered its moon."

"We didn't recently discover it. We walked on it!"

"That's what concerns me. We walk on our moons all the time and never make a big fuss about it. If I can't prove to my father that your planet has something to offer, I'm stuck with a war, most likely, and an evil wife." Griffin spreads his hands wide and shrugs. "So tell me, Kyran Gray, is the Origin Collective going to be able to help me? Will they have advice for my planet? Will they have some kind of perspective on peace that might prove useful? Will they perhaps know of developments in science and medicine that would impress an Emperor President of an advanced world?"

Kyran scowls at all of us in turn, and I can't help feeling shocked that Griffin's revealing all of this so easily to a stranger, especially after everything I went through to get it out of him. The bodyguards circled around us don't say anything, either, which seems strange. I'd think they'd feel a bit more cautious with all of this vital and secretive information.

"If you want help with important matters of science or thought, you should have just come to me," Kyran says. "The New England Chapter of North American Witches is one of the best chapters in the world. Perhaps even the best, but I prefer to remain humble." Kyran pauses for a few seconds to let his humility sink in. "Anyway, if you're looking for answers to questions about the direction of the world or want to ask for help for your planet, you want the Origin Collective."

"How will we attract their attention?" Devon asks.

Griffin sits up straight. "Bono! We need Bono, don't we?"

A car rolls by blasting Griffin's song just then, which makes him nearly leap up from the steps. Devon grabs his arm before he can do anything crazy.

"You'll need to create a spectacle... either a major televised performance or a concert event that they can't ignore, and you'll need to signal them with their symbol," Kyran says.

"Oh. This?" Griffin holds up his long, pale fingers slanted into a pyramid.

"No, no, not that. Here." Kyran holds his hands up, fingers curled to form a big circle.

I laugh without meaning to, but stop when Kyran shoots me a withering look. He's actually pretty intimidating for a metrosexual witch carrying a man purse.

"Once we make contact, it will be no problem for me to charm them and convince them to help my cause, of course," Griffin says, more to himself than anyone else. "Thank you, Kyran Gray. You've been most helpful."

"Good. Now we can discuss rates. I have to charge according to my worth, of course, and that's determined by the New England Chapter of North American Witches, so don't be surprised when you hear the figure. You have to pay for quality."

Griffin stands up and jams a finger into Kyran's neck. Kyran flops back against the steps, limp and silent.

"Oh my *God*! What did you do?" I say, and Devon shushes me. "What did you do, Griffin? *What did you do?* Is he okay? Did you kill him?"

"I just wiped his memory. He'll be fine. He'll wake up in about twenty seconds and have no idea he ever spoke to us at all." Griffin stifles a yawn, and then plucks a handful of money from the back pocket of his jeans. He tucks the money into Kyran's jacket pocket before turning around to smile at me rather brightly. "Brilliant! Shall we start planning our big event before or after my performance tonight?"

Chapter 10

GRIFFIN'S FIRST LIVE PERFORMANCE IS SCHEDULED FOR NINE PM. HE'S greeted with free water bottles, soda, wine, beer, snacks, hugs, and a full-on mouth kiss from a woman who appears to be part of the studio's official staff. A few minutes after, he's given a full-on mouth kiss from a man who also appears to be part of the studio's official staff. The man asks him to sign a neon-blue CD-R with a marker. Griffin does so while grinning widely, and then asks if the man wants my autograph.

He doesn't.

The bodyguards walk the studio again and again, silently staring down anyone and everyone who crosses their path. Devon, though he smiles and greets everyone with handshakes and pleasant words of introduction, glances around nervously more often than usual.

As Griffin is swept away, I catch Devon's arm and lean in close to him. I'm still a bit shaken after the Kyran incident, though I had insisted we stick around long enough for Kyran to wake up, just so I could be sure he was all right. Thankfully, he'd been fine, other than having no idea who we were and walking away muttering about how annoyed he was to have been stood up for a meeting. "Is something going on that I don't know about? Everyone's acting really weird."

Devon's eyes follow Griffin and the three bodyguards who leave the room with him. "Oh," he says, as if he's forgotten I was there at all. "Oh, well, we've been here for a few days now."

"Are you worried about his crazy fans?"

"No, Daisy. No, it's... it's nothing to worry about." Devon pulls away from me and chases after Griffin, leaving me no choice but to follow.

When I finally catch up to Griffin, I hear him saying, "Tech? Oh, oh... well, I have just a few things out in the vehicle." He motions at the bodyguards. "Go get my stuff, would you?"

Two of the bodyguards take off and return with a cool white Telecaster and a few other odds and ends that vaguely resemble musical instruments. And an oversized snare drum.

"I want Wanda and Devon to join me for the interview," Griffin says to the producer, who looks like she needs another cup of coffee and some under-eye concealer.

"Are they in the band?"

"Dev's my manager and Wanda's very important to me." Griffin pauses for a moment, wiggling his eyebrows. "They'll join me."

"We were only expecting to have you on the couch, Mr. Valentino."

"You can fit all of us on the couch!" Griffin says, snapping his fingers.

"Sure, sure, we'll fit all three of you. Whatever you need, Mr. Valentino. Your interview segment will be five minutes, and then your performance will be four minutes. Is there anything else I can do for you?"

Griffin smiles, and then stifles a yawn. "Nah, that's good. No, wait, I changed my mind. Dev here loves your coffee drink. Can he have some coffee? I'll have some, too."

"Help yourself to all the coffee you'd like at the catering table. You look a bit tired. Are you sure there's nothing else I can get you?"

Griffin waves her away and turns back to Devon and me. "This will be my first live performance, so I must impress everyone, of course, but the interview segment provides me an opportunity to set up anticipation for our big event. I've decided it should be a concert."

"Don't you think you should see how this goes first?" I whisper. "I haven't seen you perform yet. What if you're not any good?"

"I'm good at everything," Griffin says, then wanders off to help himself to some coffee and snacks and to oversee his equipment set up.

Just as I'm being mic'd for the show, my cell phone buzzes from deep within my purse. The incoming call name is *Mom and Dad*, which means my mother has probably finally caught wind of a famous pop star chatting amiably in public about casually sleeping with me.

Might want to skip that call for now. Or maybe forever.

The makeup artist spends a few minutes cleaning up my hastily applied makeup from earlier, attempting to tame my frizzy flyaways. It's not exactly supermodel treatment... no, that's reserved for Griffin, who seems to have attracted a herd of giddy admirers from the studio. They ring around his chair as his dark hair is touched up. When he insists on wearing eyeliner, several offers ring out to help him apply it. Ultimately, he tells them he'll do it himself, since I've 'taught him how.'

We're ushered into a holding room with purple walls, all the while watched closely by a man wearing a headset and a nervous expression. The bodyguards line the room like grim-faced vertical furniture. I'm so nervous that I stare at one of the bodyguards for a long time and then giggle a little when I catch the scowl he's shooting me.

"Twenty seconds," the man with the headset says. "By the way, I love your song."

Griffin smiles widely. "Thank you."

The man motions us to follow him through a dark hallway, onto the set, and just before we step into the light, he says, "*I love you*" to Griffin.

Griffin just smiles and continues on, welcoming his screaming audience member admirers by waving his arms wide and then pressing his hands to his lips so he can blow kisses at them.

Devon nudges Griffin with an elbow. "Go sit down," he says, but he's laughing.

I attempt to sit at the end of the couch, furthest away from Johnny Bardo, the host, but Griffin motions for me to sit in the middle, and then perches beside me on the couch.

"Well, well, well. Tonight we have a very special guest... a worldwide sensation! Only two days ago, Griffin Valentino took over the known universe with his incredibly catchy song, and now he's sitting here with us, ready to perform that song for the very first time on national television," Johnny Bardo says, his voice sounding a bit higher than I expected.

I've watched Johnny Bardo's show enough times for this whole situation to feel surreal, even without the alien connection, so I sit in stunned silence as Griffin cheerfully speaks about his music. Johnny Bardo's signature black hair swoop looks shinier in person, and I can't quite decide if he's actually handsome after all, or if it's just his thick layer of tan makeup and a hint of blue mascara mesmerizing all the viewers at home.

"Now, you've brought a couple of people with you, this evening... your girlfriend, Wanda Kirkwood, and your manager, Devon London," Johnny says. "Devon, what do you think of Griffin's overnight success?"

Devon struggles against a toothy smile, all golden hair, warm skin, and charm. "Aww, I dunno, Johnny. I think maybe Griff's just a little special."

"I'd like an Oscar," Griffin interjects.

"You're an actor too?"

Griffin considers this and glances at Devon. "No, but I'd like an Oscar anyway."

The audience laughs, and Johnny looks at me. "And we've heard a lot about you, Wanda. How does your family feel about you dating the man behind the most downloaded song on the Internet?"

My phone buzzes in my pocket, and I let out a nervous chuckle. "Oh, my mom's probably a little worried. I'm okay, Mom!" I say, turning my head to look into the closest camera. "I promise! I'm alive, and I'm alright."

"How nice, the girl wants to send a message home to her mother! I guess even fame doesn't change some things, like mothers worrying about their daughters." Johnny pauses. "Well, Griffin, how does your mom feel about the people saying you're in a special marriage with Wanda and your manager, Dev? Because, apparently, your fans are convinced of this fact."

Griffin's laughter is unbridled, surprised but delighted. "Is that what they're saying? I'm *married*?"

"Are you married? To Wanda and Dev? Or maybe just to

one of them?"

"I'm not sure," Griffin says.

"Not sure?" Johnny smiles into one of the cameras. "Now if that's not something a rock star would say, I don't know what is!"

The audience laughs, and at least two or three people let out a wolf whistle.

"Can you give us some details about this special marriage? Your fans want to hear more. Do all three of you share a room…?"

Devon clears his throat. "Griff, do you want to tell them about that big concert we're planning?"

Griffin sits up straighter, nodding. "We're going to create a spectacle, a concert like nothing you've ever seen before. And the concert will be free! So… everyone's invited!"

"Free?" Johnny says, raising an eyebrow in his trademark 'surprise' manner. "You know your fans will happily pay to see you, right? Especially if they think they have a chance of getting in on your special marriage."

"I don't need their money, just their adoration." Griffin stands up, holding his arms out wide. "You're all invited, all of you! Everyone!"

"Where exactly is this free concert?" Johnny asks.

"That will be announced soon. And we will, uh, what's the word? Stream it, online. You will be able to attend this concert, no matter where you live, directly from the comfort of your home, if you can't attend in person." Somehow, I didn't anticipate this whole streaming thing, but there's nothing I can do to stop him from saying it. I just hope he has some way to magically make that happen with his finger-snapping alien powers.

"Ambitious, but exactly what I'd expect from a man who's

taken on the music scene in such a hurry." Johnny motions to us. "And you're about to perform your single for us…?"

"Yes, yes." Griffin waves to his audience and then walks to the other side of the set, where all of his weird equipment has been set up. A few of the bodyguards rush toward him, picking up instruments and holding them at awkward angles.

The music is every bit as over the top, ridiculous, and catchy as on the recorded version that I've heard pouring from stores, cars, and restaurants since Devon and Griffin came into my life, but the 'live performance' is somehow even more colorful and outrageous. I know, even though I can't explain how, that no instruments are being played. Nothing we hear is organic or real; no one's hands make contact with strings or percussion. The Telecaster hanging from Griffin's body by its black strap might as well be a toy, for how useless it is.

The audience goes crazy, Beatles-style, and I see at least four girls sobbing with abandon into their tightly curled hands. Griffin alternatively plays coy and flirtatious with the cameras and the audience, all half smiles and inviting hand gestures, which only serves to ramp up the frenzy even more.

Through all the strangeness, I have to give Griffin one thing—he really does have a great voice. That, at least, isn't manufactured through his alien powers.

As the song fades away, Griffin bows to the audience, and I can see from the pink in his cheeks and the shine in his eyes that he's truly ecstatic. When Johnny approaches to shake his hand and say a few words before the commercial break, Griffin holds his hands up in the symbol of the Origin Collective.

Devon's already on his feet and headed toward Griffin before I can even stand.

"Was I good? Was I good?" Griffin asks, between ear-shattering yawns. "Devon, was I good?"

"You were great. Hey, let's get out of here. You need something to eat." Devon wraps his arm protectively around Griffin's shoulders.

"Do you want to stay and sign a few things?" Johnny asks. "We have some members of the audience who would really like your autograph."

Devon shakes his head, even as Griffin is nodding. "Not this time. Thank you for everything, Johnny, but we need to head out." Devon glances at the bodyguards. "Come on, let's gather everything together and leave."

Griffin pulls away from Devon, bouncing over to his audience with his arms open wide, even as the bodyguards hurriedly snatch up all the strange set equipment. As soon as everything's in hand and ready to go, Devon links arms with Griffin and drags him away. Surprisingly, Griffin doesn't fight him, and thanks to all the scary-looking bodyguards, no one stops us as we make our escape into the night.

Chapter 11

"WAS I GOOD?" GRIFFIN DEMANDS AGAIN AS WE PILE INTO THE CAR. At first, I think he's asking Devon, but then I realize he's looking at me, eyes wide and nervously inquisitive, his hands twisting together in his lap. "Wanda, was I good?"

"Yeah, I guess."

The doors slam shut, and we pull away into traffic.

"You guess? Was something wrong?" There's a note of panic in his voice that I hadn't expected. "What was wrong?"

"Well, I don't know where the music came from, is all."

"Oh." Griffin yawns again, this time for so long that it makes me as well. Did he sleep last night, after we drank? I don't remember him lying beside me, so maybe he didn't. "It came from me, of course."

"Can you elaborate on that a little? I never saw anyone playing any instruments."

Griffin stares at me as if I'm completely bonkers, and then

glances at one of the bodyguards. "I'm hungry," he says in the imperious tone he'd used when we first met. "Stop somewhere and let's get some food." He then switches to his native language and talks quietly into Devon's ear, all nervous hand gestures and furrowed brows. I turn my attention to my phone, which now registers eight missed calls from my mother. Not good.

It isn't until the car lurches to a stop at the curb that I realize where we are. "Wait a minute. Wait a minute, guys!" I say. "Hey, we can't stop here. We need to keep going."

Griffin pulls away from Devon long enough to raise an eyebrow at me. "Why?"

"Because I work just one block down! If my boss sees me, he's going to kill me. He already does everything in his power to make my life miserable as it is, and I really don't want to give him any more ammunition."

"Are you saying this man mistreats you?"

I laugh, the sound bitter. "Hmmm, makes fat jokes about me in front of customers, throws plates at my feet when he's mad, and calls me unrepeatable names? Sexual harassment? That kind of thing? I guess you could call that mistreatment. It's pretty bad when the customers in a Manhattan restaurant are actually nicer than the person you work for."

Griffin slides out of the vehicle. Several of his bodyguards leap after him, shuffling around and glancing in every direction as if they expect someone to pick him off from a sniper post. "Where is this man?" he asks, poking his head back into the car to look at me.

"Uhh… well, over there, the red awning. But we're going to—wait, what are you doing?" I demand as he turns on his heel and marches off toward the restaurant I've worked at since arriving in New York City. "Get back here, Griffin! Do not go in there!"

"I'm hungry," he says, without bothering to slow down. "So we're going to get something to eat."

"What part of my boss is going to kill me did you not understand?" I chase him, but his jaw is set and his head held high. I consider tackling him but that would lead to one or both of us getting run over by taxis, and I really don't want to get run over by taxis.

"Your employer will find it difficult to harm you with six of my father's best bodyguards standing by." He reaches the door and tugs it open. "And impossible, with me there."

As usual, the TVs blare inside the restaurant, and music loops over top of that. The restaurant stinks like burned oil and old trash, a combination I've never quite been able to grow accustomed to. It's a greasy oasis in a city of excess; an establishment that the educated know provides cheap food in an environment entirely opposite of posh.

Griffin stops just in front of the host stand, which is covered this evening by Anna, one of my pleasant but very lazy coworkers. She glances up at us, then back down at her phone, and then back up at us again, her mouth falling open.

"Oh my God. Daisy. Daisy! Where the hell have you been? Jimmy's freaking out. Last night, we were way understaffed, and he's pissed. I've never seen him this pissed," she says, and then shoots a glance at all the bodyguards who have crowded in behind Griffin. "Are we getting audited?"

"Tell him that something happened to me," I say to Anna, grabbing for Griffin's arm. "Let's go. We can eat somewhere else." Any second now, Jimmy might appear, and the scene he'll cause will be too legendary for me to live down. Or survive, maybe.

Just as I think we might be able to make a clean escape, Jimmy busts out of the back. Judging by the fire in his eyes, he already knows I'm here. He makes a beeline for me, his stiff, skinny frame moving altogether too fast and his chewed-gum face pressed into a hateful expression.

"Do you know what happened last night?" he says before he's even reached me. A customer pushes by a couple of Griffin's bodyguards and bumps into me, attempting to get into the restaurant, but even this brave person stops when he sees my boss.

"A-Anna just mentioned that you were understaffed," I say, my voice automatically turning back into the pathetic, shaky, nervous mess it always turns into when I'm faced with Jimmy.

"Understaffed? Is that what she told you? Did she mention we were slammed and that Gary's out with a bad kidney? He's in the hospital, Kirkwood, but even he had the decency to call out. But you just take your fat ass and disappear on me for two days, and then you have the nerve to show back up here? What do you want, your check?"

Several people in the restaurant stop what they're doing to turn and stare, so Jimmy lowers his voice.

"I told you the day I hired you that this is a busy restaurant in a busy city, and I don't put up with whiny little bitches who want the day off so they can play with their friends in Central Park or audition for plays." He shakes his head. "My God. You tell me, '*I don't have a life, I don't have a life*', and then you screw off just when we need you most. I hope you get AIDs."

This is actually one of his better speeches, in comparison to the one he gave my coworker, Laura, when she burned her hand so badly that she had to miss work for five days. But watching someone else get railed on this way is one thing, and getting yelled at in the backroom is another, but standing in front of a bunch of strangers while your evil, misogynistic, abusive boss says awful things to you is something else entirely.

I struggle to think of something to say.

I was abducted by aliens. Everyone should get a free pass when they're abducted by aliens.

Jimmy turns his laser-eyed gaze on Griffin. "Are you waiting for a table?" He motions at Anna, who's been standing by the whole time in silent horror. "Do your job and get these people to a table."

"Wanda," Griffin says. "Do you have anything you want to say to this man?"

Once again, I try to say something, but anxiety has emptied my mind of coherent words and pressed embarrassed tears into the corners of my eyes. I turn to leave, but Griffin reaches out and catches my hand with a surprisingly strong grip.

"No. No, I don't have anything to say to him."

"What would you like him to say to you?" Griffin asks, his eyes still fixed on Jimmy.

I shake my head, wanting nothing more than to just run away. Maybe I'll move back home, at this point. Or I'll tell Devon and Griffin to take me with them back to their planet, where I'll wear a scarf or bag over my head at all times and never speak to anyone again.

"Maybe you, Jimmy, should start by apologizing," Griffin says in a flat tone. The TVs switch off and the music stops playing overhead. The lights flicker once, twice.

Jimmy stands up straighter, as if he's been shocked. His eyes widen a little and his lips move soundlessly for a few seconds, until he finally looks over at Anna. "I'm sorry I've been such a disrespectful asshole. And I'm sorry I've been taking money out of your tips to pay for my rent and cocaine habit."

What?

Anna stares at him. She's said many times that she thought he was taking money from her tips, which was part of the reason she asked to work at the host stand. He's always denied it, of course, and threatened to fire her if she brought it up again.

Jimmy turns around and waves one of his hands in a strange, limp-wristed manner, as if he's a puppet being pulled around by invisible strings. "Everyone, may I have your attention, please?" he says. "My name is James Alan Priestley. I like to degrade my employees to make myself feel better about how ugly and pathetic I am. I frequently threaten my female employees with employment termination if they don't allow me to ogle them, call them names, and make sexual passes at them. I skim off the top of their pay, and I've cheated on my taxes for six years in a row. I have an illegitimate daughter that I pretend isn't mine, even though I know she is. I haven't seen her in two years, though, since I hit her mother for calling me a name."

The customer who had earlier tried to push past me turns and walks back out the door. Everyone else, even the elderly couple in the back corner, has turned to see what's going on.

But Jimmy's not done. He spins around, looking at me. "Daisy, I've called you names and made jokes about your ass, but it's actually because I find you very attractive and you won't give me the time of day. The only way to make myself feel better about that is to make you feel worthless, and I've always secretly hoped that one day I'll bully you into letting me fulfill my sick fantasy on you, right back there in my office."

My face feels like it's on fire, but I can't help feeling a little justified in my silent fears about his intentions.

"To apologize for my terrible behavior, no one will have to pay for their meals tonight. I vow to never say another disrespectful thing to my employees and never steal from them again. For now, I'm going to go sit in my office and think about what an awful bastard I've been." With that, Jimmy walks away.

A lot of people stand up and leave the restaurant, but Anna just stands frozen at the host station for a while before finally looking at me.

"Do you know what just happened…?"

I shake my head as Griffin shudders and the TVs switch back on.

"No idea! No idea at all," I say.

Devon steps forward then. "Anna, might you please give us a table? We're quite hungry," he says, and Anna jumps right to it. I've never seen her with so much spring in her step as she leads us to a booth table and lays out our menus.

"I dunno what you did, Daisy, but that was incredible!" she hisses, prancing off to talk to some of our astonished coworkers.

I slide into one side of the booth, and Griffin and Devon slip into the other side. Griffin is still snickering, though his delight is now tempered with aching yawns. "Thank you," I say, though some part of me is afraid I'll wake up in bed, in my apartment, and all of this will have been the strangest dream ever. "How did you do that?"

Griffin peers across the table at me, incredibly amused with himself. "I just found all of his ugly secrets and made him feel like sharing them with the world," he says, which sets off a fit of smug, quiet laughter. He pokes Devon in the side, but Devon only smiles.

"You need to eat, Griff."

"Yes, something nutritionally bankrupt, strange, and delicious, please!" Griffin says. "Wanda, what should I eat?"

"Uhhhh…" I turn my head down to the menu, looking at

it with fresh eyes. Serving subpar food is different from eating it with visitors from another planet, and my mind is distracted by the events of the last few moments. Finally, after senselessly staring at the menu for what feels like forever, I notice the burgers. "Our burgers are pretty good, I guess. It's a really American thing to eat. Well, I guess it's a very human thing to eat."

"Good, good, that sounds good. And here's our waitress."

The aforementioned waitress is a Brooklyn girl named Phoebe. Jimmy likes to poke fun at her for being too skinny. After Phoebe expresses her hearty enthusiasm for what just happened with Jimmy, she takes a better look at the bodyguards who are awkwardly standing around our booth, and then at each of us sitting at the table. "Wait, are you Griffin Valentino?"

"Yes, of course."

"Oh my God. This day just keeps getting weirder." She clears her throat. "Sorry! Sorry. We just don't get a lot of famous people in here. They tend to avoid us like the plague." She wields her notepad and pen. "What would you like to eat, Mr. Valentino?"

"I'll have whatever Wanda suggests," Griffin says, motioning at me.

"Wanda? Your name is Wanda? I thought your name was Daisy."

"My name is Daisy, but my uh, my professional name is Wanda," I say, because at this point, I can't really argue any longer. "We'll all take a house burger each. Load one of them with everything on it. Griffin's really hungry." I glance across the table at Devon, who gives me a grateful nod in response. "Is there any way you could make them on the fly?"

"Sure, sure. Be back soon!"

When I turn my attention back to Griffin, he's lying on his

side on the booth seat.

"Is he asleep?" I ask, and Devon nods. "He's been yawning a lot today. Did he stay up all night last night?"

"No. He slept in my room—like a rock, to be exact." Judging by the bodyguards' body language and Dev's nervous manner, something is going on. "He's used too much," Devon says quietly, as if he knows what I'm thinking. "Way too much, and he's exhausted himself. I hope he's not used it up entirely." Devon motions for one of the bodyguards to lean down, and he whispers something to him, before looking at me again. "As soon as we eat, he needs to go back to the hotel and rest. Once he's rested, he'll be fine, but he's... he's got to stop before he runs out."

"Runs out of what?"

Devon sighs, giving me a pointed look.

"Of his finger-snapping power, you mean?"

"We can only do so much of that without recharging. It's not infinite."

"Oh. Well... will sleeping recharge him?"

"Home recharges us. Resting will just make him feel alright again; it won't give him back his abilities. Until he's home, he'll have to be more careful, and he won't want to admit that." Dev sighs again. "Griff lost our home stone, which renews his energy, just after we landed, so we don't even have that. We only brought one, since I don't have sensitivities and don't really need one. He doesn't like to... well, anyway."

"No more finger-snapping," I whisper, wondering if they're in more danger than I'd anticipated. Somehow, I'd begun to count on Griffin's magical ability to make things happen whenever he wanted them to. "What about you? You said you don't lean toward that stuff, but can you do it at all? If you needed to?"

Devon shakes his head and doesn't say anything again until Phoebe arrives with our meal. The noise of clattering plates or the smell of food must rouse Griffin, because he sits up and rubs his eyes with the heel of one of his hands, yawning.

"Ah, sorry, I'm tired from my wonderful musical performance," he says, dropping his gaze to his oversized burger. "What's this?"

"Just eat it," Devon and I say at the same time.

Griffin watches how I pick up my burger and follows suit, taking a big bite and then thoughtfully chewing. "Hmm… this is good," he says. "It has many tastes all at once."

Devon nods. "We don't have anything like this back home."

"It's big, isn't it?" Griffin says.

"Yeah, massive."

It looks like a standard burger to me, but then, my French friend once told me that American food portions looked big to him, so who knows what they look like to aliens.

We're all munching away, and I've just remembered that maybe I should offer the bodyguards something to eat, when someone turns the sound volume on the restaurant's main television set up. Up, up, way up—loud enough to hear the jingle for breaking news—and then something about odd phenomena in the sky, a purple, yellow, and red streak of light that scientists can't explain.

"Wait, what was that?" Devon asks, dropping his half-eaten burger to his plate. He stands up from the booth and Griffin follows him, both of them drawing closer to the TV, huddling close against each other. After a few seconds of hesitation, I join the small crowd that's gathered around.

"This footage was captured by a London student, just three hours ago," the reporter says, and then the screen flashes to something that looks eerily like ripples emanating downward from a bruise in the sky.

"Looks like a lava lamp," someone says.

"Or maybe it's aliens," someone else suggests, and everyone laughs.

I wonder if Griffin's dad has popped by for a visit to check up on him. *Oh!* Or maybe the evil future wife has scheduled a date. How awkward would that be? I can't even imagine.

"You guys expecting some visitors?" I ask Griffin quietly, in a lighthearted tone. "Or did you order something through the mail and they're special-delivering it?"

When Devon and Griffin turn to look at me, I know something's wrong. Very, very wrong.

Chapter 12

WE'VE BARELY STEPPED OUT ONTO THE COLD SIDEWALK WHEN DEV wheels around on Griffin, the smile he'd held on his face while we said goodbye to Anna, Phoebe, and some fans in the restaurant long gone now. "We're not staying there tonight," he says to Griffin.

"Staying, how do you mean?"

"At the hotel. We're going somewhere different and we'll have all our belongings sent over."

"That's a bit daft, isn't it? After all, everyone knows we're at the other hotel. What if someone wants to get hold of me for a television appearance or to star in a movie, or what if they want to nominate me for an award?" Griffin asks, fluffing up his dark hair with one hand.

"Did you hear what you just said, you stupid arse? Everyone knows you're at the hotel!"

Griffin glowers at him, spreading his feet to widen his

97

stance. "Yes."

"So if someone wants to come along and shoot you through the ears, they'll bloody well just follow the fans right up to your bedroom!" Devon says. "We're getting a different hotel, Griff, and we're not telling anyone where it is."

"The groupies like to know where their idol is staying."

"The groupies can stuff themselves. I swear to the gods, if you tell a single soul where we're staying, I'll knock you out and send you home without hesitation. And that includes mentioning it on television!"

At this, Griffin springs forward, propelling himself until he's chest to chest with Devon. "We're not going home."

"Yeah, well, we might have to," Devon says, his voice quieter, but he doesn't tear his gaze from Griffin's or make any move to step away from him.

"What's going on?" I ask, but they continue to stare at each other in silence. "Should we maybe talk about this in the car...?"

"I'm not going home until I've succeeded in my mission," Griffin says to Devon, as if I'm not even there.

"Or what? Or until someone kills you?"

"I dare them to try."

"It wouldn't be too hard, considering you lost our home stone and now you've nearly exhausted your energy supply with posturing and running around making pretty girls fall at your feet, like you hadn't learned anything at all with Zorga."

Griffin shoves Devon. "That's not true! I told you, I didn't lose the damn stone. I never took it off, not even once."

"Then where is it? Where is it, Griffin?"

"I didn't lose the bloody thing. Someone's *taken* it from me," Griffin says, shoving Devon again.

"We're both helpless here, and if someone's come for you,

it won't take them long to find you," Devon says, shoving him back. "If you'd spend a bit more time thinking about that and less time putting on silly costumes and kissing strangers, we might actually have a chance."

This time, Griffin plants his hands on Devon's shoulders and shoves him hard enough to send him back a few feet. Devon regains his balance and charges for Griffin, his right fist swinging for his friend's face. Griffin ducks and tackles him around the waist, sending both of them crashing to the sidewalk.

"Stop it!" I yell, but I don't dare attempt to pull them apart.

Dev manages to roll them both over to put himself on top of Griffin, but only for a few seconds. Griffin catches Devon's neck in a lock, forcing him over onto his back. They kick and struggle against each other, landing blows, and go on this way until I see the bright flashes of cameras and hear the voices of everyone who's surrounded us to gawk.

For some reason, the bodyguards still haven't stepped in to stop Griffin and Devon from fighting, but seeing paparazzi cameras and wayward cell phones held up for pictures spurns me to action.

I rush forward, heart hammering away in my throat, and grab Griffin's arm before he can do any more damage to his friend. He tries to shake me off, but I hold on too tight. "Get up right now," I say. "Right now, do you hear me? Get up!"

One of the bodyguards steps forward, trying to pull me away, but Griffin obeys me and stands up.

"Leave Wanda alone," he says, breathing hard. He wipes blood from his mouth, thick blood that looks black, and then offers his hand to Devon. He swats his hand away, standing up on his own and crossing his arms protectively over his chest. "Where's the car? Someone get the car."

"We're not staying at that hotel tonight," Dev says, and this time, no one argues with him.

As we walk together to the car, in a bundle of frayed nerves, questions and camera flashes follow us. Griffin climbs inside first, with Devon right behind him, and then I follow, plopping myself between Griffin and Devon, just in case. The very instant the last of our entourage has sat down, we pull away from the curb.

"What's going on?" I say before anyone else can say anything. Griffin turns his face away from me, staring out the tinted window. "Devon?"

"That thing you saw on the television, that's likely an indication that someone else from our world is here," Devon says, with a tremendous, exasperated sigh.

"Is it Griffin's dad?"

"Anterys wouldn't come here to save his life. No, he told us we were thoroughly on our own through this; it's all part of this damned wager. If someone else from our world is here, they've got nefarious intentions. That much I'm certain."

"We don't know that," Griffin says, without turning his head.

Devon presses his lips together and lets out a noisy breath through his nose, shaking his head.

"By nefarious, uh, well… how nefarious exactly do you mean?" I ask, though Griffin's half-dozen bodyguards that seem to appear and disappear at random would indicate a pretty high level of danger just on their own.

Griffin shifts in his seat, still staring out the window. "They want to kill me."

Oh, that is not good at all.

"I won't let them do it," Devon mutters. "If it means we go home, then that's what we'll do. I won't let them kill you,

Griffin."

"What's the point? We go home, I'll marry that beastly woman, you'll get sent to the Fifth City, and then what? Nothing's solved. Everyone's still hungry and angry. One of these days, they'll just finish the job anyway."

Devon winces. "Don't say that."

Neither of them speaks for a long few seconds, and I'm just about to say something to kill the silence, when Griffin turns his head to us again.

"I can't lose the wager," he says. "None of us can. If we go to war again, there won't be anything left this time."

Though Dev hesitates, he finally sighs and turns his head, leaning around me to meet Griffin's gaze. "We have to be safe about it, though. I want you in one piece when your father has to admit he lost to you."

"Us. Lost to us," Griffin corrects. "I'm sorry I hit you."

"You should be, you idiot. I clocked you good," Dev says, a hint of humor finally trickling back into his voice. His posture relaxes a little and his eyes flick between Griffin and me. "Got what you deserved, pushing me around."

The thick, black blood has mostly stopped oozing from Griffin's mouth, thankfully, but quite a bit of it's smeared on his hand. "Is it your lip?" I ask.

"Yeah. Dev's a peace lover, but he's scrappy when he wants to be."

"Not the first time I've proved that," Dev says.

"Are you reminding me that you once almost broke your prince's nose?"

"I did break it, and I'm still not sorry, either."

"That's not true. You felt very guilty; I thought you might even cry." Griffin raises his voice for the driver. "Oy! Take us to a new hotel! And then someone needs to go secure our belongings. I want my clothes."

Our new hotel's a bit less posh than the other one, but when Griffin requests someone send a record player to our room, the man behind the desk barely hesitates in promising to send one up.

"Is there anything else I might get for you this evening, Mr. Valentino?" the man asks, and Griffin leans up on tiptoe, rests his elbow against the tall counter, and peers importantly over the top of his sunglasses.

"Can you send up some of those hot dogs from the street vendors? Two or three? Or, maybe five?" he asks in a quiet voice.

"No, we don't need any of those," Dev says, shaking his head. "We do, however, expect to remain under the radar during our stay, from fans or media or anyone else who might ask after us, should they catch a hint we're here. Discretion will be generously rewarded."

The man smiles. "That's not a problem, sir." He eyes Griffin's face again. "There's a full first aid kit in the room…"

"What about David Bowie?" Griffin asks. "D'yanno where David Bowie is? I need him to sign something for me."

"I'm afraid I don't, sir, but perhaps I can make a few phone calls."

"That won't be necessary," Dev says, flashing a toothy smile. He links arms with Griffin, tugging him away from the counter before he can request anything else.

Chapter 13

No sooner have we arrived in our new suite than Devon claims one of the rooms, retiring to it and closing the door without a word. At first, I think perhaps he just needs to collect his thoughts, but then I hear him speaking quietly in his language from the other side of the door.

If Griffin hears it, he doesn't say anything. He circles his room a few times, poking about and peering at the artwork hanging on the walls, and then turns his attention to one of the silent bodyguards. "Go get our things from our other hotel. Make sure you don't leave anything behind, understand? I want all of my clothes, and my Bowie record. They're sending a record player up and I need to listen to Bowie for inspiration, as I plan my concert."

The bodyguard nods and shuffles to the door without a word, followed by one of his companions.

A quiet buzzing noise, emanating from my purse, captures

my attention, and I cross the room quickly to extract my cell phone. *Mom and Dad* flashes across the screen, and I sigh.

"What's that?" Griffin asks, perched on the edge of the room's writing desk.

"My mom keeps trying to call me. She's probably really worried," I mumble, weighing the phone in my hand. I can answer it and face my mother's hysterical blabbering and fear, or I can put it off a little longer. Of course, the latter will only insure even more blabbering fear for the future. "She worries a lot about things—"

Griffin crosses the room so quickly that I barely even register that he's moved, and he snatches the phone away from me. He slides it open with ease, placing it at his ear. "Hello, hello? Hello? Kirkwood mother? Hello, yes, this is Griffin Valentino. Did you ever consider naming your daughter Wanda?" He bites into his lip, a smile creeping over his face. I try to snatch the phone back from him, but he leaps away from me easily, his footing graceful as he dodges any attempts I make to recover the phone. "Yes? I knew it! Ha-ha!"

I try again to retrieve the phone, but he sidesteps me.

"She's fine, yes, I assure you. She's a wonderful girl, very helpful and very smart. And so beautiful!" Griffin says, and then pauses. "Oh, yes, I did. We share a bed so my friend can have his own space. He's quite fussy, you know, not because of a bad back or anything, but he likes having his space. I invade his space whenever possible, but during a trip like this, so far from home, it wouldn't be very kind of me." Griffin snickers. "Yes, what? No, don't worry about that; my bodyguards look after all of us. What...?"

Growing desperate at this point, I throw my full body weight into him, knocking him back against the wall and grappling for the phone. Griffin lets out a quiet puff of air from the collision with the wall and my body slamming into his, but only responds by looping his arm around my waist.

"Give me the phone!" I say between clenched teeth, finally managing to pry it away from him. "Mom?"

"Daisy! Daisy, how on earth did you meet a rock star?"

I almost drop the phone. "Uhh, what? Mom, I'm okay. Don't worry."

"Of course I won't, he told me he's taking good care of you. But how did you do it? I thought you said you'd only seen a couple of reality TV stars since you moved to the city!"

Griffin smiles smugly at me, still holding me around the waist. I untangle myself from him and cross the room, phone pressed to my ear. "Aren't you worried...?" I whisper, and my mother laughs.

"Darling, he promised his bodyguards will take good care of you. Will you get to meet Ryan Seacrest? If you meet him, you have to tell him how much I like him."

This is insane. My mom and I haven't had one conversation since I moved that didn't involve her suggesting I buy new locks, talking to me about ratings for various pepper sprays, or relaying news stories she heard about dead bodies found in dumpsters.

"Mom."

"Griffin seems like a very nice young man, though I hope you're being safe. Having a baby with a rock star is a tricky business, what with all those months on the road and the groupies."

"*Mom!*"

"Don't be afraid to remind him about protection. In this day and age, we're allowed to speak up about that kind of thing."

From across the room, Griffin snickers, raising one hand to his face and rubbing his eyes. "Ask her about your name,

Wanda."

"You know, I think I have a coupon," Mom says. "Not for the flavored ones, but the regular ones work just as well."

"Mom, please stop talking about this." I shoot Griffin a nasty look. "What did Griffin ask you? About my name, I mean?"

"Oh, well, he wondered about us calling you Wanda. We were going to name you Wanda, but your father vetoed it at the last minute, because he thought it sounded a bit dated."

Griffin walks by me, smirking.

"Alright, Mom, look... I don't know when we can talk again, so please don't worry if I don't answer," I say. "I'll call you when I have a chance."

"Call me if you meet Ryan Seacrest!"

I slide the phone closed.

"Well now, Wanda, I guess I was right about you, wasn't I?" Griffin asks, sprawling out on his back on the king-sized bed.

"The only thing you were right about is that my mom wanted to give me a dumb name." I cast him another dark look, but he just smiles in return. "Aside from that, you were wrong about everything else. You didn't even want me along at first, remember?"

With that, Griffin's smile slips a little. "Who do you think chose you for our human escort, Wanda?"

"Devon, obviously."

"Wrong." Griffin shrugs, holding my gaze for a few long seconds. "But speaking of Dev, I think he's had quite enough time in there on his own." Griffin disappears from view and reappears across the room. He knocks on his friend's door and doesn't stop until Dev finally opens it. "What've you been in here doing, anyway?"

Dev's voice drops to an undertone, and they speak

back and forth in their language. Judging by Dev's guarded expression and Griffin's tensed shoulders, they can't be discussing something pleasant.

I shove my phone back into my purse and wander closer to them. "Did something happen?"

Dev looks between Griffin and me, as if considering if he wants to tell me anything, but he finally relents and nods. "I've just spoken with our contact back at the landing site, and he confirmed it wasn't anyone friendly. So it's either nothing or it's…" Dev stops, sifting his fingers through his golden hair. "We'll need to be careful. Very careful."

"We'll need to set up our concert event, is what we'll need to do. The sooner we get in touch with the Origin Collective, the sooner we can gather some helpful information and go shove it in the Emperor President's face," Griffin says.

Dev lets out a heavy sigh, closing his eyes. "You're running short on persuasion, Griff, and probably healing, too. Do you think you can handle something like a concert?"

"I'm not running low, look." Griffin raises a hand to his injured lip, brushing his pale fingers over the wound.

"You don't have to do that; it's no time to show off," Devon says. "We can just use the first aid kit the humans—err, the hotel staff—left for us."

Griffin motions at Dev with his free hand, as if to shut him up, but as the seconds click by and nothing happens, I can see the slightest twinge of fear in Griffin's eyes. Then, all at once, the busted lip heals up, the swelling disappears, and he lets out a little sigh.

"See? Good as ever," he says. "It's always harder to heal yourself, that's all."

"Griff."

"Don't use that tone with me, or we'll end up in another

scuffle," Griffin says, but the look they exchange is far from violent. "I'm fine! I want my bloody David Bowie record, though."

"What if you didn't have to use your finger-snappy powers at all?" I interject, and both of them look at me with something like amusement. "No, I'm serious! You want to be a real pop star, you want to dress like one, and feel like one. Why don't you learn to actually play the music? The instruments, I mean."

"Real pop stars don't play instruments. They stand behind a microphone, wear great clothes, and everyone wants to be them or kiss them. Or," Griffin says, a big smile filling his face, "sleep with them."

"Maybe you should be a rock star, then. Rock stars are better, anyway. You know, like David Bowie."

"How's Griffin going to do that? He doesn't know what he's doing!" Dev says.

"I'll teach him. I'm not very good, but... well, there's the Internet for everything I don't know."

Dev bites into his lower lip, staring at Griffin. "I dunno, Daisy."

"She's right. I can learn! I can be a rock star!"

"Yeah," I say. "And we'll set up a Twitter account so you can update your fans on progress for the upcoming concert without revealing your location. You can even post pictures of yourself and answer their questions there, so they feel connected, and you won't even have to use your magic. Or whatever it's called."

At this, Dev seems to relax a little. "Alright, we'll try that."

The bodyguards finally return with our belongings; Griffin rushes across the room with his arms held wide, demanding someone unearth his Bowie record.

I want to ask Dev more questions, mainly about this other alien who's showed up on my planet, but he rushes off to sort through the belongings with Griffin. Before long, the two of them are laughing uproariously and playfully shoving each other around, talking in their language. Griffin shoves Devon a little too hard, causing him to fall into a small dresser and upset a lamp. The lamp stops just short of hitting the ground and levitates in place, a whisper away from shattering to a million pieces, and Devon regains his feet to pluck the lamp from its airy perch and place it back on the dresser.

"You little arse," Devon says, the only warning Griffin needs to make a run for it, apparently. Griffin darts away, jumping on top of and then over our bed, narrowly preventing himself from falling onto a dresser, and then hiding himself behind one of the bodyguards. When this doesn't halt Devon's determined approach, Griffin books it across the room again, this time grabbing hold of me from behind, as if I'm a human shield. "Well, that's heroic of you, Griff. Hide behind Daisy."

I can feel Griffin's laughter vibrating through his body even before I can hear it. He releases his hold on my arms and steps out from behind me, making it all of a step before Devon charges him and knocks him clear to the floor.

"Is this really a good idea?" I ask finally, as they grapple with each other on the carpet. "Griffin, you just fixed your lip, you know."

Just as I think they might kill each other, Griffin manages to pin Devon down and hold him in place long enough to assert his authority, and then climbs to his feet with a smug expression plastered on his face. He picks up a bag with the clothes he's bought me, holding it out in offering.

"Don't you like the tops I got you?" he asks, probably because one of the sparkliest bras sits directly on top of the bag, in all its lacy pink, bedazzled glory. "I was assured they're the finest breast decorations that your planet has to offer."

A slight blush creeps up my face. Usually, the only two people in my life who talk about my breasts are my mother—worrying if I show too much cleavage—and one of my roommates—making oddly specific and somewhat hurtful analogies about my small chest. "I'll try them on later."

"But don't you like them?" Griffin continues, dangling the bag between us, so I snatch it away from him.

"You need to get some rest," I say. "It's getting late. Wrestling like a seven-year-old boy on sugar isn't going to help anything, especially when you fell asleep in a busy restaurant earlier."

Dev picks up a few bags from the floor and stifles a yawn of his own as he stands up. "I think she's right, Griff. You should get some rest. We all should. If we're in danger, we'll need our wits about us." He walks over to me, planting a quick kiss on my cheek, before saying something stern in his language to Griffin and retreating to his room.

The bodyguards shift around a bit, deciding who will stay awake and stand guard, and who will sleep. I finally feel as if I can turn the lights down in the room and get ready for bed. Despite all the excitement and tension that the boys experienced today, I've experienced just as much stress. Meeting Kyran at the library, making an appearance on a television show, sitting by for Griffin's first musical performance, and then the whole scene at the restaurant with Jimmy... Never mind Griffin and Devon's fight and the news about a possible new alien visitor...

I'm exhausted.

Placing the bag of clothes and underwear on the floor by the bed, I boldly climb up and claim my spot on the right side. When I turn my head to seek out Griffin's gaze, I find him watching me with a raised eyebrow and a half smile.

"Get over here and go to sleep," I say, with an unusual amount of authority. And, somewhat surprisingly, he obeys me, going so far as to leave behind all of his belongings without looking back.

In fact, he's only looking at me, which is a bit unnerving once he's joined me on the bed and stretched out on his side. We stare at each other until I start to feel a bit warm and uncomfortably pleased. No amount of denial could tell me I don't find him enchanting when he's so close, staring at me, especially as the remaining light dies out, seemingly on its own.

In the darkness, he's illuminated by everything that makes him foreign to this planet, to my life, so I look away from him.

"You still won't look into me, Wanda," he whispers across the slight space between our bodies.

"I don't understand what you mean."

"Where I come from, we're not as senseless and hurried as you are. We're tired. We're angry and hungry. But some things, the beautiful things, and love above all, that's sacred. Don't you look into each other here?"

"Eye contact?"

"No. No, it's… it's more than that, I guess. You don't do it?"

"Most of us try not to make eye contact at all, especially in this city," I say, thinking of advice I'd been given soon after moving to Manhattan. I'd held dear to it ever since, avoiding connections with other people whenever possible, especially of the eye-contact variety.

"How do you ever know anyone at all then?"

"I dunno. We ask questions when we go on dates. And then we just kind of accept the person and move in with them or move on."

Griffin lets out a little 'hmmmf' noise. "But what about lovers? I understand that pop stars take part in meaningless sex, but surely, the rest of you don't? Surely, you don't, Wanda?"

I shift my pillows around a little, feeling nervous. "Earlier you said it wasn't Devon who chose me," I say, hoping this will effectively steer the conversation in a more comfortable direction than my lack of a love life. "Are you trying to say it was you?"

"Of course it was. You feel our similarity, don't you? Our heritage?"

Now I have no idea what he's talking about. "Uhhh. No?"

He considers this, turning onto his back. I'm sorry for the glow of his eyes to direct elsewhere, but I don't dare say so.

"Before we exist in the way we do now, we exist elsewhere. We don't remember it, of course, but sometimes we know that someone we meet came from the same place we did. Someone's made from the same spirit matter. It's why we're drawn together. You don't seek out that similarity here?"

"We usually seek out... well, I don't know. A sense of humor? Money? Good hair? We're not looking for magical spirit stardust."

"Odd."

Even though I don't want to admit it, the idea is a bit interesting, even if nothing else. I shift around and clear my throat. "So you think you and I are made of the same magical stardust or something?"

"I believe so," he says. "It's a romantic notion, but I've always thought it was rather beautiful."

"Was Devon made from it too?"

Griffin snickers. "Devon? Nah, Devon and me, we're a different kind of match. After my mother died, my father went round gathering up the kids of nobles and politicians so he could find someone for me to play with, and I didn't like any of them. He just wanted me to bugger off from moping around him all the time while he was busy. But then there was Devon, sitting by himself in the corner with a disgusted look on his face, so I asked him a question and he told me off. We've been best mates ever since."

At this, I can't help smiling a little. "That's probably a better match than any silly stardust."

"I'm lucky, that's for certain. You know, one time..." he says, trailing off. After a few seconds, I realize he's once again fallen asleep on me, this time with his mouth still hanging open, so I sigh and pull the covers up over him.

One of these days, I'll write a memoir called, *I Tucked an Alien Prince into Bed.* You know, after we put on a massive concert event, get in contact with the Origin Collective, and send Griffin and Devon back home with good news, that is.

After I teach Griffin to play real music...

Chapter 14

My friend, Kammie, has a recording studio in Greenwich Village; the studio is cramped, ugly, and cheap because someone was murdered there about ten years ago, or maybe it's cheap because the walls are painted a sick sort of pink and green color, but whatever. It works.

Kammie meets us on the third floor, at the top of a set of narrow, death-threatening stairs, and opens a door that looks like it should belong to a bathroom in a building that's been bombed. The misspelled neon graffiti on the door is actually the most attractive part of the entrance, no exaggeration. But Kammie's all smiles, her curly, red hair pinned on top of her head, and she radiates early morning coffee-fueled energy as she bounces around us.

"There's this place downstairs that sells coffee for fifty cents," she says as a greeting. She eyeballs Griffin and Devon, and then smiles at me. "If you want to go get some, you'll probably puke, but it shakes you up. I didn't sleep last night. It's stronger than my medicinal energy-boosting tea."

"Well, I think you look very refreshed for not sleeping," Devon says, his English drawl a bit more pronounced and even posher than usual. "I might take you up on that coffee, if you'd show me where it is…?"

Kammie's nervous energy crashes to a halt as she meets Dev's gaze. "Sure, sure, of course. I'd love to show you."

Griffin snorts loudly and pats his best friend on the shoulder once before wheeling away to poke around the tiny studio. He picks up a guitar, bass, and drumstick in turn, as if to weigh each one and decide which he likes best.

"Oh!" Kammie says. "Daisy, you won't believe who stopped by this morning." She doesn't wait for me to guess. "Lillian Gale! Lillian Gale stopped by, looked at the studio, and said she might rent it out for a couple of days for a project she's working on with Leonidas Bondi. Do you even know what I'd do if Lillian Gale of Juicy Bed decided to record something here?" She pauses and snickers. "Well, I'd be able to pay the rent, for one thing. Speaking of, you're going to be able to throw a bit in the jar, right? I wouldn't think of charging you a full fee, of course, but a few bucks would be great."

"Griffin's going to pay for it," I say, and Griffin just removes a small wad of bills from his pocket and tosses them absentmindedly in my direction. The money falls at my feet, so I quickly scoop it up and hand it over to Kammie. "See?"

Kammie stares at the money, fanning it out and gazing at the hundred dollar bills as if she's never seen them before. "So who are you two, anyway? Daisy said you're a new band."

"Oh, well, actually, Griffin here is the star," Dev says, twirling a pen though his fingers. I've never seen him do this before… or smile so mischievously. "I'm his manager. The brains and business side of the thing, you know."

"Yeah, we're sort of in need of a band," I add, noting the sexual tension radiating between Kammie and Dev. Not a good time, when there's so much to do. "Think you can help us, Kammie?"

"What do you need? Bassist? Drummer?"

Griffin chooses that moment to clatter around on one of the snare drums, sounding a bit like a little boy on Christmas morning with his first drum kit.

"Uhhh... actually, I'm not sure yet. Depends on what he decides he's best at."

Kammie narrows her eyes, crossing her arms over her chest. "This seems a bit odd. He's a musician and you want to use the studio, but I have to be secretive about it and he doesn't even know what instrument he's good at yet? And there's a bunch of scary guys in suits standing around outside the door?"

Dev and I exchange a glance. "Griffin's a recovering pop singer," I say. "He wants to be a proper rock star, though, so I've encouraged him to learn an instrument and get a real band. Before this, he was playing with all... uhhh... synth. You know, piping music in."

I've known Kammie for a few years, having connected with her through the Internet and then later meeting her in person when I moved to the city. I know she, like me, respects artists who write and play their own music, but I also know she has a particular aversion for what she considers to be 'pop crap,' so her distaste for the artificial in music will outweigh her inquisitive nature. Thankfully, I'm right, and she just waltzes toward the door, crooking a finger in Dev's direction.

"Why don't you come with me, manager, and we'll go get that coffee," she says.

As much as I like Kammie, I'm all right with the idea of

her leaving, especially if she's going to get all lovey-dovey on Dev. I need to be able to concentrate on finding out if Griffin has any musical ability in that skinny little alien body of his.

"Get some coffee for me too!" I say. "Oh, and for Griffin! Take however long you need!" I push Dev toward Kammie, and he shoots me a huge grin just before disappearing with my friend.

Huh. Even aliens love redheads.

Griffin, meanwhile, stations himself behind the drum kit and makes a terrible clattering while twisting his face into what he probably considers to be serious rock expressions. I shake my head as I approach him and reach out for one of his slender wrists. "Stop, stop. I don't think you're a drummer."

"But I like it!"

I want to say he's god-awful at it, but that might cause a scene. "You'll have a hard time singing from behind a drum kit," I hedge. "Besides, don't you want everyone to be able to see your great clothes? You shouldn't hide fashion sense like yours behind a drum."

Griffin vaults out from behind the set, drumsticks flying haphazardly over his shoulder in his wake.

His attempts on a keyboard are promising, but he seems to give up on that rather quickly. "What's this?" he asks, picking up a banjo. "Why does this guitar look so strange?"

"That's a banjo. You should try this instead." I pick up a blue Ibanez electric guitar and offer it to him. He stares at it for a few seconds before abandoning the banjo and snatching the guitar away from me. At first, I think we might really be screwed, but then I hear something remotely music-like coming from the guitar. "Do you want a pick?"

He shakes his head and continues noodling about on the guitar.

Maybe he'll be an unnatural guitar genius. Maybe he'll turn into full-blown rock star after only a few moments of thoughtful concentration and alien magic. Maybe I won't even have to look up instructional videos on the Internet or embarrass myself with my minimal guitar knowledge.

After about fifteen minutes of him playing around with the guitar, I realize that's not going to happen. He's got some natural talent, but it's definitely going to need nurturing and instructional videos on YouTube. Oh well.

"All the best rock stars play guitar," Griffin says without looking up.

"Most of them, yeah."

He fishes his small, phone-like device out of his back pocket. "Here, take a holopic." I turn it around and around in my hands, trying to find anything like a power button. "How does this work? What is this thing, anyway?"

Griffin impatiently taps the top of it, and then presses his finger against the screen. It lights up and I see a fuzzy, moving image on the screen, something that looks like a field of glowing flowers, all of them swaying gently back and forth. Before I can ask him about it, Griffin hits a small, pink spot in the center of the screen. All at once, the display switches to what appears to be camera mode. "There now, take the holopic. Make it a good one."

Surprisingly, his device is quite similar to a cell phone, complete with a clicking noise once the photo's been taken. Of course, once it shows up as a preview, I realize the differences in our technology. His 'photo' is more like a 3D gif, rising off the device and playing in a loop.

"That one's alright, I suppose," he says, taking it away and turning it around on me. Before I know what's happening, he takes a picture of me. "Hmmm. That's better. Very nice, Wanda."

I watch as a little holographic gif of my surprised face floats above his device. "You wanted a picture of me?"

Griffin pushes the device back into his pocket and returns to playing around with the guitar. "Of course I do; don't be daft. You're my friend, aren't you?"

Warmth creeps up my neck and into my face. I have to smile a little, even though I try to hide it from him. "Errr, speaking of friends, I wonder where Kammie and Dev are? They've been gone a long time."

"Probably in the stairwell, snogging," Griffin says with an amused snort. "He fancies her, I can tell. He's never very subtle about it when he's got his eye on a woman."

Great. "Maybe we should go find them? I need to ask Kammie about finding you a band."

With immense reluctance, Griffin lays the guitar down and follows me out of the studio, then rushes in front of me so he can walk first. He trails his fingers along the cool, graffiti-splattered wall during our descent back to the first level of the building, casting a few half smiles over his shoulder at me here and there.

Griffin's bodyguards fall into step behind us, their loud footsteps making them sound like an army.

"Kammie?" I call out as we reach the bottom of the last staircase. The first floor of the building looks a bit like a murder scene, but thankfully, Kammie and Dev are very much alive, standing close together by an oversized coffee machine. It's the sort of coffee machine you might find in a post-apocalyptic wasteland.

"Daisy, Daisy! Come get a cup of this stuff! There's a little jar, and you just leave your money in it. Make sure to leave your money in it, though, or else a leprechaun or a thug might beat you up," she says, waving me over. As I approach, I can't help noticing her dark pink lipstick has migrated all over Dev's neck and shirt collar. "I was just telling Devy about how you can pour coffee grounds on soil, and it's like magic."

I shake my head with a little sigh. "Kammie."

"No, it's true! This isn't a myth; it's a scientific fact. Some of my friends conducted a big experiment with coffee grounds and determined that the whole thing is completely true." She takes a sip of coffee, and then waves her cup around in Dev's direction. "So, Devy tells me that you guys were on Johnny Bardo's show last night! I'm gonna have to look it up when I get home tonight. Daisy, I told you that you'd get a really great job in the music industry, if you tried hard enough! Good thing you happened to be at that swanky party with them and introduced yourself."

Ah, so this must be the version Devon has told her. I force a smile and nod. "So lucky, right? Almost like aliens orchestrated it."

Griffin pokes a finger into my back just hard enough to hurt, and then shoots me a thin-lipped warning smile as he takes his place at my side.

"We'll need to use your studio for a few days," Griffin says to Kammie. "Don't worry about compensation. I have a lot of money."

"I noticed that. So, are you an heir or something? Oooh, or a runaway duke? Do you still have dukes in England? Earls? Do you know Prince Harry? Do you know Tom Hiddleston?"

"We also request your assistance in acquiring a band. I need the best of the best, because we're going to put on a concert event like the universe has never seen. If you can contact David Bowie, that would be helpful."

Kammie laughs. "David Bowie? Look, the most famous thing about my studio is that someone got stabbed eight times in it. I don't know David Bowie. I know a lot of second-rate bands from Queens."

"Doesn't *anyone* know David Bowie?" Griffin demands, but after rolling his eyes dramatically, he sighs and continues. "Anyway, I suppose we'll accept whoever you can find us, then, in substitute of David Bowie."

"Maybe I could get you a second-rate band from Queens," Kammie says.

Griffin and I exchange a look. A second-rate band from Queens is better than no band at all.

Chapter 15

About an hour later, we descend upon a favorite bar of Kammie's, not far from the studio. Kammie rang a band called Frog Snout and asked them to meet us for a late lunch, which they've agreed to. Griffin wanted to bring the Ibenza to the bar with him; I can't help thinking that's a good sign, but ultimately, we convinced him to leave it behind.

Outside of the bar, which looks almost as rundown as the studio, a girl runs up to us and says, "Griffin! Griffin Valentino!" and asks Griffin to sign a piece of paper she digs out of her pocket. He obliges with a hammy smile. She takes a few pictures with him on her cell phone, before stepping aside and staring at him in silent, open-mouthed amazement.

"We should get inside," Devon says to Griffin, loud enough that I can hear, and tugs on Griffin's arm. We all walk into the bar together just in time to hear Griffin's song playing.

I shoot Griffin an inquiring look. "I thought you couldn't

do the...?"

"It's playing," he whispers. "It's actually playing. I'm not doing it!" His face lights up so much that I think he might start levitating. Come to think of it, he's an alien, so that would be possible. "Dev, do you hear it? Dev. Dev! D'ya hear it, Devon?"

Though Devon remains quiet, I can tell by his smile that he's proud, too. He pats Griffin on the back and then motions for me, speaking in an undertone, "You said you have a way for us to make announcements without giving away our location, right?"

"Yeah, Twitter."

"I've no idea what that is, but that sounds like a good idea." He glances over at Griffin, who's dancing wildly to his song, jumping up and down. "We just heard that the other visitor may be in America now. We need to keep things moving along."

I can hear the nerves in his voice, so I nod. "Yeah, no problem. I'll set up the Twitter account now."

"Thanks, Daisy."

I fish my phone out of my purse as we choose a table in the back corner, setting up a Twitter account in Griffin's name, connected to one of my old email addresses.

"What do you want to say to your fans, Griffin? On Twitter, I mean?" I ask, and he rambles off about a thousand sentences at once, still flushed and bright-eyed from his excitement. "No, no, it has to be a bit shorter. Maybe a sentence."

"A sentence?" Griffin whistles. His whistle sounds odd and sends shivers down my spine, though I can't quite explain why. He sits down next to Devon, prodding him in the shoulder with one finger. "Hmm, Dev, what should I say? You're my manager."

"You should tell everyone about your concert."

"I'll tell them about my concert!" he says, as if he just got the idea, and dodges Devon's elbow with a laugh. "Alright, where do I say it? Into your phone?"

"No, it's typed. I type what you say, and then everyone can read it online."

"Fine, you type it then. Say, 'I'm planning a concert like the world has never seen and you're all invited to attend for free.' How's that sound?"

"Sounds good." I type his message in and send it.

Kammie, who had disappeared off to the bathroom as soon as we arrived, joins us at the table. "Just got a message from the band boys. They're running a bit late, but they'll be here as soon as they can. We should order without them, though, and let them have their own tab. They're bad about not paying for things."

So Griffin's band will be made up of pirates from Queens. *Fantastic.*

A waitress approaches us and Devon flashes his trademark toothy smile, ordering bar food off the menu like a professional. "And I'd love a vodka cranberry," he adds, handing his menu off to Griffin.

"I want whatever Wanda's having," Griffin says, without even looking at the menu.

"May I see your ID, sir?" the waitress asks Devon, and Devon's eyes widen a little.

"Oh, I don't... I don't have it on me. Why do I need it?"

"We ID anyone who appears to be under the age of thirty. Unfortunately, I can't serve you alcohol if you don't have identification," the waitress says, tapping her pen against her notebook.

I hurriedly put in a food order for Griffin and myself, and then let Kammie order her food, waiting until the waitress is gone to say, "They sort of forgot their passports."

Kammie seems a bit suspicious, but she nods.

My phone buzzes on the table and then just keeps on buzzing until I finally pick it up and check the notifications. Griffin's Twitter account already has almost a hundred followers and a few tweets from fans.

"They think you look young," Griffin says, elbowing Dev. "You know that, right? That's what it means. Guess all your years avoiding the red stones and black dust has finally paid off, eh?"

"Black dust?" Kammie repeats.

"They mean coal," I say quickly. "You know, England's all about coal!"

Kammie glances between Devon and Griffin from her spot at my side, and then looks at the bodyguards standing around our table. "Why do you have so much security?"

"Someone's trying to kill me," Griffin says. "I'm not joking; someone is actually trying to kill me. I'm sort of important back home, and there are certain groups who have conspired to bump me off, you know?"

Dev clears his throat, an uncomfortable smile on his face. "It's a precaution more than anything, Kammie. We hope we won't have any trouble during our stay here."

The doors to the bar open, loud enough that all of us jump in our seats from fresh paranoia about our topic of conversation. Thankfully, it turns out to just be a few young women making a dramatic entrance. They eyeball us from across the room and station themselves at the bar, shooting glances over their shoulders at us.

"Wow," Kammie whispers. "English musicians have such a crazy life. Are you afraid?"

Griffin shrugs. "I'm used to it by now, I suppose. I'm more worried they'll try to hurt Devon or something, since he's my best friend."

"Don't worry," Devon says. "With any luck, it's all just fine. And they're not going to come after you, since you're... American."

Kammie hesitates, still looking back and forth between Griffin and Devon. "You're secret agents, aren't you?" she asks, narrowing her gaze. "You have to be. I mean, you're English, you won't show anyone your IDs. You're both really attractive, you have a ton of money, someone's trying to kill you, and you need help pretending to be musicians. This is like James Bond." She nods a few times. "It's okay, though. You can use my studio. I like James Bond."

"Yes," I say. "They... actually may be secret agents. But we can't tell you anything else about it, Kammie, so you need to stop asking. Pretend we never had this conversation."

"Wow, your names are probably fake too! I knew Devon London seemed like an odd name for an Englishman. Do you carry a gun to bed, Dev?" she asks, wiggling her eyebrows.

"*Kammie.* You have to stop asking. They can't tell you anything more. It's all classified, okay? You have a big secret to keep now, so please... please just help us out."

With a few more enthusiastic nods, Kammie sits back in her chair. "You can count on me. I knew there was something weird about you two. My skin tingled when you walked in the room, and the lights flickered a little. I should have known."

"Kammie."

"I won't tell a soul, I swear."

With that, I redirect everyone's attention to the Twitter account, which gains new followers with every passing second. Griffin's first tweet has been retweeted by a few major celebrity gossip sites, which means fans and followers are pouring in.

"What are they saying?" Griffin asks, moving so he can

stand behind me and peer over my shoulder at the phone. "Wow, they really like my song, don't they? Ha! Someone wants to marry me. What's that one? What's that mean, Wanda? No, never mind; look at that one! Below it. That person says, 'your song is out of this world.'" Griffin laughs uproariously at this, and Devon laughs, too, though quieter. "Now, what's this one? 'Wave to us. We're sitting at the bar.'"

Wait.

We all glance over at the bar and realize the three young women are expectantly smiling at us. One of them waves to Griffin, and he waves back.

Only seconds later, the door opens again and a few more girls spill inside. Like the others, they head to the bar, but these giggle and shoot glances at us with a bit less subtlety.

I run a search for Griffin's name on Twitter and find a tweet from the girl we met outside the bar, telling everyone she'd just met Griffin and tagging our location. "We might have quite a few fans show up," I say, more to Devon than anyone else. Griffin has already started easing in the direction of the fans, with a couple of his bodyguards in tow. "The girl we met outside told everyone where we are, before I even set up Griffin's Twitter."

Devon sits up straighter, his eyes darting around. "Can we hide what she said?"

"No, she's the one who posted it, so there's nothing I can do."

Several pictures and a lot of laughter later, Griffin says goodbye to the fans and rejoins us at the table, just in time for the food to arrive.

"None of them are assassins in disguise, are they?" Kammie whispers across the table to Devon.

"I should certainly hope not."

"Nah, they're fans! I have loads of fans," Griffin says, poking at the burger I've ordered him. "Everyone likes me a lot better here than they do back home. It's nice. Sort of makes me want to stay forever."

"Oh, do you have to go back home soon?" Kammie asks.

"Eventually, yes," Griffin says. At the same time, Devon says, "Soon."

We eat in silence after that, even as more fans arrive and station themselves at the bar. Eventually, after what feels like forever, three young men arrive. All of them are rather tall and sport shoulder-length hair of varying degrees of shagginess. Even at a distance, I can tell they must be related, and up close, they look remarkably similar. They introduce themselves as Frog Snout, a stupid band name if I've ever heard one.

Griffin stands up to shake their hands, looking quite small in comparison to them.

"Wow, man, do you have a lot of lawyers...?" one of them asks, motioning at the bodyguards.

"Don't ask questions!" Kammie says. "No questions at all, unless they relate to the upcoming concert that Griffin and Devon are putting on."

"Yeah, yeah," the guy says, looking down at Griffin. "What's this about a concert? We haven't really booked for anything since the fire in that club in Chinatown. Which we didn't start, by the way."

I resist saying anything to Kammie about these people, though barely.

"We're going to put together a massive concert and invite everyone in the world to watch it for free," Griffin says with a humble shrug.

"Oh." Frog Snout exchanges a meaningful look and then collectively nods, curtains of shiny, light brown hair bobbing along. The one who seems to be the spokesman clears his throat and says, "I suppose we can do that. It won't be early in the morning, though, right? We're kinda rock n' roll, man. We don't wake up until two pm. Sometimes three. But usually two. Well, two thirty, to be safe."

Thankfully, Griffin doesn't seem to be fazed by them, not even when they sit down and help themselves to some of the food at our table without asking. They ask very few questions, which is good, and we set up a time the next afternoon for them to meet us at the studio for practice.

"We'll be there, man, barring alien invasion," the spokesman says, shaking Griffin's hand again. Griffin stares blankly back at him. "Oh, you saw the news, right? We're like probably getting invaded by aliens. I knew this day would come! My friend thinks there's like some hierarchy of ancient beings ruling us and giving us nightmares, but I think it's aliens. And if it is, the first place they'll go is New York City. We're like the epicenter for all things cool and weird."

"Maybe they'd come here to look for David Bowie," Griffin says. "None of you know David Bowie, do you…?" This time, he doesn't seem as surprised to hear that they don't.

As we exit the bar, my mind is busy calculating how exactly we're going to manage this concert. We'll need a proper venue, although Kammie swears she can arrange something. We'll also need to promote it beforehand. Somehow, it will need to be filmed and broadcasted, although Griffin swears *he* can arrange something. That's assuming anyone in this 'band' can actually play music worth a damn, and that Griffin can write a bunch of songs in the meantime.

We're greeted by a crowd of people standing outside the bar, mostly girls, all of them eagerly waiting for Griffin. One of them is even wearing a shirt with Griffin's face screen-printed on it. They all chirp for him, voices rising like a chorus of excited birds, saying, "*Griffin, Griffin, Griffin, Griffin!*"

"Now, now, you need to make an orderly line," Dev says, nearly shouting to be heard over the noise. He grabs hold of Griffin, stopping him from diving right into the center of the crowd. "If you want to speak to Griffin, you'll need to get in line."

"Don't be silly, Dev, they don't want to hurt me," Griffin murmurs, pulling away from his friend. "They love me." He smiles at his audience, holding his arms wide, and then saunters toward them.

Dev bounces about, his hands curling in and out of fists, barely able to stay in one place for more than a second, as Griff meets the fans. The bodyguards stand close by, although they don't seem quite as nervous as Dev.

"Alright, alright," Dev says, after some pictures have been taken and Griffin has signed a lot of items and body parts. "Come on, Griff, we need to get going."

"You all *must* come to my show!" Griffin says. "Twitter. I'll tell you about it on Twitter! Who wants to come? I want everyone to come!"

He gets a lot of cheers, but Dev finally drags him away, arm flung around his shoulders to keep him close. I say goodbye to Kammie, who seems genuinely impressed by the crowd of fans.

"I like those boys," Kammie says. "Especially Devon. He's a tiger! I'd like to take that tiger back to my place."

Of course.

"Alright, Kammie, talk tomorrow!"

"Be careful, though, okay? I mean it. If you're friends with them, you might be in danger. You know what happens to the girls in the Bond movies!" she says, and then I have to run to catch up with my alien friends, all the while wondering if Kammie's right.

Maybe I'm in danger, too.

WE RETURN TO THE HOTEL LATE, HAVING STOPPED A FEW TIMES FOR supplies for the upcoming concert. Even in the hours since the Twitter account was set up, Griffin has received countless messages from fans, leaving me unable to do anything but scroll in open-mouthed amazement through all of them. He inspires a lot of love and adoration, with very few nasty messages in the mix. It's incredible.

At the hotel, Devon disappears into his room, taking all the bodyguards with him; he strictly instructs us to leave him alone. Griffin picks up his white Telecaster as if he's never seen it before and sits on the bed to strum it. My inquiries about his plans for the rest of the evening are met only with silence, so after a while, I give up and turn on the TV.

As I flip through the channels, I find an old black-and-white science fiction movie about an alien invasion. I watched it as a kid and remember feeling vaguely uneasy about the fact that most of the characters didn't even notice the aliens around them until too late.

I cast a sidelong glance at Griffin, who freezes immediately and looks back at me. "What's that?" he asks.

"What?"

"That, in your movie. What's that supposed to be?" he demands, pointing at the extreme close-up of an alien on the screen.

"That's an alien, of course. According to Hollywood in the 1960s."

Griffin scowls at the screen as a woman in an absurd blonde wig screams and faints. "How ridiculous. I've never seen anyone who looks like that, not even on some of the less educated planets. Not even on Z23, and they have some of the ugliest beings I've ever laid eyes on." He glances at me, almost apologetically. "Well, they have a lot of arms and I suppose they can't help it, but it's not my thing."

It's really not my place to scold him on racism toward beings with more than two arms, so I just shrug. I'm still trying to catch up with the idea that there are tons of other beings living out there in the universe.

The movie turns very serious when one of the aliens walks into a grade-school classroom and all the children stop what they're doing and lie down silently on the floor. Griffin, however, laughs uncomfortably and then starts laughing harder and harder until he's red in the face and doubled over his guitar, coughing and spluttering.

"Oh, this is ridiculous! What a load of rubbish," he splutters. "Well, what happens? What happens in the end?"

"The humans round up all the aliens, kill them, and then burn their bodies, just in case," I say, without really thinking about it. "But they're bad aliens," I add quickly, looking at him.

"They're not like you and Dev. Besides, this was probably just a hidden commentary on the Russians or something. America was obsessed with hating the Soviets then."

I switch the channel to an advertisement for an exercise bike that also tones your facial muscles via a special helmet.

"What's Dev doing in there, anyway?" I say, trying to change the subject away from humans slaughtering aliens.

"He's telling the guards not to bother with protecting him if we're attacked," Griffin says in a flat voice, still staring at the screen. "I'll order them to disregard that later."

"Uhhh… oh. That's… How do you know that?"

"Why do you think he didn't invite me to his security meeting?"

"Dev told me the other alien might be in America now. Is that why he's acting so nervous about everything? Or is there something else that I don't know?"

Griffin casts me a grim smile. "Once, we were walking through a crowd together after one of my father's speeches, and someone threw a bag of poisonous red dust at me. I was sick for ages. They'd called me names before, but they'd never done anything that malicious. I thought they might like me, if they realized I was on their side. And another time, an angry citizen cut my arm clear open. I bled all over my white shirt and made such a mess that some of my blood ended up on Dev's clothes."

I shiver a little. "So you're in real danger."

Griffin sets aside his guitar and glares in the direction of the TV. The screen goes black and the lights flicker around us. "I want to listen to Bowie right now."

I watch him as he climbs off the bed, all tense energy and electric charge.

"Look, that movie was stupid," I say. "We've always

pictured aliens as being scary. I mean, honestly, before this week, I thought the same thing."

"Thought what?"

"Oh, you know... that aliens are these frightening, dangerous beings that would abduct us and experiment on us. Or murder us."

Griffin slides his Bowie record slowly out of its sleeve, leaving it naked in his hands, and then he slides one pale finger down the side of the shiny, black vinyl. "Maybe you're not wrong, Wanda," he says quietly, without looking at me. He drops the vinyl into place with the careless grace of a lover, and then finally peers at me with those strange eyes.

I've never felt so turned on by someone playing a record.

"Of-of course I'm wrong," I say, standing up and nervously winding my fingers together. "You're not like that at all."

"I'm not, but maybe the others are?" he asks, as "Five Years" by David Bowie fills the charged space between us.

I walk toward him without even really meaning to. "You're an annoying little man with... with designer clothes and an obnoxious laugh. That's not what we expected from an alien invasion." I'm standing in front of him now, with no idea how I got there, and I reach out to grasp one of his jacket lapels in my shaking fingers.

"Are you finally going to look into me, Wanda?" he demands, a sneer forming on his face. "After all this time?"

"Please just shut up," I say, snaking one hand up so I can twist my fingers deep into his soft hair and force his mouth to mine. Not surprisingly, he responds with vigor, pulling me in hard against his body and returning my kiss. It's been a while since I've kissed anyone, and he's certainly new to me, so I bump noses with him and it takes a bit of fancy—okay, not so fancy—maneuvering around his high cheekbones and my nose and whatever, but he coaxes my lips apart for a deep, claiming sort of kiss that sends shockwaves to my toes.

Speaking of my toes, I realize one of my feet is nearly crushing one of his feet, so I step off him, but this makes me almost lose my balance. Griffin takes advantage of the situation by snarling a little and spinning us around, crashing my hip into a table in the process. I gasp from the pain, but he covers my lips with his again, kissing me so hard that I dig my nails into the back of his shirt in response.

Griffin presses my back to the wall, his hands dancing down my sides, down my hips. "My father said if I came here, all of you would hate me," he says in little gasps between kisses. "You'll try to kill me, just like those—those aliens on your movie."

"That was not my movie," I say, tugging at the bottom of his shirt, attempting to move it in the direction of up, up, up, over his head and off.

"I think he's wrong."

"I think you should stop talking about him right now, before I force you to strip naked and put another record on," I say, finally managing to remove the shirt from him and toss it on the ground. "Do you have any idea how hot you looked with that record in your hands?"

Griffin kisses the corner of my mouth, my chin, the most vulnerable part of my throat, my collarbone, and then he bites my jaw, which is almost hotter than him holding a vinyl record in his hands. Almost.

"Is that all I needed to do? Hold a record?" he demands, before moving his teeth to my collarbone. "Or did you want me to do this?" He hitches up my skirt just enough to run one finger up my bare thigh, much the same as he ran it over the side of the record.

I restrain any loud noises, but barely.

"Look, the wall is too advanced for me," I say, pushing him back, but not too much. I slide out of my dress in a mess of flailing arms, leaving it behind as I grab his wrist and tug him toward the bed. "Even if you could make me levitate or something, this is better for me. Okay?"

Griffin nods, all but tackling me to the bed and catching us up in another feverish kiss. After a few seconds of kissing nirvana, I grab a handful of his dark hair and pull hard enough to force his lips away from mine. "You should lock the doors."

"The…?"

"Your best friend and about half a dozen oversized bouncers are in the next room, remember? Go lock the door to that room and the door to our room."

Though I'm disappointed to lose the warmth of his body against mine, I'm glad that he obeys me and runs across the room to lock the doors. He returns almost before I know he's gone, climbing back onto the bed with me.

We tangle, and I do my best not to embarrass myself or hurt either of us. His arms are pleasantly wiry and muscular, more than I would have guessed, and his shoulders are good and strong for how slender he is. My hands explore this new territory a little at a time, savoring the glowing heat of his skin.

"You're beautiful, Wanda."

Somehow, even I'm starting to believe my name is Wanda. "Well, you have strong arms," I say as he presses kisses down my front.

"I was in the military."

"What? You? In the military?"

"Yeah, yeah, we all have to put in two years." His lips have reached my belly, and I try not to knee him in the face or something, but my reflexes are still dodgy from years of misuse and the occasional tray-tipping scare at the restaurant. "But I wasn't very good at murder."

"Oh. Oh, Griffin, please don't use that tone right now."

He looks up at me, raising one eyebrow in surprise.

"No, no," I quickly say. "Sorry, by that I meant, please keep using that tone. You were all growly. Please tell me more about that. If you used a gun, you can tell me about that. Or talk about music."

Griffin snickers and returns his face to mine, kissing me again and then whispering something in my ear that I don't understand. It's definitely something in his weird alien language, but it sounds snarly and delicious right now. "I only had a gun when I was in the military. A citizen has no use for a gun," he says, in English again. "Our guns are quite different from yours."

"Whatever, whatever. We'll pretend you're James Bond right now, okay? And I'll be a somewhat clumsy Bond girl who didn't get the perfect blowout and makeup job." I trace my hands over his back and shoulders. "My hormones must be really bad right now. I shouldn't be doing this. I should not, *should not*, be doing this."

"It's because we're made of the same stuff," he says, wriggling around to remove whatever else he's wearing. Once he's sent the last of his clothes over the side of the bed, Griffin bites my earlobe gently and whispers, "Why don't you look into me, Wanda? Do it. Just do it." When he meets my eyes again, I let out a quiet sigh and nod.

"Alright. Whatever this is, go on."

He leans down, and we stare into each other's eyes. At first, I don't see anything besides thick, black lashes and bright blue eyes, but then I feel as if I'm levitating. Some part of me is lifting away from the rest, floating into a universe of painted memories, many of them not my own. I can see a little boy with yellow hair laughing, and I see a tall, graceful woman dancing about in a white dress. I see a tiny, green plant poking up from black soil. I see ugly red, green, blue, and yellow colors swirling together in the sky. I see Dev's face, twisted into a panicked expression, I feel my lungs burn with something painful, even more painful than a strong sense of betrayal that goes along with it, and I see red-black blood on my fingers. I see the tall, graceful woman folded into herself and bloodied on the floor, arms splayed wide and eyes closed. I see rows of uniformed soldiers, I see Dev laughing about something. I feel confused and lost and happy and lonely and drunk and hopeful and hopeless all in turn, emotions washing through me, sewn together with my own memories. High school photos, the first time I rode a bike, my mom's embarrassing lecture about boys…

I feel excitement, warmth, pleasure, and just a touch of tenuous doubt. And then, all at once, I can see Griffin again, though the memories and visions continue to exist around me like ghosts.

"Do you see now?" Griffin whispers, his eyebrows drawn together, and I nod. I still feel dazed.

"Don't doubt yourself," I say at last. "You're doing just fine. Just show me why your—uh—why the women on your planet don't need blush, okay?"

Wait, is he vibrating a little…?

Yes. Yes, he is.

When I was younger and still imagined that my life would be full of romantic adventures, grand trips to exotic locations, and a record collection to rival that of the most serious collector in the world, I had often fantasized about rolling around on a beach with a handsome man to some sexy David Bowie songs.

We're not on a beach, and technically, Griffin is an alien, but this is close enough to be satisfactory.

"It's been a while, so please—" I start to say, but he nibbles on my neck, and I find it difficult to remember how to talk, never mind what I was saying.

"Daisy," Griffin whispers against my ear, and I shiver to hear my real name. "There's nothing to feel nervous about. You've seen me, but I've seen you, too. I know."

His mouth moves over me in claiming waves, lower and lower, past my belly this time, until he's reached territory no one's gone to in that way before. I've read about this kind of thing in magazines, usually from the safety of my bedroom while wrapped up in pajamas with frogs on them, but it's all been theory up until this point. Griffin's got me squirming helplessly before I've even had enough time to process what's happening.

I raise my head to look down at him when he stops, already thinking of about two hundred ways to scold him, but he's grinning back at me in the most evil manner. When he leans over me, I wrap my arm around his neck, pulling him down against me. He kisses my neck once, twice, and then works his fingers down over me. He's better at that than I've ever been, the jerk. "Are you ready for me yet?" he whispers, snickering when he draws a gasp out of me. "Good girl, Daisy."

Just as I start to tense up again, I hear him say, "Don't think about that. Don't think about him." I'm not sure if he said it out loud or in my head, but somehow, it works. I stop worrying so much about what I look like or what's going to happen or what happened before or the bodyguards over in Dev's room or anything in the world except for myself and Griffin.

"I've abducted your mind," he says, with one last very deliberate flick of his finger, and a dark laugh. "And now I want the rest of you."

Oh, God.

"Alright," I manage to say. "Alright, Griffin. I have not known you long enough at all and shouldn't be doing this but... alright." This is all the permission he needs to fully take me. He draws noises out of me that I hadn't thought possible, and he makes a few noises that I'm sure actually *aren't* possible—for humans. He's attuned to me, through it all, patient, confident, and just fervent enough to leave us both a pleased wreck by the end.

And then, maybe ten minutes later, I'm on my way to the bathroom, wrapped in a blanket and clutching some clean clothes, and the door between our room and Dev's busts open.

Like, all the way off its hinges.

Somehow, I manage not to scream, but I definitely gasp and pull the blanket up and around myself better.

Dev's the first through the doorway, his eyes wide. "Is everyone alright?" he demands, and then his eyes stray to Griffin, who's lazily stretched on his back on the bed, propped up on his elbows. "Griffin, did you—?"

"You could bloody knock next time, mate."

"You locked me out! I was worried about you!"

Griffin doesn't seem all that bothered as the bodyguards spill into the room, and Dev shoots me a few embarrassed glances. "Well, you should be worried. I can't find that menu they gave us for room service," Griffin says. "I'm hungry enough to eat a full grown balak."

Dev looks at me again, and then clears his throat, dropping his gaze. "Sorry, Daisy. I'm just... I was a bit worried is all. Sorry. I shouldn't have barged in like that."

"I-I would appreciate it if everyone would just walk away and pretend this never happened," I splutter.

This isn't quite the most mortifying thing that's ever happened to me, but it's close. Thankfully, all the bodyguards return to the other room, leaving Dev behind with Griffin and me.

"Well, don't just stand there gaping like a fish," Griffin says. "Where's that menu?"

"You could have told me," Dev says.

"Told you what?"

"That you needed some time alone. I tried to open the door and... look, I was worried."

I wave one hand around. "Nothing was planned, alright? And to be fair, it was kind of my fault. I jumped him." My face warms to the approximate temperature of Texas blacktop in July. "Can we please follow my earlier suggestion and pretend this never happened?"

"Nah, he needs to find the menu. You had it last, Dev. Where is it?" Griffin asks, shifting around casually on the bed so his back is to the backboard. A corner of the sheet is barely draped over his lap, precariously close to slipping out of place.

"I'm going to go into the bathroom and try not to die from embarrassment. When I return, I'd like the door to be put back where it belongs and for everyone to have learned their lesson about knocking first. Goodbye."

With that, I spin around and all but run into the bathroom, slamming the door closed behind myself.

My original plan had been to take a shower and then climb back into bed—wearing one of Griffin's expensive T-shirts—and cuddle up to him for the rest of the night. It shouldn't be too much to ask, really. But that's just not how my life ever seems to work.

After a quick shower, I shuffle over to the mirror for a full assessment. My skin doesn't appear to be glowing and my hair hasn't turned into a shampoo ad, but that's all right. It was all a bit of a surprise and I'll just have to deal with the fallout from it, awkward eye contact with Dev included.

Once I'm finished brushing my hair and composing myself, I exit the bathroom with head held high. Okay, not high, but with *some* confidence at least. Mercifully, for the sake of my hormones and sanity, Griffin has put some pants on and settled himself in the middle of the bed with his guitar. The David Bowie record has finished playing, so the music I hear is… Griffin's.

It sounds good, too—nice little guitar tune and his melodic humming over top.

"That doesn't sound too bad," I say, looking around and noting that Devon and the bodyguards have managed to prop the door back in the doorway, even if it's not really fixed. "Aren't you… tired, though?"

Griffin shrugs and continues playing, lost in what seems to be a song in progress. He looks energized, rather than tired, and when he finally raises his head to me, I see a gleeful expression. "Got some ideas for songs," he says.

"From David Bowie?"

He rolls his eyes. "From you, of course. From our experience together."

Ah. Great. Hopefully, he won't add graphic lyrics with details about everything that happened between us. My mom is only going to be able to take so much.

"It was a pretty nice 'experience', up until the door came down," I say, settling under the cover on the right side of the bed. "However, I am tired."

"Go to sleep, then." He strums the guitar for a few seconds, and then glances over his shoulder and smiles at me. "Don't worry, I'll find you in your dreams."

I want to tell him that I wasn't worried about finding or losing him, but that actually sounds kind of nice. And when I drift off to sleep, I do see him once or twice in my dreams, but he's being pulled further and further from me, no matter how fast I run toward him…

Chapter 17

I WAKE UP FEELING A BIT SORE BUT DEEPLY RESTED, SITTING UP WITH A loud, exaggerated yawn.

Griffin is nowhere to be seen, once again, but he's left a stack of scrap papers and musical equipment in his wake. I lean over his side of the bed and pick up one of the papers, finding unfamiliar scrawling all over it.

A voice floats to my ears from the other room, Dev's voice, but he's not speaking English or any other human language. I hear Griffin's voice, too, so I slide off the bed and head toward the doorway.

"Uh, what's all the paper...?" I say, and Griffin leaps up from his spot on Devon's bed to greet me with an enthusiastic kiss on the lips. He's wearing his Union Jack T-shirt and some loose-fitting pants that look suspiciously like women's yoga pants. But all in all, he's looking quite snuggly and cute, especially considering how rumpled and messy his hair is.

"I wrote twenty songs last night," Griffin says. "Do you like cupcakes? The staff sent up a dozen cupcakes this morning. I've just had three of them."

"You wrote twenty songs last night?"

"Yeah, I've got loads of them! They're all amazing, and everyone's going to love them. They're going to be the most popular songs in the world."

"How did you write that many songs in one night, though? Did you sleep at all?"

Devon and Griffin both angle their bodies toward me, almost in synchronization, and stare as if I've just said the most ridiculous thing ever. They exchange a look, and then Griffin says, almost gently, "Well, no. We... Last night, we..."

"Alright, someone spit it out. Why are you looking at me like that?" I demand when they've weirded me out enough.

"I suppose things are a bit different here, for you, than for us," Dev ventures, before trailing off. "We're rather energized by certain events."

"Like what happened last night before everyone barged in?"

"Yeah, I'm all charged up!" Griffin says. "Do you feel charged, too?"

"I haven't had coffee yet, so I'll get back to you on that later," I say, struggling not to laugh. "So you're telling me that on top of everything else, the men of your planet gain energy from sex? Do you also keep your rooms tidy? Cook? Remember birthdays? Because I'm starting to think we should turn the tables on this abduction thing and keep a bunch of you here for the ladies of my world."

Griffin and Dev seem to have no idea why this is funny, but whatever.

"Alright, one of you can get me some coffee," I say, pointing between them. "And then we should probably get ready and go meet up with Kammie at the studio."

After a bit of rummaging around, I find one of the dresses Griffin bought me, along with the bag of bras and underwear. I'm halfway through changing into the dress when I realize something all at once.

Last night was a bit unexpected. Okay, very unexpected. And...

My gaze falls to the mirror's reflection of my belly, which looks the same as always... just a little rounder than it needs to be. Nothing's grown, my skin hasn't changed color, and I don't see any bulging veins or anything, but... but the danger could be real. *The danger could be real!*

What if he's planted an alien baby in me? What if Griffin's whole purpose on our planet was to find a human woman and put an alien baby in her? What if I'm going to blow up? Or what if the baby is going to grow gigantic, gangly, and terrifying... and then eat my guts?

I've never felt quite this panicked before. A few seconds of mental torture later, I decide to go right to the source and stomp out of the bathroom. Griffin's close by, thankfully, fiddling with pedals and humming to himself. I grab him by his shirt and shake him just a bit harder than is strictly necessary. He reacts by grabbing my wrists in a crushing grip, tensing up, and letting out a defensive puff of air.

"Tell me right now, Griffin Valentino. Did you put a chestbuster in me?"

"A-a what?" he says, releasing his hold on me.

"If you put your alien spawn in me, and it's going to gnaw me from the inside out, I swear I'm going to murder you before it finishes me off. And I'll call my mom and have her murder you when I'm done."

He looks so confused that I relent and let him go, though I don't step away. "I'd better not be pregnant, mister! Admittedly, I forgot to make you use a condom, but whatever. Is it going to kill me?"

Griffin's eyes narrow a little, the weird blue color darkening. "What's that? What's a condom?"

"Oh, great. No one ever told me I'd have to give an alien a sex education class." I pinch the bridge of my nose and close my eyes, trying to think how to explain it. Memories of bananas and awkward giggles in the classroom come to mind. "It's something you wear to keep us from making a baby."

"Why would anyone want to wear something to stop them from making a baby?" he asks in a very slow and deliberate manner, as if I'm the crazy one here. "Do you have any idea how seldom children are conceived on my planet?"

Hmmm. I do sometimes forget he's not just from England. "Alright, well, around here, they're certainly not scarce. How are your babies born?"

With this, Griffin yells for Dev. "Oy! Dev! Get in here and help me with something!" he says, and Dev wanders into the room. He's clutching a steaming cup of coffee in one hand, which he offers me. "Daisy here has some questions about... errr... childbirth. Right, well, enjoy that. I'll be in the washroom, having a bath."

He's gone so quickly that I can't help wondering if he teleported, and Dev stands in front of me with bright pink cheeks, stammering as he asks me exactly what I need to know.

"The babies on your planet don't claw their way out of their mothers or something, do they?" I demand, and Dev continues stammering, explaining in very polite and flowery terms that their babies are born from the same place they're conceived. "Oh, okay. Thanks, Dev. I got it; you don't have to say anything else. It's the same here."

Dev shoots me a relieved smile and suddenly has something very, very, very important to do in the other room.

"Someone bring me some juice!" That's Griffin's voice, echoing from the bathroom. I take a deep breath and push open the door, only to find Griffin propped up in the bathtub like a smug king on a bubbly throne. He's probably quite proud of himself for escaping an uncomfortable conversation. "Oh. Daisy. Where's my juice?"

I close and lock the door behind me.

"Why're you doing that? I want my juice!"

"Your juice can wait," I say, sitting down on the edge of the bathtub. "You need to answer some questions for me."

Griffin pulls a face and slips down into the bubbles until everything below his nose has disappeared from my view.

"Dev's already answered the worst of it for you, you coward, but you need to tell me if I need to worry about something gnawing me alive from the inside out."

"That's ghastly; where in the cosmos would you get such an idea?" he demands, raising his mouth above the waterline long enough to speak, before submerging again and peering up at me with narrowed eyes.

I grab my cell phone from the bathroom sink, where I'd left it, and find a clip from *Alien*. "There now, see?" I say, holding it in front of his face. He watches it silently, barely blinking, and as the clip ends, he bursts into hysterical laughter.

Griffin sits up in the tub, doubled over. "What kind of tripe is that? Your people have the damn strangest ideas I've ever heard of! I—I don't even think that the... Well, maybe that could happen on Alscos or its moon. Maybe there. Everyone says you shouldn't do anything dodgy with them, but I've never seen anything like that! What film is this? Really, I think

Dev and I'd better watch the rest and have a laugh."

"So, nothing like that's going to happen to me?"

"Not unless there's something about your human gestational period that no one's ever told me!" he says, slipping back down under the bubbles.

Sliding my phone closed, I let out a relieved sigh. "No, no. Pregnancy here is already scary enough without fear of anything busting out of your stomach and eating you alive."

Griffin muses on this. "There are some holopics of me as a baby, and I didn't have any teeth at all. You know, I got 'em later. They never quite grew in exactly right, but that's pretty common in the royal family. And my mother was quite well alive until she was murdered by terrorists."

"As long as nothing scary is going to happen to me, we're good," I say, and then hesitate. "I'm sorry about your mom. I, uh, I think I saw her last night when we... when we did that thing. The eyeball thing. She seemed really wonderful."

He looks away from me. "Yeah."

"It's awful that someone would actually... you know..." I don't know what the delicate term is. "Murder her. You were really close with her, huh?"

Griffin shifts around a bit. "You have so much water on this planet," he says, as if we haven't just been talking about anything serious at all. "We have one small bathtub in the royal home, about half the size of this one. It's one of the only ones in the city. Maybe in the world. I don't use it often, because it's a disrespectful waste of water, but someone started this rumor that I take baths every night." His eyes flick up in my direction. "I take regulated showers like everyone else. I've used that tub twice in my adult life."

"I see."

"Once they believe something like that, though, they'll

believe anything. They'll believe every mistake I've made is a million times worse than it really is. Maybe they believed things like that about her, too. Maybe they thought she was frivolous and didn't care about them." He glowers, and the water in the bathtub ripples, moves, even though he's completely still. "But they never really knew her at all. Not like I did. She was always so kind, and she looked for the best in everyone, tried to find peaceful solutions to things. And they've never known me for anything besides a privileged brat with a big house and a white uniform, making a poor choice in his lover and painting a silly message on the side of a building."

The lights flicker a few times over us. "Whoa, alright. Dark mood." I slip out of my clothes, climbing into the bathtub with him. His face registers something like shock, rather than just surprise.

"What're you doing?"

"There's room for me to join you, so why not?" I say, angling around so I can sit in front of him and lean my back against his chest. After a few seconds, I feel him relax. He settles his arms around me. "You're on my planet now, and we can waste water sometimes if we want. Just don't tell Sting."

"How odd," he says, but I can almost hear him realizing how cozy and convenient this situation is. "We'd never do something like this back home."

I glance over my shoulder at him, unable to hold back a laugh at his surprised expression. "Listen, I know you've been through a lot, and it sounds like things are even worse on your planet than I could possibly imagine. But things aren't quite so bad here. My phone's constantly buzzing with notifications of all the people on Twitter talking about how much they love you. You've noticed how much people like you." I hesitate, but then shrug and just say it… "What if you stayed here?"

"Stayed?"

"Yeah. Instead of going home to your dad and crazy fiancée and people who throw poisonous dust at you, you could just stay here, play shows, and buy nice clothes for us to share. It'll be fun. And even my mom seems to like you. That's huge."

For a long time, Griffin remains silent, but he finally says, "I could write songs."

"Yeah, you could."

"And make music videos and appear on important television shows."

"You could totally do that. And you could actually go to England, you know, for research and stuff. Maybe I could come with you."

"Of course you'd come along; don't be daft!"

I laugh a little, feeling his fingers dance up my legs beneath the water. "There are so many foods you could try, too. I'd love to see your face if you ate a hot pepper."

All at once, though, Griffin sighs heavily and his hands fall away from my legs. "They need me, Daisy. Even if they hate me… I need to do this for them."

"You're right," I admit with a heavy sigh. After all, I have no idea what it would be like to live on a planet in as much trouble as his, and I certainly can't imagine the embarrassing moments in my life turning into something even uglier and scarier, like some of his memories. But I still can't help wishing it were possible for Griffin to just stay here. I'm starting to kind of like having him around.

I turn around carefully, slipping a bit here and there, but finally settle with my knees on either side of him, my hands on his shoulders. "You need to promise me something, Griffin Valentino."

He stares up at me, a rapt pupil now that I'm facing him,

though his gaze slips to my chest once or twice.

"Promise me that you won't just disappear. I know you're in danger, I know you have a mission to complete, and I know you're from another planet and whatever, but you have to promise me you won't leave without saying goodbye."

Griffin nods, taking his time in answering. "I won't leave without saying goodbye."

"Good. And—"

He cuts me off with a fierce kiss that almost convinces me to spend a lot of time in the bathtub, but then I hear Devon calling for Griffin and gently untangle myself.

"You should finish getting ready," I say, standing up on shaky legs. "We don't need any more broken doors."

Once I'm dressed, I exit the bathroom in a hurry. Otherwise, I'm afraid I might climb back into the bath with Griffin and give myself even more reason to worry about alien babies.

Chapter 18

I PROBABLY SHOULDN'T BE SURPRISED BY KAMMIE SHOWING UP TO THE studio decked out in a nice dress and greeting Dev with a kiss that lingers a bit longer than is strictly necessary, or by the fact that Frog Snout arrives fifteen minutes late, clutching coffee cups and moaning behind sunglasses about what a late night they had.

Griffin moves about the studio like a little dictator, bossing everyone around about what he wants done. "Here, look through these songs I wrote," he says, handing off the stack of loose papers he's left his notes on.

"Dude, what language is this?" the unspoken leader of Frog Snout asks. His name is Bill, I think; he likes moonstones, and he's been to Sweden a few times. That's really all I know about him. "I've never seen this before."

"It's an ancient language," Griffin says, propping his hands on his hips in a haughty manner.

"Oh. Cool. How do I read it, though...? I didn't pay much attention in school when we studied Greek and German and stuff."

Griffin snatches the papers away from Bill. "Whatever, you don't need to know the words anyway. Just listen and then play along."

Frog Snout shares a collective shrug before taking their places around the studio. Dev stands with Griffin for a while, peering over his shoulder at the notes and whispering to him, until Griffin waves him away.

"I need some space; I need some space," he says. "Go stand with Kammie; you know you want to." Griffin picks up his guitar, looking a bit like a fluffy purple chicken thanks to that ugly sweater he's insisted on wearing again. "This is one of the best songs ever written, so don't ruin it."

From my spot in the corner of the room, I can't help snickering a little. But the song isn't bad, really. In fact, between Frog Snout's surprising talent and Griffin's soaring voice, it sounds... well, really good! I'm tapping my feet and nodding along, and the second song is even better.

The third song they practice, though, is much slower. Griffin shoots me a meaningful look before lyrically articulating, in a deliberately enunciated manner, how impressive last night was. His description is quite blunt. All I can do is sit, frozen, and try to will my face not to be so warm. When I catch his gaze, he smirks at me, apparently mistaking my reaction for pleasure rather than embarrassment.

I imagine him singing this in front of the world... and my mother hearing it.

I imagine never speaking to my mother again, just in case.

They run through five more songs, and then Griffin abruptly declares they're finished.

"We've only practiced them once each," Bill says, and the rest of Frog Snout nods, long sheets of shiny hair flapping about as they do so. "We usually practice about fifty times before we perform a song live. Sometimes, we just skip performing it live. You know."

Griffin shoots Bill a look. "You don't need fifty times to learn my song. Our concert will be the night after tomorrow."

"Wait, the night after tomorrow?" I say, at approximately the same time Dev and Kammie echo my question. "Griffin, that doesn't give you much time to prepare!"

"I'm prepared. I could perform it right now!" he says.

"You've just written the lyrics and you guys just jammed a little, but how is anyone going to remember how the songs go?"

"Night after tomorrow," Griffin says again, with a tone that doesn't invite argument. He and Dev lean their heads together, Dev even going so far as to slip his arm around Griffin's shoulders to close them off into a private bubble. They converse quietly, and then shoot a few meaningful glances in my direction before announcing they're going to step outside. I can't help feeling like I should go with them, but Frog Snout stands around in the doorway, patting themselves down for cigarettes.

"Weird guy, huh?" Bill says, glancing over at me. "Real weird."

"Maybe he's an alien," another of them says, and they laugh, high-fiving each other. "You saw his eyes, right? Weird eyes."

"Yeah, weird eyes. Weird guy."

"They say we're ripe for an alien invasion any day. Like, any day. We could already be invaded and don't even know. He could be the alien." Suddenly, they're all shooting nervous glances about, twitching, and clearing their throats.

Kammie elbows me with a wink and a smile, as if we're

in on a special secret, and I just offer her a half-hearted smile.

Frog Snout decamps outside to smoke, and I angle myself closer and closer toward the door. "We should go find Griffin," I say.

"Yes, yes, and Devon. We need to keep an eye on them," Kammie says, falling into step with me. She doesn't seem to be in such a hurry, but I can't help quickening my pace a bit more with every new stairwell.

What if Griffin and Devon sensed something? What if they're in danger? What if they decided to go home and Griffin broke his promise to me? Thankfully, the bodyguards are so tall that I spot them right away, ringed protectively around Griffin and Devon. I approach without hesitation, for once, pushing right between two of the hulking aliens.

"What's going on? Did something happen?"

Devon raises his head from Griffin's weird, phone-like device, which both of them have been staring at, but he doesn't seem to know what to say.

"My father's gone and given us three sodding days," Griffin says. "Three days! He's decided there's a—a deadline now. Didn't even send the bloody message himself. I tried reasoning with him earlier, but his secretary's sent me a message back and signed it off with 'have a productive day.' I'd like to give her a productive day!"

For a second, I think Griffin might dash his device against the sidewalk, but then he lets out an angry puff of air and pockets it instead.

"It's alright, Griff," Dev says quietly, cupping his hand around the back of Griffin's neck and leaning their heads together. "We'll figure it out."

"We can't bloody figure anything out in three days! If the Origin Collective doesn't contact us immediately, we're lost."

"Is that why you want to have the concert so soon?"

Griffin closes his eyes and shudders. "Even that's not soon enough now. Can we do it tomorrow night? Nust. Nust!"

It sounds like he's saying noost. "Nust…?"

"Yeah, nust; it's the worst word I can think of, and that's not even enough. My mother's probably turning in her grave right now." Griffin pulls away from Devon, waves his hands to the bodyguards like he's parting the Red Sea, and stomps away from us.

I hang back with Devon for a few seconds, but his exasperated sigh tells me he has no idea what to do or say. He glances in my direction, a certain level of pleading in his dark eyes.

"Alright," I say, without Devon needing to say anything. "I'll go talk to him."

Griffin's got his arms crossed over his chest and a scowl on his face when I approach. I can hear a faint buzzing noise radiating from him, frightening and pulsing in the air around us. Part of me warns to back away, reminding me he's not human, no matter how much he might appear to be, but I take a deep breath and step closer anyway.

"Can we find a venue for tomorrow night?" he asks, before I can open my mouth.

"I'll talk to Kammie. Look, even if we can't take over Madison Square Garden or something, we can get our hands on the biggest venue available and just wing it. Do you have any of your finger-snapping magic left? Brainwashing? Maybe you could seduce someone…?"

"It's not magic," he says, but I can hear the slightest humor in his tone. However small it may be, and however grim his face still is, I'll take it.

"Do you think you have enough for this?"

Griffin stares into the distance for a few seconds, and then flashes those strange blue eyes in my direction. "I have a little left."

"Well, let's talk to Kammie about it," I say. "And you need to reserve every bit of your energy, power, magic, or whatever it is, alright? You'll need it for this." After a long pause, I lower my voice and say, "If you can't do it for some reason, though, just stay here. You're trying so hard to help your people and your dad doesn't even appreciate it. So just stay!"

"Sounds like he'll arrest me before he'll allow that to happen," Griffin says. "I'm the last in our family line, and he wants me to hurry up and marry that dreadful woman. Makes everything all neat and tidy for him, looks good for the public. And then we can spend the next ten years trying bitterly to produce an heir." The air ripples around him, and the hairs on my arm stand on edge from a static charge.

"Griffin." I reach for him, but he catches me by the wrist before I can touch him. Warm shockwaves run up my arm, and not from some silly, romantic moment. He's humming with dangerous energy that reflects clear to his eyes. "Calm down, Griffin."

For a moment, I'm afraid he'll lose his temper and electrify the city, fry a bunch of people like some bad *Carrie* remake, and then government agents will show up, haul him off, and open him up like a classroom anatomy experiment.

With caution, I turn further toward him and gently pat his hand that's grasping my wrist.

"You're not a bad alien," I say, quietly, forcing myself to stare back into his eyes. "You're a really funny, weird alien who likes to wear ugly sweaters and shop for designer clothes. You can pull this off, Griffin, I believe in you. But you can't get all scary right now, okay? You can't. Everyone needs to love you, not fear you."

I can feel rage, sadness, and frustration seeping out of him, leaking into my brain through our eye contact, but then Griffin's shoulders slump and his grip on my wrist loosens a bit.

"You okay now?" I ask, and he nods. "Good. I'm gonna bring Kammie over here." I feel a little nervous to leave him alone, so I turn and catch Kammie's eye, waving her over. Frog Snout has set up a smoking post not far from us, and all of them are staring at Griffin with suspicious looks on their faces. *Oh well.*

"Is everything alright?" Kammie asks as she approaches. She eyeballs Griffin and then raises her eyebrows to me, as if in some kind of secret signal that I don't quite catch. Dev follows her closely, taking his place beside Griffin. The two of them exchange a look, although I'm pretty sure they know exactly what the other is thinking, without needing words at all.

"Griffin needs to do the concert tomorrow night," I say. "We need a reasonably sized venue, someone to film it, and a way to broadcast it online."

"Um, hello, Daisy, don't you remember about Lillian Gale? I can ask her to help us out. I bet she'd get us booked for anything we wanted!"

"Madison Square Garden?" I ask, and Griffin perks up as he waits for her response.

"Well, we'll see. But she left her cell phone number with me, so we could discuss the terms for her renting the studio. Want me to go call her?"

Griffin nods, leaning against Dev's side. "You will be repaid for your kindness and assistance, Kammie. I'll make sure of it."

"Oh!" Kammie says, tossing some of her red hair over her shoulder. "I'm happy to help, and you don't need to worry about paying me back with money or something. I'm not materialistic… If I was, I wouldn't live in this horrible place! All I'd really like is a bit of time alone with Dev, honestly. Your friend is quite the gentleman, and one doesn't come across single men like him very often."

Dev's face tinges a light pink, and he smiles, wide and bashful. "That's very nice of you, Kammie. I think you're lovely, too."

"You two are ridiculous," Griffin says in a gruff voice, poking Dev in the ribs. "Just take her out tonight, won't you? You've been making eyes at each other all day, and I can't stand it anymore."

"I can't leave y—"

Griffin stands up a bit taller. "I'm commanding you, Devon. You'll take her out tonight, and you'll have a good time doing it. You never think of yourself."

Dev acts as if he might argue again, but Griffin cuts him off with a wave of his hand, turning his attention back to Kammie.

"How soon will you know if your friend can help us?" Griffin asks.

"Oh, she's a famous musician; she's not exactly my friend, but I'll call her right now."

"She's famous, you say? Ask her if she'll perform with me. That'll get us even more attention."

Kammie glances between Griffin and Dev, and then at me. "Alright, let me go call her. Someone had better talk to the Froggy boys, though, before they mutiny. They're convinced the two of you are aliens." She shrugs one shoulder rather daintily before leaning closer to Griffin and Devon. "Don't worry, though. I won't tell them that they're right." With a wink, she's off, headed inside to run back up to her studio.

"What did she say?" Griffin and Devon ask each other at

the same moment, exchanging a pointed look.

"Uhhh... I think maybe she knows," I say at last.

Griffin pokes Dev in the side. "I suppose that makes tonight a bit simpler, eh?" he asks, laughing to himself before he puts on his best pop star face and walks off to talk to Frog Snout.

Somehow, maybe because I've been around him long enough now, I sense a change in the air even before I hear Griffin's finger snap.

Chapter 19

IT TAKES A LOT OF PRODDING, BUT DEV FINALLY AGREES TO GO ON HIS date with Kammie, so long as all but one of the bodyguards remains with Griffin. Lillian Gale has promised to help us, because she took such a shining to Kammie. She thinks Griffin sounds like an 'interesting creature' and has even booked us for the Bowery Ballroom tomorrow night. I've set up a simple website with Griffin's name as the URL, so we have somewhere to direct people to the livestream of the concert. Lillian will join Griffin on stage at the end and perform one of her songs from the classic Juicy Bed days. She does not know David Bowie.

And all of this has put Griffin in a much better mood, thankfully, even though he still has no leads on the Bowie thing.

Griffin and I take his car back to our hotel without really speaking, but once he's climbed from the car, he turns and offers his hand to me.

"Suddenly so chivalrous," I say, trying not to laugh. "Shouldn't I be the one helping you out of the car, Mister Pop Star?"

"Ah, shut it."

"Awww, that's more like the Griffin I know. I was worried the alien pod people had abducted you."

He pulls me against him. "Are you asking to be abducted, Daisy Kirkwood?"

"You already abducted me, remember? In SoHo?"

Griffin presses a kiss to my lips, and I can't help slipping my arms around his neck. I'm not sure how long we stand there being amorous with each other, but just as it starts to feel like a rom-com come true, a bright flash of light all but blinds me.

"Mr. Valentino! Mr. Valentino!" someone shouts, and I glance over Griffin's shoulder to see a group of photographers, cameras drawn and at the ready. With mighty *click-click-clicks* and lightning-like circles of flashes, I have to blink back stars.

"How did they find out where you're staying?" I whisper. "It's hurting my eyes…"

Griffin turns toward the photographers, stepping in front of me. "Hello, everyone!" he says, waving one hand. "If you'd like to take my holop—errr, picture, you may do so now."

"Mr. Valentino, what do you think about legendary rock musician Robert Zuma calling your music 'pathetic English vomit'?" someone asks, swooping in with a video camera.

Griffin steps back a bit, his foot lighting on mine, and I feel his fingers flutter back over me, but he regains his composure and leans toward the reporter. "Did he? Well, I dunno who he is, so what's it matter?" Griffin says, which just prompts the reporter to wolfishly grin.

Dating an Alien Popstar

"How is your boyfriend, Devon London?" the man asks, and we endure another painful round of camera flashes.

"Dev? Dev's fine," Griffin says, reaching back again and finding one of my hands. He squeezes my fingers, even while standing up a bit taller and raising his chin for the pictures. "Tomorrow night, I'll have a concert at the Bowery Ballroom. You may start queuing now if you wish. Lillian Gale will join me onstage at some point, and the whole thing will be filmed. You'll be able to watch at, errr…" He stops and looks back at me. "Where is it, Daisy?"

"You'll be able to stream it on Griffin's website, which is his name." I rattle off the URL.

Griffin turns his attention back to the reporters. "That's right. I hope all of you will come. It will be the best concert in the universe." He holds his hands up in the symbol for the Origin Collective.

"How do you feel about the British prime minister's sister calling the president a monkey? Are you angry about that?"

"A monkey?" Griffin says. I realize all at once what's about to happen, but before I can stop him, he nervously giggles and says, "Well, that's funny, isn't it? Nothing to get angry over." Suddenly, all the reporters are yelling at Griffin, asking him leading questions to get inflammatory answers, so I lean up, hands on either side of him, and bite his earlobe to get his attention. "Let's go inside," I say, and he nods.

"Alright, goodbye!" Griffin says, and his bodyguards take this as a cue to spring to action. They clear a path for us, and we escape into the lobby of our hotel, cameras flashing behind us. "They really love me, don't they? And to think, I always assumed the people of your planet were idiots," Griffin says as we head toward the elevator.

"They were baiting you, Griffin. Oh, God, you shouldn't

have said anything to them about the British prime minister's sister."

"Well, I don't know her, but she sounds like good fun if she likes monkeys. Those are the cute, furry things, right? I've called Dev a balak more times than I can count. One time, he elbowed me hard enough that I dropped a glass of nutritional liquid on my foot."

"Griffin."

"No, it's alright, I had it coming. And my foot's fine."

A member of the hotel staff runs for us, cutting across the lobby with such vigor that he slides a few paces as he stops in front of us. "Sir, I'm so terribly sorry. I have no idea how they found out you're staying here! I called for someone to get rid of them, but there's nothing we could do…"

Griffin nods and waves him away. "It's alright. Nothing we can do now."

"Are you… you're, uh, you're alright, sir?"

"I'm fine, thank you. Just make sure that anyone who asks after me knows they can find me at my concert tomorrow night at the Bowery Ballroom."

Griffin pulls me into the elevator and steps aside while all the bodyguards pile in after us.

"There's going to be some fuss about what you said," I quietly say.

"Fuss? What do you mean? About what?"

"There are still a lot of racism issues in this country." I close my eyes, wincing. "They wanted you to say something controversial, and you don't know any better, so you played right into it."

"Racism?"

There's no easy way to explain the situation to him, but Griffin just presses into me, trapping me against the elevator wall. He whispers something in his language, in a sultry tone. When I eyeball him, he apologizes and switches back to English. "I liked it when you bit my ear," he whispers. "You should do that again."

It seems like all the bodyguards are staring directly at me right now, and the music playing in our elevator is just a bit too chipper. I take a deep breath and force a smile for Griffin. "We'll talk about that later, alright?"

"You know what we should do?" he whispers against my ear. Tingles run clear through me.

He's making it hard to think. "W-what?"

Griffin traces his fingers down my side, and I shiver. "We should order a bunch of hot dogs from a street vendor and try on the Dior clothes I had sent over this morning," he says.

"Oh." Not what I was expecting. "*Okay...*"

"That way, I can choose my stage outfit for tomorrow night. After all, for the rest of time, everyone will look back on this concert! I have to look fabulous."

We reach our floor, and the doors to the elevator slide open.

"Can you show me what this Lillian Gale sounds like?" Griffin asks as we walk into our suite. "Video or something?"

I pull up a video of her singing at a charity event and hand my phone to Griffin. He stares silently at the screen the whole time, as if he's memorizing everything he sees. When it's over, he hands the phone back.

"I like her," he proclaims, and then walks away from me. He speaks for a while with two of the bodyguards, in his native language, with a lot of hand gestures included. They seem to be negotiating something, because one speaks rather defensively, and then Griffin's voice turns stern.

I receive a text from Kammie that is nothing more than

a 'thumbs-up' emoticon. Well, at least things are going well for her. I tweet from Griffin's account, telling everyone the plans for the concert tomorrow night, inviting them to join us. Within seconds, there are excited replies and retweets.

Wow.

Griffin returns to me a few minutes later, already tugging his shirt off. "Alright," he says, "Help me find the perfect outfit."

Rolling my eyes a bit for good measure, I dig around through his bags of clothes. There are so many pieces that I'm a little overwhelmed at first, but after a moment, I gather together a pair of black skinny jeans, a white dress shirt with black piping, and a knee-length black jacket.

Griffin strips off his pants and tosses them aside, diving right into trying the outfit on. "Hmmm, how do I look?" he asks as he's adjusting the jacket.

"You look very nice. Can you move around in it?"

He tests it out by dancing around a bit, twirling, kicking his legs out, almost knocking a lamp over in the process. "Yes, I think I can move quite well." He spins one more time, throwing his hands up in the air with a flourish at the end. "Will everyone like it?"

"Everyone? I don't know about everyone. I guess it's never really possible for everyone to like something. Or someone." I shrug. "But I like it."

"I like it, too," he says, trotting off to inspect the ensemble in the mirror. I follow after him, without quite as much enthusiasm. "I wish they could see me this way, back home."

Somehow, I know Griffin means something deeper than wishing his fabulous Earth wardrobe could be seen and worshipped on his planet. "Maybe they'll see you differently when you win this bet against your dad," I say, finding his gaze in the reflection of the mirror.

He stares back at me for a long time, so long that I almost forget everything except for the enchantingly unfamiliar essence of his blue eyes.

"I don't want you to forget me," he whispers, but I never see his lips move.

"Why would I forget you?"

Griffin's eyes turn down and his shoulders droop. "It might not be safe for you to remember."

"If you think you're going to wipe my memory or something, Griffin Valentino, you are very much mistaken. I have no intention of forgetting you, even if you think it's for my safety. This brain is mine, and I'll keep all the memories I want to keep."

Maybe he smiles, a little, but it could just be a trick of the light. "I can't ever win an argument with you, can I?"

"That would be a great big *no*."

He looks away from me, as if debating something, and then says, "At home, we have two words for love. One means… we like something a lot. Maybe a certain taste, color, or feeling. But the other word means that our soul would break, that we would cease to exist, without the being of our affection."

"That makes a lot of sense. People would be less confused when I was talking about my inordinate love for spaghetti or chocolate. They'd know I don't actually want to marry chocolate," I say. "I mean, sometimes I want to marry chocolate, but that's usually hormones talking."

"The word for love, for powerful and life-altering love, in our language, is waandaa."

There are so many things I want to say, but Griffin closes up as palpably as a flower closes its petals, rearranging his collar before walking away from me.

"Is that why you always called me Wanda?" I ask, trailing

after him.

"When we first met, I sensed your name was Wanda."

"Well, what's your name? Your real name. It can't really be Griffin Valentino."

He hesitates, but then he says, "Griffin Tamanoc Anterysli. My family name is Tamanoc. Anterys is my father, so my father-name is Anterysli."

His name sounds foreign and certainly too wordy for me to repeat on command, but somehow, I feel as if I can see him now, in a way I never could before.

"Your name is really Griffin?"

"There are animals on our world called griffins. Or rather, there was, a long time ago. Not sure there are any of them left now, but my father named me after them. They're symbolic of power, so of course he likes them."

I cast a half smile in his direction. "That's cool. We have ancient stories about those, too. I guess our people really are connected, in more ways than we thought."

"Well, I always thought it was a little silly. I'm not very powerful at all." He inspects a shirt before tossing it aside.

"So, Griffin Tama-what Antler-y... do you, uh, do you still think of me as Wanda?" I whisper.

Griffin sorts through his pile of errant clothes for a few seconds before glancing over his shoulder at me. "That will always be my name for you."

With an unusual degree of authority, I order all the bodyguards to guard the suite from outside our room, make sure Griffin's stage costume is carefully removed and set aside for tomorrow night, and then abduct my alien to the nearest horizontal surface.

I've only got three days left with him, after all, and you can't ignore a deadline like that.

Chapter 20

WE ARRIVE AT THE VENUE IN THE MORNING, AROUND TEN, AND WE'RE whisked inside by several intimidating men and a talkative, middle-aged woman wearing a headset. Griffin's treated like royalty in residence, and we're led directly to Kammie and Devon. Dev's in good spirits, all self-satisfied smugness and smiles as he greets us with coffee and cheerful banter. I catch one look at Kammie's slightly rumpled hair and have a good idea of why Devon never returned to our suite last night.

Almost immediately, Devon pulls Griffin aside to speak to him in hushed tones. Judging by the way Griffin slings his arm around Devon's shoulders and leans into him, the two of them aren't used to being apart for very long.

"Lillian Gale will be here later," Kammie says. "And Frog Snout's here already. I think they're having a third smoke break. They're a bit nervous."

My eyes stray to Griffin, Devon, and their circle of

bodyguards. "You think we can really pull this off?"

Kammie pats at her messy hair and shrugs. "I should hope so, considering the boys need to get back to their planet in two days. On the other hand, a part of me hopes they'll just decide to stay here."

I turn to look at her, dropping my voice to a whisper. "You… he told you…?"

"Well, of course he told me! And showed me some pictures, too." Kammie shoots me a pointed look. "Honestly, Daisy, you, of all people, should know I'm very careful about the people I associate with."

Now I struggle with laughter. "You? Careful of who you associate with? Have you met Frog Snout?"

"Alright, well, I'm very particular about the people I go on dates with. Devon's wonderful, but I wanted to get to know him a bit better before I made any firm decisions on him." Kammie lets out a little sigh, and then quietly says, "I'm not sure I could ever go back to dating anyone that *isn't* from his planet. He's so polite, well spoken, and knowledgeable. He actually likes to treat a woman right. And cuddle. That alone makes him a superior being."

She has a point, but it's not going to do either of us much good. Griffin's mission is too important to him; he won't change his mind about leaving, even in the face of really great cuddling sessions.

A few hours of set up and rehearsals later, Griffin's bouncing around on the stage like he owns it, showering all of us with ridiculous guitar riffs and delighted laughter. Frog Snout behaves quite amiably, and not even one member of the band mentions anything about aliens. Apparently, Griffin's finger-snapping persuasion has left them with a lot less questions.

Dating an Alien Popstar

Lillian Gale arrives late, as might be expected. In person, she's even taller and more striking than I'd imagined. She's always been a legendary figure in my mind—the leader of Juicy Bed, a songwriter and queen among the male-dominated music field of her time. She's mythical, although not as outwardly eccentric as Bjork, and she's powerful, though not in the snarly manner of Kim Gordon. Standing in front of her, even briefly, is enough to make me almost dizzy with excitement, but she's surprisingly unfussy and swoops in to kiss Kammie on the cheek in greeting.

"Now, now, who do we have here?" she asks as Griffin approaches her. She sounds considerably younger than a woman in her late thirties should. Her orange hair has been pulled neatly back into a braid, but nothing else on her is tidy. She's a tangle of sumptuous fabrics and jangling gold bracelets, and her eyes wander almost as much as her hands float through the air as she speaks. She circles Griffin a few times, and then nods as if she's made a very important decision. "Yes, I'm glad I've lent you a hand. You don't belong around here, and we must always treat our visitors well. Always, always, if we want to keep it all spinning the way it should, in this big universe."

It might be my imagination, but I could swear that Griffin blushes a little. He smiles shyly up at Lillian when she grasps one of his pale hands between both of hers, and he's quick to answer all of her questions.

I can't help wondering if Kammie told Lillian that the boys are from another world, but I don't dare bring it up.

"Thank you for your help," Griffin says, half-bowing to Lillian, and then motioning for Dev. As soon as his friend is close enough, Griffin pulls him in tight against his side. "This is my best mate, Devon London."

"Have you been to England yet?" Lillian asks, confirming

my suspicion that she knows. *Oh well.* At least she got us the gig. "You simply have to go during your visit. I'm from England, you know, or part of me is. Sometimes, I think I'm actually from something a bit less... physical than that, you know? Might be from the darkness or the light or a beautiful lake somewhere."

Griffin's confused smile kind of makes me want to hug him, but then he and Lillian walk away from the rest of us, talking about the song she'll perform with him. I take this opportunity to all but pounce on Devon.

"Have you heard anything new from back home?" I demand as quietly as I can manage.

"No, Griffin's father hasn't sent any correspondence." Devon glances in Griffin's direction. "Knowing him, he expects to win the wager and won't bother contacting us again."

"Did you tell him that there might be someone else from your planet here?"

Devon hesitates in his answer. "Daisy, you see... Griff and his father have a very difficult relationship. I'm not sure that telling him that would be good for the situation."

"You mean, he wouldn't send help if you needed it?"

"Help? It would be his idea of a hard lesson, if anything. He never wanted us to come here."

Griffin and Lillian practice their song together, and the music fangirl in me does cartwheels to witness something like this, especially from the side of the stage, but when it's over and Griffin's bouncing back toward us, I can't help returning my attention to Devon.

"There were a lot of reporters outside our hotel last night. We managed to slip out this morning without anyone seeing us, but our hotel location has definitely been compromised," I say, and I can almost feel Devon's worry trickle back into his mind. He pulls away from me and propels himself toward Griffin, catching him up in a congratulatory hug and then whispering in his ear.

I almost lose contact with them for the rest of the afternoon, because Griffin's got a million things to go over and a billion reasons he needs this whole thing to work out. Eventually, I feel so awkward and unsure of my place in the fray that I step outside to the designated smoking area and suck in a few deep, second-hand-smoke-laced breaths.

A quick look at my cell phone reveals I've missed a few calls from home and two from my day job. What must they think of me now? I've all but disappeared from my life, whisked off into a world of expensive clothes and interplanetary intrigue. And what will happen in a couple of days? Succeed or fail, Griffin and Devon will return home. I'll end up unemployed… and possibly homeless. It wouldn't be horribly surprising if the roommates decided my absence was a good excuse to throw my stuff into the street and rent my room to someone else.

All at once, I imagine asking Griffin to take me with him. Would he be able to? Would he want to? Maybe he'd say that there wasn't enough room in their spaceship or pods or whatever it is they used to get here. Maybe he'd tell me that his planet would kill me. And if he loses the bet, maybe he'd say no on the grounds that, technically, he's betrothed to someone else, however horrible she happens to be.

But I can ask.

With a renewed sense of confidence, I hurry back inside and allow myself to be caught up in the head-spinning circus that is concert prep.

Half an hour before the concert's set to start, the venue is already packed. I hear a lot of murmured amazement on the part of the staff, especially since Griffin is such a "new sensation." Griffin's escorted about like the prince he is, offered water bottles, and asked a lot of questions about his career. He's wise enough to keep tight-lipped on the matter, though, and in place of telling them anything, he just smiles at everyone in a rather sneaky manner.

Someone takes a lot of photos of Griffin and Lillian together, and Griffin tugs Devon into the pictures with him, pulled tight against his side. The two of them grin like kids on Christmas, but then Griffin looks to his left and right, his smile falling away.

"Where's Daisy?" he demands, his brow furrowed. "Someone find Daisy, would you? She should be here."

I step out of the shadowy safe spot where I've been hiding and wave to Griffin. His face lights up again and he motions for me, completely insistent until I'm close enough that he can press a quick kiss to my cheek and show me off to the cameras. Dev holds his hand out for Kammie, who takes it and steps onto the white backdrop with us, and suddenly, we're all part of some strange, beautiful photoshoot.

Just before the concert, Griffin finally starts to show a little nerves. He paces back and forth, a short distance each time, his pointed features cast with shadows. Someone announces that stage time is two minutes, and Griffin fiddles with his guitar a bit, muttering to himself.

"You're gonna be great," I say, and he captures my hand a bit too tightly. His fingers feel colder than usual. "You okay?"

"She always told me to never give up."

"Who…? Your mom?"

Griffin nods.

"Well, I'm sure she'd be really proud of you right now," I say. "Go out there and show everyone in the universe who you really are. This time, they'll all see the truth. I know they will."

I can feel the air around Griffin warm up, as if the chill has been melted away from him. He leans in to catch my face between his hands for a kiss. Even with his guitar hanging from its strap between us, I pull him as close as I can and drink him in. With one last gentle ruffle of his hair, I let him go and step back.

"Twenty seconds!"

Griffin and Frog Snout walk together toward the ramp that will lead them up to the stage. From the angle I'm standing, the ramp looks eerily a bit too much like it might lead into a bright spaceship in some cheesy science fiction movie. When Griffin steps onto it and turns one last time to smile at me, silhouetted against blinding lights, I have to struggle to just wave goodbye to him and not chase him up it.

I've never felt more left out than in this moment, especially when I hear a roar of cheers and screams from the crowd gathered out there.

"He'll be back," Dev whispers from beside me. When I don't say anything, he drops his hand to my shoulder. "Thank you, Daisy. None of this would have been possible without you."

I shrug a little, struggling with something that feels suspiciously like tears. How tired am I? How overwrought and exhausted am I really, after all of this? "It's no trouble," I say, but then I can *hear* the tears, gathering in the back of my throat.

"Thank you for being so good to Griff. He's not one to let many people in, but when he does, there's no letting go. He really cares for you." Dev quietly sighs. "I'm glad we found you. And I'm... eternally grateful that you stuck around even when we hadn't done anything to deserve it."

My eyes remain on the ramp a little longer, but then my vision blurs from tears. I struggle for a few seconds, because it's stupid to feel this way, but then Dev pulls me into a gentle hug.

"Wanna go up there?" he whispers.

"On stage, you mean?"

"Yeah, wanna go up? I think we should be up there with him."

"*Yes!*" I say, and he laughs. "Of course I want to. Can we do that?"

Dev wiggles his eyebrows at me. "According to everyone here, I'm his manager and you're his girlfriend, so I don't see why not, right? Besides, Griff's guards are going to panic if they're not up there." With that, Dev reaches for Kammie's hand and leads us up to the side of the stage.

All of that overwhelming emotion remains and just seems to grow when I'm finally standing off to the side of the stage, watching something I helped orchestrate. There's a sense of pride, of course, but also a sense of loss; we've finally achieved this moment and time marches on, closer and closer to the end of our adventures together.

Kammie elbows me gently, smiling. She raises her hands and claps along to the song, so I join her, clapping, swaying, and finally, smiling. I peer out at the crowd, and I sweat under the bright lights; a longtime dream fulfilled in the strangest way. Eventually, I even find myself laughing as Griffin attempts some banter between songs.

I'll have to coach him on that, later.

Lillian joins him on stage, near the end of the set, and she twirls around him like a green-and-blue impressionist painting. Her dress trails out behind her, and she throws some glitter dust on the people in the front row, on herself, and then on Griffin. I catch his slight wince as she tosses the remnants of her glitter bag over his head, but then he seems to realize there's no danger. He becomes a sparkly, grinning mess, coaxing the crowd into loud cheers for Lillian.

"Good night, people of Earth!" Griffin shouts, his voice amplified throughout the venue without need of a microphone. "Thank you for your love! Here is my love for you in return." He holds his arms open to them, letting out a delighted laugh at the screaming response he gets. "Please be good to each other, and try not to believe the evil of... of someone else. Find the good in them whenever you can." He moves so he can stand directly in front of one of the cameras and holds his hands up in the symbol of the Origin Collective.

After a bit of searching, I locate my phone in the deep recesses of my purse, and though it means taking my eyes off the scene before me for a few precious seconds, I snap as many pictures as I can. The last one is Griffin offering a sweeping bow to his adoring audience, and I email it to myself immediately, just in case. No use taking a chance with a moment like that.

Griffin and Lillian walk toward us at last, both of them sweaty and laughing, and then Frog Snout offers their own shaky, dumbfounded bow to the audience. As they exit the stage, I can hear Bill say, "So that's what it's like to play for an audience!"

"That was bloody amazing, Griff!" Dev says, pulling his friend into a backslapping hug that sends a bit of glitter floating into the air around them. "You were incredible; I'm so proud of you."

"We were all good," Griffin says between heavy breaths. His cheeks are pink with exertion, and his eyes blaze with blue electricity. The air around him crackles a little with warm, pleasant energy as he looks from Dev to Kammie, Lillian, Frog Snout, and then to me. "Great job out there, mates."

"A real audience," Bill says, shaking his head. "It's different than we expected."

"Yeah, louder!" another member of Frog Snout says. I never learned his name, but tonight, he smells even more like cheese than usual. "It's much louder."

"For all your hard work…" Griffin pats Dev's butt a couple of times with a mischievous look on his face as he removes his friend's wallet. The stack of money he hands Bill sends a lot of happy exclamations throughout Frog Snout.

Bill clears his throat. "Will you be, err, offended if we say that perhaps we're retiring from music? Tonight was basically the apex of our career," he says, and his band members nod. "I've always wanted to paint houses. I think Andy here wants to be a scuba dive instructor. And besides, this is enough bread to buy us food and medicinal magical plants for a long time." He pauses. "Hey, you don't mind if we go hit the catering table, do you?"

Griffin offers them a little bow. "Good luck, my friends, with everything. I will never forget you."

A few sloppy hugs are exchanged, and then Frog Snout leaves us, talking happily among themselves about their plans for the next few days.

Lillian kisses Devon on the cheek, and then holds Griffin's hands for a few seconds, as if saying a prayer over him. "Be brave, Griffin Valentino, be very brave," she says. "And keep an eye on what's closest to you."

With that, Lillian leaves us. Griffin leans close to Dev, speaking to him quietly. I'm about to say my own congratulations to Griffin when a man wearing a headset approaches and motions me closer so he can tell me something.

"You might want to see what's happening on TMZ," he says in an undertone. "And think about getting someone to kill it, quick."

"Why, what's happening?"

He gives me a serious look, so I fish my phone back out and type Griffin's name into a search engine with shaking fingers.

The first link that comes up has the headline *Rowdy Rock Star Gets in Fight and Makes Racist Comments*. The preview for the link ponders *Might recently famous Griffin Valentino be on drugs?* Another link calls him violent, and still another comments that he's still got a rabid audience despite his 'serious' faults. All of them are hooked up with a video clip from last night outside the hotel, when Griffin answered the 'monkey' question.

"The video went up about two hours ago. They must have wanted to time it with the concert, to get the most attention," the man says, and I feel like I can't even speak. I'd known that Griffin would get backlash for his remarks, but I hadn't realized how ugly it would actually look once it happened.

"He didn't mean to say that," I splutter at last. "He didn't understand what they were asking."

"Look, I'm just saying… you need to do something about it fast before it gets out of control."

I glance at Griffin, who's still busily talking with Dev. "How?"

The man shrugs. "Say he was sick, or he'd had too much to drink. Don't blame it on drugs, though. That'll make it worse."

My legs feel weak as I scroll through links to gossipy websites around the Internet. They're calling him racist, and someone's uploaded a video of Griffin and Dev's fistfight from the other day. Several of the links refer to him as bisexual and inquire if he's hurting the gay cause by beating his boyfriend. One link is from a blogger who claims he snorted coke with Griffin in a bathroom stall. *Ugh.*

Even though I don't want to, I pull Twitter up to see if

anyone's tweeting Griffin about the videos. Sure enough, mixed in with adoring tweets about the concert, I see people calling him awful names because of his comments last night.

One social justice blogger has tweeted Griffin, "We don't need racist, violent cis white men speaking for the gay cause! *There, I said it!*"

"What's wrong, Daisy?" Griffin says, and I nearly drop my phone in my rush to keep him from seeing the tweets. He pulls me into a tight hug. "Are you alright?"

"Y-yeah…" Oh, I can't tell him. I can't! It'll break his heart. "It's nothing."

He presses a kiss to my lips. "Yes, it is. You looked really sad."

"I'm just… you know, fried. It's been a long day, and we didn't get a lot of sleep last night."

Griffin's eyes narrow a little, and I try to avoid his gaze. "You're lying, Daisy. What's going on?"

Another man wearing a headset approaches us, holding a phone out to Griffin. "It's for you, Mr. Valentino," he says. "It's urgent."

Griffin takes the phone and presses it to his ear. His facial expression changes quickly from confusion to elation. "Alright, yes, when? When? Yes, hold on, please." He turns to Dev, wildly motioning him closer. "Here, please tell Devon everything you've just told me. We'll meet you there immediately. Or, well, the very moment we can get there. Yes, thank you so much, yes, yes. Yes, here's Devon." He hands the phone off to Devon and turns back to me, shaking all over with excitement. "We're going to England, Daisy! The Origin Collective has invited me to meet with them!"

After slipping out of the venue and Griffin signing things for the fans gathered there, we pile into our car and head back to the hotel, Kammie with us. Griffin's flying high on adrenaline from the show and his excitement about the Origin Collective, his hands moving nervously as he shifts around again and again in his seat.

"It's a good thing we bought tuxedos," Griffin says as we approach the hotel, prodding Dev. "Did you get the plane tickets for tomorrow morning? Dev?"

"The hotel staff should be able to help us with all that," Devon says, his head leaned over his phone-like device. He clicks away at it without looking up. "We'll have to get everything packed up fast. And I'll need to find our passports."

"You have passports?" I ask. "How did you get those?"

Dev shrugs. "We made them before we arrived. Better to blend in."

"You do realize you could have used that for getting your drink the other night at the bar?"

"Could I? Well, damn." Dev smiles, rather wistfully. "Next time, yeah?"

Kammie glances across the car at Griffin and me. "Daisy, do you have your passport with you?"

"It's... no. I don't have it with me." I let out a nervous chuckle. "It's at the apartment, in a box under my bed. You know, back with the roommates and all of that. My other life."

Griffin and Dev exchange meaningful looks.

"You two go on," Griffin says. "Make the arrangements for our tickets and pack up. We'll go get Daisy's passport and meet you back in a while."

Dev puts down his device. "Are you sure, Griff?"

"Of course! It's fine. Come on; don't be daft, Dev. D'ya reckon Daisy's roommates are going to try to kill me?"

I laugh, but Dev's face remains serious. "You'll need to take the guards with you."

"Yeah, yeah, yeah, whatever."

"And be careful."

"It's alright! I'm just gonna pop in and see what Daisy's place looks like before we have to go, you know?" Griffin says, and then all of us fall silent as the car pulls to a stop in front of the hotel. Griffin stammers a little, looking at Dev, but shooting glances in my direction. "I mean, we're not leaving right now. You know. I just mean... I just meant it might be nice to... well, since we're not staying forever..."

With a shake of my head, I wave to Dev. "We'll be fine," I say. "I'll keep a close eye on him, I promise." The idea of a little time alone with him isn't so awful, anyway, considering that he's right. They won't be here forever.

Besides, I need a chance to ask him about my idea.

Dev and Kammie exit the vehicle together, but Dev turns back to look at Griff. "If you feel at all unsafe…"

At first, I think Griffin might just wave his friend off, but he says, "I promise I'll be careful," and leans out of the car long enough to hug Dev.

Before I know it, we're pulling away from the hotel again and I've given the driver my address, leaving our friends to prepare for the upcoming trip. I haven't thought a lot yet about Griffin seeing my apartment, but the trip over allows me just enough time to sufficiently start to freak out.

"Okay, so my apartment…" I say, meeting Griffin's gaze. It's hard to concentrate on anything when he looks at me that way, so I force myself to look away. "My apartment isn't just mine. I share it with a couple of other girls. You have to understand that a bunch of girls in their late twenties, living in the city… well…"

"What?"

I suddenly realize that this potential meeting-the-roommates thing is a two-way street. What are they going to think when I show up with Griffin Valentino? "And they might ask you a lot of questions. I don't really bring guys over. Ever."

Griffin considers this, shadows moving over his face as we drive along in the dark. Before we left the venue, he'd taken a quick shower, but some of the glitter had stuck to his hair, and I can see it shining like tiny stars when the passing lights catch it just so. "Well, then, I suppose they can all gape like fish when you walk in with me on your arm."

"They're probably going to be surprised that you're there with me."

"Why? Why would they be surprised? Would you prefer me to sex it up a bit before we go in?"

"While that sounds extremely inviting, I'm not sure—"

Before I can finish speaking, Griffin moves closer, coaxing me over until I'm sitting in his lap. "You know, we really don't have to sex it up." After a kiss, I whisper, "Unless you want to."

I can feel that he wants to, loud and clear, but we're close enough to my neighborhood by this point that I don't want to get him started just to shut him right down again.

"Griffin," I whisper, my lips brushing his cheekbone. "I want to talk to you about something."

"Would you rather me wait in the car? Because I will, if that would make you feel more comfortable."

"No, no, it's not that." How do I tell him that I'd like him to take me back to his planet on his… spaceship? Pod? Laser beam…?

"You should never let anyone make you feel like less than exactly what you are, Waandaa. You're magnificent, and you smell wonderful. And you're quite clever with wardrobe choices, even if a bit too safe at times."

I've never had a guy say he loves me. Well, except Creepy Jerry, but that doesn't count. However, it seems worth the wait right now, just to hear someone call me his beloved in an alien language.

"Griffin…"

The car stops, and a quick glance out the window tells me we've reached my apartment.

"Alright, look," I say, scrambling off his lap. "I've only lived here for three weeks, so these girls aren't terrible people or anything. They just assume by now that I'm either a closet lesbian or a hopeless case."

Griffin laughs. "Are you asking me not to do anything dodgy to them?"

"Yeah, kinda."

"Don't worry, I won't. Not unless you ask me to."

We, meaning Griffin, five bodyguards, and me, head up to my apartment together. Unlocking the door with a pounding, painful sense of nerves, I imagine a wide variety of increasingly awkward outcomes to this situation, but it turns out that only one of the roommates, Nina, is home. She springs up from our small red couch once she sees all the bodyguards. "W-what's this? Who...? Wait, are you Griffin Valentino?" she demands, seemingly all in one breath.

Griffin stands up a bit straighter. "I am."

"Your song..."

"It's wonderful, yes."

"It's my ringtone!"

Griffin glances at me, and I cover his confusion by loudly announcing, "I need to get something from my room!"

Nina stands rooted to the spot, staring at Griffin with wide eyes. Given her pajama pants and sleeveless shirt, she must be sick or in the middle of a breakup. The latter is very possible, considering she's had at least ten male visitors since I moved in. She's easily the nicest of my roommates, but even she's been suspicious of my relative inability to join in on the apartment-wide conversations about relationships and boys.

"How do you know Daisy?" she asks, probably calculating her chances at throwing him down on the couch and becoming a professional Valentino groupie.

"She's been my friend since I arrived, actually, and my lover, more recently," Griffin says, folding his hands behind his back and smirking. "I'm lucky to have found her."

Nina glances over at me, surprise evident in her expression, but then she finally offers me a slow nod and gives me a thumbs-up.

I'm not sure if I should be embarrassed or proud, so I duck into my room and search for my passport instead. After tearing through the box I'd thought the passport was in, I move to my small dresser, and barely hear Griffin step into my room.

"So this is your personal space?"

I stop everything to take a good look around and try to imagine what he sees. A teddy bear. A framed autograph from one of my favorite musicians. A pile of clean clothes that haven't been folded or put away. A box of pads. *Oh God, how embarrassing.* Two boxes of cheese snack crackers.

Oh, and a stack of magazines that range from music magazines to the kinds that say things like *Ten Best Secrets for a Mind-Blowing Night.* Griffin immediately picks up one of the latter and leafs through it.

I return to my search and finally locate the passport, just as Griffin pauses on one page and frowns a bit. "Hmmm, your publications have the strangest advice…"

"Let's go," I say, taking the magazine away from him and pushing him out of my room. With one last glance back at my teddy bear, CDs, and that small photo of my parents and me that my mom had insisted I bring to NYC, I'm ready to go.

Actually, on second thought… I run back into the room and grab the picture of my parents.

If I'm going to another planet, I should bring that along.

"Goodbye, Jagger," I whisper to the teddy bear, and then hurry out of the room, nearly colliding with Griffin in the hallway.

"You got everything?"

I nod and lead him back to the front door. "Bye, Nina."

"How long will you be gone…?" she asks, stationed by the television once again. "We all wondered where you were."

"Could be a bit, but I'll let you know," I say, hesitating. "We're going to England."

"*England?* Wowie, that's amazing! Wait until the girls hear;

they'll be so jealous, too. Well, have fun, alright? And be safe. And send me a message immediately if you meet Prince Harry."

I can't help laughing, especially when Nina goes so far as to spring over and give me a hug.

As we leave, Griffin looks at me and asks, "Think she knows David Bowie?" and I just laugh even harder, because the day has been strange, wonderful, and exhausting, and I have no idea what's even happening in my life.

We arrive back at the hotel after a ride that puts Griffin to sleep and even makes me nod off for a bit, leaned against his shoulder. As we pull up near the front entrance of the hotel, I realize there are a lot of people standing outside.

More than a lot. A full-sized crowd.

"Wonder what's going on at the hotel?" I say, waking Griffin. We stare together out the window, and I hope silently that the crowd is for someone else. "Maybe a famous actor is staying at our hotel."

"Nah, it's probably for me," he says, and I sense something almost like anxiety in his voice. "Look, someone's got a sign with my name on it."

Sure enough, I spot a couple of handwritten signs with Griffin's name on them.

One of the bodyguards steps out of the car first, holding the door open for Griffin. I expect him to hang back, to let someone clear a path for him, but instead, he takes an audible deep breath and leaps out of the car. His posture says he's confident, maybe even arrogant, but I can feel the static around him that tells a different story.

"Hello, everyone!" he says as I'm climbing out of the car. I haven't told him yet about the gossip websites or the mean things people are tweeting at him, so all I can do is desperately hope no one brings it up. "I'm flattered and honored that you came out here to see me. Tonight's show was wonderful, and I invite all of you to watch it on my website. I'm very tired, though, and I'd like to go to my room to get some rest. I have a lot of very important work in the morning. If you'll be kind enough to allow me through, I would appreciate it."

Before I can stop him, Griffin steps out into the crowd.

It really seems almost like they swallow him. One second, I can see his wisps of hair sticking up at haphazard angles, and then, he disappears from my sight in a crush of arms, faces, and screams.

I press into the crowd, pushing and shoving my way toward Griffin. From behind, it looks as if he's being devoured, hands grabbing at his clothes, head, and hair. I can tell by the tension in his shoulders that he's closing in on himself, even as I see him batting uselessly at the sea of strangers around him.

As I fight my way closer, I call for Griffin, but I don't think he can hear me. He raises his hand, snapping his fingers, but nothing happens, so he snaps them again and then again. He sways sideways and loses his balance. I reach him just in time to catch him from falling and cling tightly to him. One of the bodyguards follows at my heels and walks by Griffin and me, clearing a path toward the hotel.

"Racist!" someone yells, and I pray they'll shut up. "Racist!" A few other voices join in, hurling insults, though thankfully, most of the crowd seems more interested in touching Griffin rather than hurting him, as we struggle through.

It's just as we reach the entrance to the hotel, where a couple of doormen rush out to help us, that someone says, in a very clear voice, "You're nothing but an over-privileged brat, Valentino. Go back to England, you racist bastard!"

Griffin shudders, craning his neck to try to find who said it, but we tug him into the safety of the hotel.

As we burst into the hotel lobby, two members of the staff approach us with terrified looks across their faces. "I'm so sorry, Mr. Valentino," one of them says. "We called for security, but they're... they're on their way. They—they—"

Griffin, for his part, pushes away from his bodyguards and me, saying "Don't touch me!" as if his life depends on it. After a few deep breaths, he casts a wild look at the apprehensive hotel staff members. "It's alright," he says with a jerky nod. "I'm going to my room. Just see to it that there's not... not a crowd in the morning, would you?" With that, he turns and walks to the elevator without another word, managing to catch one alone before any of us can join him.

I have to take an elevator ride with a bunch of nervous bodyguard aliens. Never a fun time, I'll tell you that.

As soon as the doors open, I burst from the elevator and run to our suite, knocking on the door until Kammie opens it. I can hear Dev's voice and feel his concern even before I can see him. "Did something happen to your eye, Griff?"

Griffin's stationed close to the bed, the heel of one of his hands ground against his eye and his whole body rigid, as if he expects to be jumped at any moment. Dev, conversely, is in motion, orbiting his friend around and around.

"My eye's fine," Griffin says, though he hasn't stopped rubbing it.

One of the bodyguards crosses the room in two long strides and takes hold of Griffin by the head, placing one huge finger on Griffin's eyelid so he can inspect his eye.

"Get away from me!" Griffin shouts. The lights in our suite flicker out, the furniture shakes, and little blue-and-green sparks dance through the air around him.

"Let him go; he doesn't like people touching his eyes," I say, taking a few blind steps in the darkness. I hear the bodyguard say something about needing to be sure he's not injured, and I hear a dangerous hissing that could only be Griffin. "He has bad memories about it—you're going to give him a panic attack, especially after what just happened out there. Let him go."

The lights turn back on, and Griffin slips away from the bodyguard, glowering. "Don't touch my eye. Don't you ever bloody touch my eye without asking; do you understand?"

Dev, for once, stands by with his mouth slightly ajar and his eyes wide, at a complete loss. "Griff, what's wrong?"

"He'd better not bloody touch me again."

"What's Daisy mean—bad memories?"

The furniture shakes, though not as violently this time, and Griffin covers his face with his hands, stepping backward. When he finally looks at us again, he takes a few quick breaths before speaking. "Dev. Did you get the plane tickets for tomorrow?"

"Yeah. Kammie and I got 'em. But, Griff, what's going on? Are you alright?"

"When do we leave?"

"Seven in the morning." Dev seems about to say something else, but Griffin's already walking away, toward the bathroom. "Griff, wait…"

"We should finish packing, you know? If we're leaving at seven." Griffin closes the bathroom door on us before we can say anything else.

Dev turns to me. "Does he know about the videos?"

I don't even want to answer this question, but I know there's no avoiding it. "I don't think so. How do you about them?"

"Kammie and I saw them when we were buying the plane tickets. She said it's 'trending' or... or something like that." Dev lowers his head. "Please, Daisy, what did he tell you?"

"Tell me...?"

"About a bad memory, regarding his eyes."

In a million years, I'd never have guessed that there could be anything, anything at all, that Dev wouldn't know about Griffin. Sure, Griffin has some obvious evasion issues when it comes to serious matters, but it's hard to believe that could encompass his best friend, too.

"Daisy," Dev says, his eyes taking on a pleading level that usually only puppies can achieve.

"He-he said that someone tried to blind him, when his mom was... you know."

"Blind him?"

"I don't know the full details, obviously, but he said something about someone trying to blind him. And a few minutes ago, we got mobbed outside. It was insane! So he's probably having a panic attack."

Dev lets out a heavy sigh and turns away, rushing off to lean against the bathroom door and quietly ask Griffin to open it. After much coaxing, I hear the bathroom door open and Dev slips inside with his friend, closing the door behind himself.

Kammie hugs me, without a word, and I find myself happy to return it.

"The crowd was pretty scary," I say against her shoulder. "I've never seen that many people swamp someone before."

"You've never seen Madonna then! Talk about swamped. Personally, I'd be afraid to come too close to her, in case she drank my youth to aid in her mission to live forever."

Despite myself, I can't help chuckling a little. Leave it to

Kammie to say something like that. I'm about to attempt a comment of my own, when I hear an insistent, strange beeping noise emanating from the bed. "What's that?" I whisper, though I'm not sure why I'm whispering. "Is that your phone?"

"Nah, my phone's in my bag."

We walk together, slowly, toward the bed. For a few seconds, I consider that it might be a bomb or something, but then realize that's completely bonkers. Instead, we find Griffin's little phone-like device on top of the comforter, buzzing, shaking, and beeping.

"Is he getting a call?" Kammie says. "I saw Dev answer his. Here, hold on."

Before I can stop her, she's picked up the device and hit a button. The device stops shaking and buzzing all at once, and a holographic image of a woman appears in front of us, almost life size. When Kammie drops the device in her surprise, the holograph flickers in and out of view, but it doesn't disappear.

Oh, great.

Chapter 22

THE HOLOGRAPHIC WOMAN IS BEAUTIFUL, BUT IN THE MANNER OF women who can look good while driving a railroad spike through your head. She casts an accusatory and condescending glance in my direction, and then smiles very slowly and asks me something I can't understand.

"Are you one of Griffin's friends?" I ask, noting she's pale and dark-haired like Griffin. Maybe she's one of his relatives? His father's secretary?

"Friends?" she repeats, and I hear a loud garbling noise as her mouth continues to move. Then I can understand her. "I am Mali, the Queen President-to-be, Griffin's future wife, and, one day soon, the mother of his offspring. Who are you?"

The crazy *fiancée*? This is the crazy fiancée? I'm in *huge* trouble now.

"My name is Daisy Kirkwood, and I'm helping Griffin win his bet against his father," I say, in as brave a voice as I can manage.

If Griffin could face down my evil boss for me, I can face down his evil fiancée.

The evil fiancée raises one thin, black eyebrow. "Griffin will return in two of your days, marry me, and take his rightful place as Emperor President-to-be. And someday, maybe, he will even be worthy of his title." She smiles at me, even wider this time. "Now, run along and find him, will you? Since he's clearly not standing here with the two of you, he must be preoccupied with some other similarly useless female he'd like to waste his seed on."

I know enough about this woman to already hate her, but seeing her and interacting with her calls for a bit more useful actions than just standing by and glaring at her.

"You shouldn't talk about him that way," I say, stepping a bit closer to her flickering, ghostly visage. "Griffin's a better person than you or anyone else on your planet deserves. He cares about your people enough that he's planning to come back to you, even when he could stay here and be... be adored by everyone! And by me."

She remains silent for a long few seconds, considering me. "By you? By a dull-minded, lower lifeform? Aww. Don't you know nothing ever holds Griffin's interest for very long? As soon as he's had his fun experimenting with you, he'll run back to his father and say he's made a tremendous mistake. And then what? He'll go back to wasting his days with the only true love of his life—Dev." She pauses, for effect. "Or did you think he might actually care for you?"

"He does care for me," I say, although my voice shakes. "And he loves his people."

"Griffin hasn't the faintest idea what it means to be a leader. Leaders don't love their people. They protect them, and many times, they protect them from themselves. Has he told you anything about our world? Has he mentioned that we have very little left in the way of natural resources? Did he mention that our last war wiped out more than half of our population? Did he mention that infertility has prevented us from rebuilding as we need to? Or did he just tell you how much he loves his people? How he pours over everything he can learn about your stupid little planet, in hopes that he might get to wear costumes, dance around, and make everyone magically happy?"

"He has compassion. And he's brave. And he *does* make people happy."

She shakes her head. "You poor little thing. It's very dangerous to fall in love with an Emperor President-to-be," she quietly says. "They don't tend to live very long, especially the foolish ones."

The bathroom door creaks open. Griffin has barely stepped into view before he sees the holograph and runs forward, scooping his phone-device from the floor. He says something to his fiancée in their native language, but she just laughs and points in my direction.

"Too late for that, Griffin. I've already spoken to your little human toy. She's fiercely devoted to you, this one. However did you manage that? Did you snap your fingers enough times?"

Griffin stands up a bit taller, his shoulders rigid. "I'd never do that to her."

"No, I suppose you don't even need to. She's not as bright as your other lover was, just by heritage, so controlling her wouldn't be difficult."

"Don't talk about her that way," Griffin says, and I can feel static in the air around him, buzzing dangerously.

"Well, I suppose we'll see if she's as good as your other girl at giving away all of your secrets," Mali says. "But then, I don't know if we all need to hear the details of your skills as a lover again, do we?"

Dev emerges from the bathroom, taking his place by Griffin's side. "You're not supposed to contact Griff until we finish the wager," Dev says in an even, reasonable voice. "You know that."

"I heard you might not be alone out there, and I wanted to make sure you were safe."

"Why do you care?" Griffin says. "Whether I'm dead now or after I marry you, it's the endgame, isn't it?"

"Your paranoia concerns me, Griffin. Perhaps we should talk to a doctor about that when you return."

"Seeing as Griff and I will return soon to collect our winnings from his father, it might be the Emperor President and you who will need to visit the doctor. The shock of losing might prove too much for you," Dev says, and then he smiles. "Goodbye now. We have work to do." He snatches the device from Griffin's hands and switches it off, effectively making the evil fiancée disappear.

No one says anything for a long, painful few seconds.

"She's unpleasant," Kammie says at last.

Griffin sighs, rubbing his face. "She's bloody insane, is what she is. I have to win this bet against my father. Why don't we all get some sleep now? Tomorrow's a big day."

Dev opens his mouth, and maybe he means to argue, but then he just nods and reaches for Kammie's hand. "We'll see you in the morning, Griff. And if you need me, just call, okay? I'll only be in the next room."

Griffin hugs his friend and quietly says something I don't understand. He turns back to me, leaving Dev and Kammie to slip off to the other room. "Dev told me about Twitter," he says, squaring off his shoulders and raising his chin. "He doesn't think I should see it, but I want to see. Will you show me?"

I hesitate, but the determination in his eyes says it's useless to argue with him.

"It's stupid," I say. "They're just… people are stupid when they're online. They think they can say whatever they want, because it's not in person, and they have this false sense of security and bravery."

"Show me, Daisy. Please."

I pull up Twitter on my phone, glancing through the most recent interactions first, hoping that maybe they won't be so bad. Much to my relief, the negative tweets are scattered with happy tweets from fans. As I scroll, however, I spot several especially incendiary ones, including one that says, with no context, "*Kill yourself.*"

Griffin holds his hand out for my phone, and I reluctantly hand it over to him. He scrolls through the tweets for what feels like forever, silently, and then hands the phone back to me.

"Do you need help packing your things?" Griffin asks in a very quiet voice.

"No, it's okay. It'll only take me a minute to pack. You know… it's okay to be upset about this, as long as you don't let it stop you from your mission."

Judging by the downward tilt of his mouth and less vibrant color of his eyes, he's upset, but Griffin propels himself around the room, gathering items and pushing them into bags. Just when I think he's not going to say anything at all, he turns back to look at me.

"This happened to Ziggy Stardust, too, didn't it?" he whispers.

"What?"

"It all went wrong."

I've never really thought deeply about Ziggy Stardust as anything other than a classic rock album from a really cool musician. In fact, I'm not sure I even remember the story behind the album.

"He got caught up in himself." Griffin seems as if he wants to say something else, but he thinks better of it. Instead, he crosses the room to me and places his hands on either side of my face, his skin colder than usual. He looks at me imploringly, brushing our noses and leaning in closer until I think he wants me to look into him again. "Even if nothing else happened, even if the concert had gone all wrong and everyone in your world hated me, I would know that I was supposed to come here and meet you."

Maybe it's the dark energy crackling around him like a near-silent symphony, or maybe it's the strange depth of his eyes, or just the softness of his words, but I feel as if we're alone in the room, alone in the world… alone in existence for a few seconds. I slide my arms around his neck, and Griffin presses a gentle kiss to my lips.

"But the concert was great," I say. "You did it; you totally pulled it off. And tomorrow, you're going to find out everything you need to from the Origin Collective."

He shakes his head, dropping his gaze from mine. "I wish I had more time, Wanda, all the time I needed to know every secret of your body, every keyhole, every pressure point and switch, the same way I knew your mind when I looked into you," he whispers, his voice breathy with melancholy.

I settle my arms around his waist. "Well, you have tonight."

Griffin's eyes flutter closed and he kisses me again, this time with an element of desperation I wasn't expecting, his mouth coaxing my lips apart without hesitation. A deep growl emanates from somewhere in the back of his throat, sending shivers chasing through me, and he bites my lower lip just hard enough to hurt. We stand together for a long time, until he quietly tells his security team to wait outside, and he leads me across the room to the bed.

When Griffin's helped me out of my dress and I've helped him out of his jacket, he leans over me on the bed, tracing one warm finger over my shoulder.

"You wore it, finally," he says, slipping a finger under my bra strap. "Do you like it?"

"Oh yeah. It's not every day I get to wear a bra that costs as much as my rent for a week." I pause, thinking. "Well, back home. In New York, my rent would be a lot more than one Victoria's Secret bra a week."

He smiles, but I can tell he really has no idea what I'm talking about, so he just kisses my shoulder instead, kisses my chest, kisses me all over.

I hold to him tightly, as if I can keep him here, and beg my memory to hold on to the sound of his breath against my neck, his fingertips ghosting across my hips, the union of our bodies, and the heat of his mouth against mine as he exhales my name.

"Let me see?" he says, breathlessly, and I let him look into me again. This time, I can almost feel him sorting through me, drinking in as much as possible, and I seek him out as well. I glimpse flashes of memories and emotions, much like last time, but this time, the greatest intensity of emotion seems to revolve around disappointment and hope in turn.

Griffin's faced crowds and crowds of angry citizens, he's faced humiliating arguments with the recurring tall, authoritative figure that can only be his father, he's faced a crushing realization that a lover had revealed the details of their time together to the public, he's struggled to find his way here, and he has been bodily dragged into a crowd and almost beaten under the fists of vengeful, hungry, and exhausted men and women back home. And yet, through all of that, I can hear a resonating admonishment... *don't give up. Don't give up, my little one.* The voice must have belonged to his mother, and the memories of her light up around his mind like sparkling lanterns.

She must have been his friend and muse as a child, gentle, curious, and enthusiastic about life, showing Griffin reasons for hope and challenging his thinking.

I see just enough of his memories of her death—a brute of a man pulling Griffin from his mother and hitting him, threatening to slide a blade across his eyes and then shove his eyes into his mouth to shut him up. Griffin's father arriving too late and sending his son away in favor of falling down beside his dead wife—to feel his long-held pain, but then, I can't look anymore. It seems too intimate, more so than any of his other memories, even.

And then I see something else, something familiar and surreal... I see myself from outside, at the concert, and though I look harried and a little scared, the overwhelming sensation surrounding the memory is one of amusement, rampant curiosity, and fondness. And something else, something like a deep despair, a sensation you only feel once you've had to say goodbye to someone you desperately love.

When I ease back into the present, Griffin and I are floating in the air, about a foot off the bed.

"*Griffin!*" I say, which snaps him out of his heavy-lidded trance. "Griffin, we're floating."

"Oh, I'm sorry."

We fall back to the bed, a tangle of arms and legs, and I can't help laughing at how red his face turns. "You made us levitate, like the aliens always do in the movies," I say.

"We… we do that often, back home." He sits up, running a hand through his heavily tousled hair, hair that I've just messed up several times in my electric-charged enthusiasm.

"I'd like to see that," I say, before I can stop myself, "So why don't you take me back to your planet with you? Take me in your spaceship!"

Griffin frowns. "Spaceship? We didn't travel in a spaceship, Daisy."

After setting our alarm for only a few hours from now, I pull the bed blankets back and slip under them. No use taking a chance in someone busting the door down again and finding us in a compromising position. "Well, how did you get here then?"

"Dimension doors, and space walking." He pauses, as if about to explain, and then shakes his head. "Dev understands the details better than I do. I'm not really the science-y one."

Oh. What if he doesn't want me to come back with him? What if the evil fiancée was right… and I'm just a fun phase he's going through? What if he plans to go home and forget about me? Am I his Earth vacation fling?

"Alright, well, is that a no?" I ask, my voice shaking a lot more than I'd like to admit.

"I've never tried traveling with anyone who doesn't know how before. It's quite strenuous. Dev's real good at it, for some reason, the little bugger, but I always get sick from it. There's no telling what it'd do to you."

"Well, what's the worst that could happen? I'd disintegrate? Get put back together wrong on the other side?"

"We can ask Dev."

"You didn't tell me those *weren't* possibilities, so now I feel a bit nervous about the idea, but sure. We can ask Dev if I'm going to blow up, fall apart, or arrive on your planet in a new body."

Griffin moves closer to me on the bed. "You'd really like to do that, though? Come back with me?"

I shrug. "I don't want to get messed up on the way, but otherwise... I could try. We could go on a few dates over at your place. But only after you win your wager and get to return home triumphant. I don't want your evil fiancée having any more excuses to make your life miserable." I pat the pillow, and he stretches out beside me. "Do you want me to come with you, though?"

"Of course I do! I don't want to leave you." He's struggling now, his normal articulation lost in favor of nervous spluttering. "But what if they... what if they wanted to hurt you, because of me? Because of you being a stranger? What if they wanted to... to...?"

"Like your mom?"

Griffin nods. "As the Emperor-President-to-be—"

This time, I'm the one to cut him off with a kiss. "I saw, Griffin. I saw your mom; I saw what happened. I have no idea how something like that would feel, to have a loved one taken away like that, but you've become a brave and good man. I'm sure she's very proud of you."

It seems as if his eyes shine with tears, but by the time he drops his gaze from mine and looks at me again, I can't be sure. Even so, this is a very different being than the one who first bossed me around in SoHo. This is a being who I'm quite certain very, very few souls have ever seen. "I would do my best to keep you safe, of course," he whispers. "But it is dangerous. Life with me is dangerous. And sometimes, it's boring—horribly boring."

"If we're comparing notes on boring, my life has been pretty dull up until this point," I say, reaching over and brushing his bangs back from his forehead. "As for the dangerous part, I'm not a cool superhero in a cat suit. It does sound scary, but I think for right now, you should go to sleep, Griffin. You have a big day tomorrow and a bet to win against your dad. We'll talk about the rest of this later, okay?"

Even as I say it, I know that 'later' isn't all that much later now. By tomorrow, I might say goodbye to them forever, depending on what happens.

"Have you ever looked into her?" I ask. "Your evil fiancée, I mean."

Griffin shifts closer to me and shakes his head against the pillow. "No. Sometimes you don't need to, because someone wears all of their secrets on the outside."

"Good. She doesn't deserve to see your memories, anyway." I close my eyes, but I can't help asking one more thing. "But you know, sometimes, even if you saw everything inside of someone, you'd still want to ask them questions or hear them say something aloud, wouldn't you?"

He nods, and I lean my forehead against his.

"Even if it means flying halfway across the galaxy," I say, "I don't want to say goodbye to you, Griffin Valentino."

Chapter
23

Thankfully, there's no crowd waiting for us when we escape the hotel in the morning, and we're able to take our car to the airport without incident. Inside the airport, Griffin orchestrates us with commands and insistent hand motions, marching about in his fluffy purple sweater, black jeans, and a pair of oversized, red sunglasses.

Only after we've checked our bags does someone approach Griffin for a picture, which he poses for with a smirk and a hand propped on his hip in the campiest way possible. We meet a small group of fans before boarding our plane. During the flight, I notice a few people taking stealthy cell phone snaps of Griffin. Surprisingly, he doesn't seem to notice. At some point, he leans his head against my shoulder and falls asleep for the rest of our extremely long flight. I follow suit, despite mingling nerves and excitement.

Of course, the plane decides to go all borderline suicidal

on us during our descent into London, shaking hard enough to not only wake me, but also to convince me we're all probably about to die.

Griffin's fingers curl over mine, a bit too tight, and when I glance at him, I find him closed-lipped and grim. "You'll be fine," he says, just as the plane shakes again.

I close my eyes and force in a deep breath. "This feels a bit too much like the first episode of *Lost* for my taste."

"*Lost*?"

"Plane crash. Island. Monsters. A million storylines. Hot but troubled rock star guy."

"Don't be daft, Daisy, I'm not going to let the plane crash," Griffin says. He's still got his sunglasses on, so I can't see his eyes when I look at him again, but I can feel the air buzzing and crackling around him. Dev, who's sitting in the row behind us, puts out a similar static charge. When I look around, I see the bodyguards are all sitting up straight and alert.

This isn't any ordinary turbulence, judging by my alien friends' reactions.

The plane jolts so dramatically that I gasp out loud, and someone else lets out a scream. Then, all at once, the shaking stops and the plane becomes frighteningly still.

Griffin takes off his sunglasses, twists in his seat, and looks at Dev. They stare at each other for a few seconds, silently, before Griffin turns back around in his seat, and the plane moves again.

"Did… did the plane just stop?" I whisper to Griffin, though it sounds absurd to ask out loud, even to an alien who can make people do things just by snapping his fingers.

"Do you think it stopped?"

"It kinda felt like it stopped."

Griffin turns his very serious gaze in my direction, blue

eyes blazing behind his contacts, and a slow, deliberate, and somewhat grim smile on his face.

"Oh my God. Griffin. Why did you stop the plane?"

"I didn't stop it—something else did. I kept it in the air."

"Something else did...?" Now I feel panicked, especially when a stewardess walks by us with her hands clamped into tight fists and her face the approximate color of toilet paper. I can hear other passengers talking amongst themselves about how strange the flight has been. "Griffin, what's going on?"

Griffin stares ahead for a long time, as if he didn't hear me, and just when I'm about to elbow him and repeat the question, he says, "I think we traveled through the entry door of... whoever else is here." He shoots me a rather intense look, and then he turns his attention to the window.

Entry door? I want to ask him more questions, but then the pilot's voice announces, with a bit of a distinguishable tremor, that we'll be landing soon and everything's fine. That the passengers shouldn't worry about the turbulence.

I don't bother trying to ask about what's going on until we've landed and gathered our bags. The bodyguards carry most everything, leaving Griffin and Devon to whisper between each other as Kammie and I follow them across the airport.

Kammie, for her part, seems far too quiet for my liking. When I catch her eye, she shakes her head and leans in close to me. "Something happened to the plane, didn't it?" she whispers. "They did something to the plane."

I don't think she's afraid, really, but I can tell she's nervous. "They'll tell us later, I'm sure, when it's safe to talk about it."

She lets out a heavy sigh. "I just don't like it. Something feels strange."

A shudder runs through me, but I force a smile. "Hey,

we're in England now. How cool is that? How many times have we talked about wanting to come over here and check out all the cool places of musical importance? Come on, how many of our favorite bands are from England?"

Kammie's smile is probably as unconvincing as mine is, but at least she nods. We drop the conversation about the plane in favor of reminiscing about plans we'd once made for what we'd do if we could make it to England together.

Griffin nearly loses his mind with excitement once we're actually outside, pointing, gasping, and bouncing on his heels. "Look, Dev! Look, look, Dev, look! Look! Dev, we're in England!" he says, fishing his device from his pocket and snapping some pictures of the sky. He drags a deep breath in through his nose and then winces a little, though he covers it with a smile. "Dev, we've done it."

"Blimey. Yeah."

I can't help laughing a little, if only because they sound so English and Griffin's about to jump out of his skin just from setting foot in England. I take a few pictures of the boys, including one rather perfect snap of Griffin hugging Dev with childlike glee.

"It's beautiful; it's so beautiful," Griffin says.

All of my long-anticipated excitement about coming here is a bit eclipsed by Griffin's reaction, and I find myself laughing even harder as he holds his device out at arms' length so he can get a picture of himself with Dev.

"We've done it," Griffin says again. "We've sodding done it! Now we just need to win this wager. Right?" He glances up from his device and smiles in my direction. "Have you ever been to England, Daisy?"

"No. I've always wanted to visit, though."

Griffin's smile slips just a bit, replaced by a wistful

expression. "Too bad we don't have more time."

"Yeah. Too bad." As much as I want to suggest he reconsider my offer and stay on Earth with me, I know we're too close to our goal now to lose sight of it. "Where and when are we meeting the Origin Collective?"

Griffin holds a hand out in Dev's direction. "Time and place," he says. "Dev!"

"Yeah, yeah, hold on," Dev grumbles, but he's smiling. He searches his pockets for a few seconds before pulling out a piece of paper. "We're meeting them at ten tonight. I've no idea what this address means. You people here have the weirdest methods of explaining your residence."

"We'll check into a hotel first, of course," Griffin says. "Something five star. Is that what you call it? Five star? Something posh."

Dev raises an eyebrow at his friend. "Why the bloody hell do we need a posh hotel, Griffin?"

"To get ready for the meeting, of course. I need to look my best to meet with the Origin Collective." Griffin fluffs his hair a little. "Find us a posh hotel, yeah?"

With a few good-natured grumbles, Dev turns to Kammie. "Might you help me look up hotels in the area, love?"

Dev and Kammie put their heads together over Kammie's phone, which leaves Griffin to position himself beside me and press his face against mine for a picture. As soon as he's finished snapping it, I catch him around the waist and hold onto him, pressing my lips to his ear.

"What happened with the plane?" I whisper. Although he wiggles a little for good measure, he doesn't try to escape.

"What do you mean? I told you, we might have passed through something."

"Is the bad alien around here?"

"Could be. But don't worry; we've got loads of protection. And whoever it is, they haven't bothered us yet."

I still can't help feeling uneasy about the idea of the other alien being so close to us, especially at this crucial juncture. Griffin and Devon need to complete their mission with the Origin Collective soon, or risk losing the wager and wasting their whole trip here. I feel almost as invested as they do, by now.

And, let's be honest, the idea of an assassin alien on the loose doesn't exactly fill me with warm and fuzzy thoughts.

A few of the bodyguards leave us. Moments later, they return in a big, black vehicle. I can't help wondering if they acquired it by somewhat illegal means, but I don't say anything as we pile inside. Griffin sits nearly glued to the window as we head to our hotel, letting out excited yelps, exclamations, and gasps as he points at things. One of the particularly crazy exclamations shakes the windows of the car in an alarming fashion, which just makes Dev laugh. At that, Griffin laughs, and then both of them laugh hysterically until they're almost crying.

We check into a hotel, and Griffin spends most of the registration time dashing around the lobby and taking pictures of things like a full-blown tourist.

Our room isn't nearly as swanky as the ones we had in New York, but Griffin doesn't seem to notice. Running to the windows immediately, he throws open the curtains and gasps in delight at our view. He takes a few pictures of that, too, and then stands very still and silent for a long few seconds, staring into the distance.

"Griff," Devon calls. "We need to get going if we're going to stay on schedule."

After a bit more hesitation, Griffin spins around and

waves his hand in Devon's direction. "Alright, where are our tuxedos?" He strips his clothes off without further ado, tossing his shirt, pants, and socks in a messy pile around himself until he's standing before us in nothing but his underwear, which he seems ready to tug off as well.

Kammie eyeballs him before casting me a cheesy wink. *God.*

Devon opens a bag and carefully removes two tuxedo jackets, both of which are quite wrinkled, and two matching pairs of fancy black pants. If I'd known they'd packed them that way, I would have suggested they transport them a bit more carefully, but there's no use saying anything now.

"Help me, Wanda," Griffin says. "Errr, Daisy."

I just roll my eyes at him and wave Devon away from the clothes. Sorting through everything, I turn around to say something, instead finding Devon similarly stripped down to his underwear with his arms crossed. He's standing next to Griffin, waiting for me, too.

Really, I need to visit their planet. Or maybe just live on it.

Chapter 24

THE ESTATE IS HUGE, ABSOLUTELY ENORMOUS, BUT IT'S NOT ALL DARK, goth, and scary like I'd expected it to be... rather, it's painted a very plain eggshell sort of color and sits in the middle of a lot of neatly trimmed bushes and some tasteful fountains.

A servant rushes out to open our car door for us, greeting Griffin and Devon by name. Griffin ambles out of the car first, casting the servant a big smile.

"Thank you for having us, thank you," he says, and then turns back to watch his best friend climb from the car. "We're not late, I hope?"

"You're quite on time, Mr. Valentino. And you've brought some friends...?"

"Daisy Kirkwood, and this is Kammie. Errr, I... Kammie...?" Griffin says, extending his hand for me while squinting at Kammie.

"Kammie Sophia Glorianne Rosemary Wooldridge."

Kammie climbs down from the car and curtsies, which makes her sparkly red dress look worthy of a princess. "But you can call me Kammie, of course."

"Wonderful, wonderful. I'll mention to the Collective that we'll need room at the table for two extra guests." The servant glances around at Griffin's bodyguards. "But perhaps not more than two...?"

"No. They're my security team. We don't want to inconvenience the Collective."

The servant smiles. "No inconvenience, sir. Please follow me?"

Despite the innocuous outside of the Origin Collective's headquarters, I expect the inside to be creepy. Maybe full of torture devices, strange symbolism, and monks in red robes, chanting in a foreign language. Instead, we're greeted by a gentle floral scent in the lobby, a brightly lit hallway just after that, and smiling servants who offer to take our jackets.

"Oh, I'll keep mine," Griffin says, his pale hands straying idly down his front, over the buttons of his tuxedo jacket, and then back up to his lapels. He stands up on tiptoe and turns a full spin in his attempt to take everything in. "Beautiful home. I love all the color, especially the yellow. I've never seen yellow walls like that before."

The servant who met us outside just smiles and nods his head once to Griffin. "Please follow me," he says, leading us from the lobby.

Griffin slides his arm around Dev's waist and whispers to him as we make our way down the lemon-yellow hallway.

I pull at the waist of my silver dress, dropping my gaze briefly downward. Griffin had pulled the dress out of one of his bags like some sort of stage magician, grinning proudly when I said I liked it. Of course, liking an expensive designer dress and actually wearing one are very different things, and this particular designer dress seems to be made of glorified silver tissue paper.

You've never known true fear until you've worn glorified silver tissue paper to a meeting between your alien friends and a secret society.

We're escorted to a huge, wood-paneled room with red curtains, red cushions, glass chandeliers, a long table, and high-backed chairs. Bowls of fruit and a few candelabras sit atop the table, which is covered in a white tablecloth and set with shiny silverware and fancy plates.

The servant stops us in the doorway, motioning behind us. "The Collective is quite private. As discussed earlier, I think perhaps it's best if your security team remains out here."

Griffin hesitates, considering. "Alright, of course. Daisy and Kammie—"

"They're more than welcome to join you."

"I'll be just here," Griffin says to his bodyguards, turning to look at them. None of them say anything, but between the tingling sensation on the top of my head and the way one of the bodyguards nods, I have a feeling that they've communicated with Griffin in some other manner.

"Please, follow me." The servant leads us to the table, pulling a chair out for Griffin and one next to it for me; he seats Devon and Kammie across from us. "The Collective will join you shortly. Until then, tea?"

"Oh yes, please!" Griffin says, then clears his throat and slumps a bit in his chair. "That would be nice, thank you."

The very instant we're alone in the room, Devon leans forward a bit and locks eyes with Griffin. "Shouldn't we at least have a few of them with us?"

"We're fine."

"Once we reveal the reason for our visit, it might be best if we're not alone."

Griffin shakes his head.

"Griffin…"

"They're just in the other room," Griffin says, and a man and woman arrive just then with a teacart, effectively cutting Dev off from saying anything else. That doesn't stop him from shooting Griffin a lot of serious looks, and then looking at me as if he thinks I can do something about it.

I offer a helpless shrug as we're served tea and cucumber sandwiches. Griffin's too busy accepting his little cup to listen to anything I might have to say, and besides, there's no way I could speak to him in this quiet room without being overheard.

The teacart has barely been wheeled away when a group of five men walks into the room, all of them probably over the age of fifty and wearing similar black suits. If I didn't know any better, I'd think they were a bunch of pleasant English bankers and lawyers, sitting down for dinner and cigars.

Griffin leaps out of his seat, standing tall and sucking in a deep breath. "Sirs," he says. "Thank you for your invitation here."

One of the men, visibly the eldest, waves a veiny hand and takes a seat at one end of the table. "Please, sit down and enjoy your tea, Mr. Valentino."

Griffin remains in place for a few seconds, stiff and watchful, but then he finally slides back into his seat as our hosts do the same.

"How was your journey?" one of the other men asks, his tone casual.

"Errr, good I suppose." Griffin twists in his chair so he can turn more fully toward the old man at the end of the table. "Your invitation—"

"And your concert? How was that, Mr. Valentino?"

"Probably the best concert this planet has ever seen." Griffin clears his throat. "Well, not only because of me, of course. Daisy and Kammie helped out a lot."

"Yes, yes. And England? How do you find England?"

"Wonderful, quite as I expected, though I haven't seen Mick Jagger or David Bowie yet, anywhere. I'd rather hoped to meet David Bowie. Do you know where he is?"

"Bowie? No, I'm afraid I don't."

Our meal arrives then, carried by smiling men and women wearing white shirts and black pants. We're served a full plate of assorted foods, none of them even slightly familiar, except for the orange slice that sits atop a blob of gray stuff. Griffin stares at everything with his hands held up, palms out, as if he's about to be arrested.

"Please, enjoy your meal," one of the old guys says, which makes me wonder if he's blind or crazy.

Or maybe all the food will taste surprisingly delicious. I pick up one of my two forks and try to convince myself to actually eat something.

Griffin takes my lead and picks up one of his forks, so Devon does, too. Kammie shoots me an extremely unimpressed look and crosses her arms over her chest.

After a bit more hesitation, Griffin takes a bite of the gray blob on his plate. His expression changes from cautiously disgusted to vaguely confused. He polishes off the rest of his food before I can force myself to eat a first bite.

"I've heard very positive things about your organization," Griffin says. "Your dedication to improving your world, for instance, and your secret acts of charity for those in need. It's admirable."

A subtle ripple of uneasiness flows around the table, and

the oldest of the Collective offers Griffin a grim nod and smile. "Your compliments mean much to us, friend, but it is us who are honored by your presence."

Griffin sits up taller in his chair. "Yes, but—but you—but you—if I were to ask you about… well, what if—I wondered—"

Dev clears his throat, pushing food around his plate with his fork. "Griffin means to say we're both thankful for your invitation, but there's something important we must tell you."

"We need your help, actually," Griffin says, leaning forward in his seat so he can look around me at the old man at the end of the table. "What we're going to reveal to you must be held in the upmost respect and—and confidentiality. I've chosen to trust you with this information."

The old man gazes silently back at Griffin, and then glances at me.

"We must insist on the confidentiality," Dev adds.

"I can assure you that anything that takes place within these walls will never be revealed," the old man says, and I feel uncomfortable laughter bubble up in my throat. It sounds so creepy that I kind of want to grab Griffin's hand, wave for Dev and Kammie, and immediately run out of the room.

"You know, I thought you'd look a bit different," Griffin says, all at once, and then he lets out his own nervous laughter. "Well, you're all so… You're like fathers, or grandfathers."

"Bankers," I mutter.

"Not a bunch of big, frightening men in robes, chanting about death and blood. In fact, it feels so homey here, I could fall asleep." Griffin shrugs. "Dev and me, we're not really pop stars, you see. We need to tell you the truth."

The doors to the room open then; several of Griffin's bodyguards approach us, two of them taking their places behind Devon and two behind Griffin.

"Well, what's this about?" Griffin twists in his chair to look at his bodyguards. "You're supposed to wait in the hall, remember? That's quite rude."

"No, no, I asked them to join us," a voice says, and a sturdy-built, black-haired man steps into the room. His dusty-red uniform seems to be a size or two too big for him, and his hair looks as if someone has recently shorn it all wrong. "After all, they're here for you, aren't they, Prince Griffin?"

"No!" Griffin leaps to his feet, nearly knocking his chair over in the process and filling the air with panicked static. He grabs for my hand, but the bodyguards behind him force him back down in his chair, and the two behind Dev act just as quickly, hauling him from his chair. Before I can process what's happened, Dev's held with his back against one of the hulking, silent guards. He has a knife pressed tight against his throat. The blade of the knife glows, casting eerie blue over Devon's pale, fearful face. "No, leave him alone. Leave him alone!"

"Griff—" Devon says, but his words are cut off by the knife cutting into his neck just enough to make him bleed a little. He gasps and wheezes out Griffin's name again. "Get out of here, Griff. Go!" As Devon's dragged away from us, Griffin breaks free of the grip holding him and twists around, hitting one of his bodyguards hard enough to make the man stagger backward.

Griffin makes it all of a few steps before he stumbles and falls to his knees.

"How much did he have?" the man in the red uniform asks, and the oldest member of the Origin Collective waves one of his wrinkled hands.

"He ate it all."

"Of course he did, greedy little bastard. And of course, his friend—what do they call him here? Devon?—only ate what was required of him. So polite, as always." The man in the red uniform strolls toward Griffin, who's kneeling with his palms pressed to the carpet and his head hanging low, gasping and spluttering. "Have you enjoyed this little planet as much as you thought you would? It's made up of everything you love, of course. Wastefulness. Whores. Gluttony…"

I do the only thing that you *can* do in this situation. I jump out of my chair and position myself in front of Griffin.

"Look, I don't know who you are, but I'm assuming you're the other alien," I say before I can stop myself. "Maybe you're friends with the evil fiancée, and maybe you're all pissed off about your planet, but you are not going to hurt my aliens. This is my planet, and they're—they're under my protection, as a citizen of this planet!"

The bad alien smiles. "My name is Taug," he says, bowing to me. "I've heard a great deal about you, Daisy."

"Good! Then you know that I'm—I'm not to be crossed. I command you to return to your planet. You have no right to anything on my planet. I can call the president for backup if I want to. And Will Smith. And Jeff Goldblum."

"All of these wonderful men before you are citizens of your planet as well, Daisy. And they all believe in preserving the integrity of your people. More importantly, they believe in your planet continuing to circle slowly around its sun, in one decaying, ugly little piece."

I look toward the Origin Collective, glimpsing only fear mirrored back at me.

"So, that's how you did it? You threatened them?" I ask, and Kammie takes her place at my side.

"I simply informed them of our superior weapons. Threats were unnecessary," Taug says. "We have no quarrel with your planet—not yet."

"And Griffin's bodyguards? Did you put them under some kind of spell?" I demand.

"Spell? No, no, I don't think you understand. We are a unit, a team, the last hope there might be for our planet, given the direction it's headed. Unlike the citizens of your world, we won't sit back and watch everything we've done come to nothing." His voice rises a bit at the end, a sinister edge to it that I haven't heard up until this point. "They've been very helpful through your trip, keeping me updated on your location." He hesitates. "Well, not all of them. A few had to be removed from their posts, just now."

A sick, sinking feeling spreads through my insides. All this time we've been in the company of traitors? "You—you need to leave," I say at last.

"We'll leave soon enough; don't worry. But first, we have a little task for Prince Griffin."

"Bring Dev back in here!" Griffin says, and I turn to find him struggling to his feet. "Where is he? Bring Dev back, or I won't do a sodding thing for you."

You know when people say they lost their balance? Well, that's exactly what it feels like when Taug fixes his glowing, green eyes on me. I fly backward and fall against the hardwood floor with enough force that I lose my breath, and it takes a few seconds for me to regain my wits and sit up again. Kammie, across the room, has also been thrown to the ground.

"Leave Daisy alone!"

"I can snap her neck from here, if I want to. But, luckily for you, I don't want to do that. Not now! That would upset you greatly, wouldn't it? I want you unharmed and unmarked, because you're a—what do you call it? Superstar. A superstar with an extremely important task to complete."

Griffin's head and shoulders slump, as if he's very tired.

"Let. Them. Go," he says in a quiet voice.

"So tired, Prince Griffin! Perhaps you should take a nap. You'll need your strength for later."

Griffin growls something in his language, and most of the members of the Origin Collective jump from their seats and run out of the room. The last of them, the old man, leaves when Taug responds to Griffin.

Taug's garbled words rattle the windows and send a wave of crackling, cold energy around the room. I have to fight the powerful compulsion to run away.

"Daisy," Griffin says, faltering and falling to his knees again. "Daisy, go. Take Kammie and go."

Taug smiles in my direction. "He's right, Daisy. You may leave."

Oh, God. If my mom were here right now, she'd have plenty of advice. She'd probably tell me to make a run for it, right? To run as far away as possible and then call the cops or Ghostbusters or whatever, whoever. Someone bigger, stronger, and more qualified than me.

Griffin crumples forward, his eyes closed even before his cheek hits the floor, and Taug stands over him for a few seconds before motioning for the bodyguards.

"Get him off the floor. He won't be out for long." Taug steps over Griffin, glances down at Kammie, and then turns back to me. "You're still here? Collect your friend and get out of here while you still can. You're lucky I'm letting you live."

My mom's voice runs through my head, telling me to get out, to run and get help, but I shake my head. "I'm not leaving," I say. "And you're not going to hurt Griffin, Devon, or Kammie."

And just like that—

Chapter 25

UGH, WOW, MY BACK HURTS. WHAT ON EARTH WAS I DOING LAST night? Did Griffin and I have another epic sexy session?

Wait, why am I on a concrete floor in the dark?

I sit up, everything flooding back to me all at once, but I receive an intense wave of headache as reward for moving so quickly. After a few seconds of waiting for the headache to stop creating stars in my vision, I desperately search for any clue as to where I am.

The small room is dark, windowless, and the walls are covered in a variety of handcuffs, small switches, whips, hammers, and other tools. Below me is bare, cold concrete, and the only light in the room radiates from two flickering bulbs that look as if they might die at any moment.

Great. So I've been kidnapped by good aliens, and then kidnapped by bad aliens in cooperation with a bunch of old dudes who run a shady secret society in a boring London mansion. Now I'm probably going to be tortured in a dark dungeon with an assortment of farm equipment and adult toys.

This is really not what I planned for when I moved to New York City.

A quiet groan draws my attention to the corner of the room, which seems to be occupied by a small, awkwardly positioned lump of skinny arms and legs.

Griffin.

I crawl across the room to him, gently rolling him onto his back so I can get a better look. He hasn't sustained any new physical damage that I can see, but he's trembling all over as if he's freezing cold.

"D-Dev...?" he says, those strange alien eyes opening and glowing in the dark as he looks at me. "Daisy?" He lets out another groan and forces himself up until he's propped on his elbows. "Daisy, I told you... I told you to go."

"Yeah, well, you also said I was free of the kidnapping ordeal, so I decided to use my freedom however I wanted," I say, even though my voice betrays my nerves more than I'd like. "And that meant staying with you. It would be pretty crappy of me to ditch you now, after everything we've been through together. Champagne, bad movies, Frog Snout..."

"Kammie!" he says. "What about Kammie. Do you know where she is?"

I shiver. "I-I don't know. I just woke up."

Griffin sits up, dropping his head into his hands. He's still shaking, maybe even harder now than before.

"Are you alright? What happened to you? Did they give you some kind of sedative?" I think he nods, but it's hard to tell. "They just want you to do something, right?" I whisper. "Then they'll let us go."

"I know these people, Daisy. Not these particular people,

but their group, I mean. They're the ones who killed my mother. They won't let Devon go. They'll kill both of us as soon as they get whatever it is they're after." He raises his face long enough to look at me. "You should have run while you could, Daisy."

Oh, God, are those tears shining in his eyes? Up until this point, I've managed to keep myself together, somehow, but seeing Griffin's sadness makes me want to cry.

"What do you think they want you to do?" I ask, my mind already whirring with half-ideas and useless solutions. "In action movies, the hero pretends to go along with what the bad guys want, and then tricks them to escape!"

He takes a shuddering breath, blinking hard enough to force a couple of fat tears to escape and roll down his cheeks. "It could be anything. I just—I just hope I get to see Dev again."

"Of course you will."

"He's been through everything with me, most of my life. I never should have brought him here. Everyone said it would be dangerous, but Dev wouldn't say anything, because… because he… he doesn't do that! He goes along with things, if he knows they're important to me." He wipes savagely at his eyes with one of his sleeves. "He should be home, working on his experiments or complaining about my stupid ideas. After everything he's done for me… Gods, Daisy, I wish he'd never met me at all! I wish neither of you had!"

I wrap my arms around him as best I can, holding him close while he silently shakes.

"It's going to be okay," I say after a long time, mostly to convince myself of it. "We're gonna get out of here. Can you call your dad for help?"

Griffin shifts around enough to pat his pockets. "They took my communicator."

Of course. "Well, is there another way to call him? Don't

you have telepathy or something?"

"He couldn't hear me from here. We're too far away."

The whole room feels as if it's been plunged into winter, uncomfortably cold and crackling with depressing energy. Sparks of blue and gray fall around us like rain before fading entirely from sight.

"What is this stuff?" I whisper, holding out a hand and collecting a few of the sparks. "You feel like you're buzzing. Is your magic coming back?"

Griffin doesn't answer for so long that I think he didn't hear me, but he finally says, "It's just from being around them, because they brought home stones with them. I had one, too, but I lost it. Someone took it from me, I think. Who knows, maybe those... those traitors who called themselves my bodyguards."

"But you're recharging your magic by being around someone with magic stones? Maybe we can steal one of them! What do they look like?"

"You wear them around your neck, close to your heart." He looks at me then. "I'm sorry, Daisy. I'm so sorry I dragged you into this."

"Hey." I kiss his cheekbone, the side of his head. "I meant it when I said we're getting out of here. There's what? Five of them? Maybe six? There are four of us, between you, me, Dev, and Kammie."

He considers this and then nods, even if only once. "They took my Dev."

"You can get him back. I'll help you. We'll get out of here, and you'll still have won your wager against your dad. Think positive." I don't feel even slightly positive, but there's no use in both of us losing hope right now. "Do you think you could fight them better with one of the stones?"

Griffin nods again, so I press my hand against his chest, over his heart. I'm about to say something really inspiring and helpful, but a loud noise startles both of us, and we turn around to find the door to our room swing open with a creak. Griffin's on his feet before I can even react, crossing the room at lightning speed.

"Where is Devon?" he says. "Where is Devon? Answer me!"

"Your friend is waiting for you, as always, Prince Griffin." It's Taug's voice, but I can't see him until I stand up and dare to move closer. I stop just behind Griffin, peering around him at Taug and three of Griffin's bodyguards. They seem altogether scarier than ever before, thanks to the grim set of their faces and the crackling energy emitting from them. "Perhaps we shouldn't keep him waiting too long, though?"

"If you want anything from me, you know you'll have to let Devon, Daisy, and Kammie go," Griffin says, his voice steadier than before, even if I can feel the slight tremble remaining in his body.

Taug simply smiles at Griffin, and then motions for us to follow him. The bodyguards fall into step beside us, watchful of our every movement. I'm equally watchful, my eyes scanning them for any signs of necklaces that might hold the home stones.

We're escorted past a series of doors and up a dark staircase, into the light of the surface level of the mansion. I recognize the Origin Collective's headquarters immediately, both by the cheerful interior colors and the faint floral smell.

A man wearing a spiffy uniform and white gloves walks by us, takes one look at Griffin and me, and averts his eyes, hurrying on past.

"We're being kidnapped here!" I call after him, but he

doesn't slow down or respond, and I receive a hearty elbow in the ribs from one of the bodyguards for my effort.

"Leave her alone," Griffin says, in a low, dangerous voice. "She's not one of us, remember? And she's under my care."

From somewhere up ahead, I can hear Taug let out a snicker. Eventually, we're escorted into a large room that is mostly empty, save for a chair, a large camera, and another bodyguard. Judging by several impressions on the carpets and some furniture lined up against a wall, this room doesn't normally appear this way. It's been set up especially for us.

"What do you think?" Taug asks, waving his arms wide, moving so he's standing in front of Griffin and me. "Is it grand enough for you, Prince Griffin? I know you're a famous celebrity now, known all over the galaxy for your music and your ability to sleep with almost anything that moves across your path. But this was the best we could do for you."

Griffin glances at me before stepping closer to Taug. "You told me that Devon was waiting for me. Where is he?"

"He'll be brought into the room as soon as you've completed our task."

"No. I won't do anything until I see that Devon is alright."

Taug cocks his head to the side. "Making demands as always, I see, Prince Griffin. Unfortunately, your days of demands are over. Back home, you held some semblance of power, but here, you are nothing. Here, you are only a toy for me to play with and discard at my whim. Here, you are beneath *me*. Here, you are crushed under the mighty boot of the very souls you held prisoner for all these years."

Griffin stands up a bit taller. "Let me see Devon."

Three of the bodyguards lay hands on Griffin and bodily lift him off his feet, depositing him roughly into the empty chair set up in front of the camera. He springs back from the chair immediately, hitting the floor and rolling away from them.

Before I know what's happening, someone's arm slides around my back and I'm tugged into a rough, painful embrace. Taug's voice fills the room as if it's been amplified by an impressive speaker system. "*Would you like me to snap her neck?*" he demands.

Griffin lets out a heavy, angry huff of air. "Leave her alone."

"You'll record our message, and then I'll consider your request."

"It's not a request. I want Dev brought to me immediately and Daisy unharmed, or I won't do a damn thing you ask me to."

The bodyguard holding me reeks of something spicy and strong, now that I'm up close to him, and I can't help wincing. Unfortunately, Griffin looks at me just then and must think I'm wincing from fear or the crazy, muscular arm clamped in front of my throat.

"It's not difficult, what we're asking you to do. We just want you to record a message for everyone back home," Taug says, in a supremely annoying and smug voice. "Tell them that you've fallen in love with this little planet, and you want to forfeit the crown to us."

Griffin hisses, making the air buzz and waver around him. "My father will never believe that. He and I made a wager, and he knows how much I want to win it."

"Your father?" Taug repeats. "Oh! So you must not have heard. I'm sorry to be the one to tell you the news, Griffin, but your father is dead."

The buzzing intensifies, and Griffin's eyes narrow to slits. "What?"

"By now, Mali should have taken care of him. And that

leaves you next in line, but everyone knows you're a reckless and irresponsible choice for leader. You've been obsessed with this planet for as long as anyone can remember. Of course, you'll want to stay here. You love it! And that leaves room for someone to step in and repair all the damage that's been done. Wonderful, isn't it? Everyone's happy."

Griffin shakes his head, opening his mouth to speak, and then closing it again. After a few long seconds, he sucks in a deep breath and looks at me first, then at Taug. "Bring Dev to me, and I'll record your message."

Taug must feel as surprised as I do by this statement, because his smug smile falls away briefly, but then he motions to one of the bodyguards. "Bring him out here. Bring the girl, too."

Though it's probably less than a minute before Kammie is dragged into the room, it feels much longer. It would seem that it took two of the traitorous bodyguards to hold Kammie, who does her best to shake them off as she arrives.

"How dare you!" Kammie shouts. "You're traitors, is what you are. Traitors! Showing up here and hurting Devon and Griffin. Daisy and I, we're their human escorts and companions. Daisy and I are going to talk to the president about this. And maybe the Queen of England, too!"

Taug walks slowly toward her. "You humans... you're fierier than you were the first time we visited, aren't you? I suppose a few thousand years should make a difference. But at the core, you're still as weak-minded and breakable as ever."

"Visited before?" I say, before I can stop myself. Muscle-arm guy tightens his hold on me a little, so I launch into dramatic coughing splutters until he loosens his grip again. "What do you mean, you've visited before?"

"You've forgotten now. Maybe your ancestors didn't want

you to know your true heritage. Maybe they were ashamed of our blood running through their veins. Through your veins."

I cough again, this time for real. "What, are you gonna try to tell me you helped us build the pyramids, Stargate-style?"

Kammie, for her part, stops squirming and shoots me a rather smug look. "I told you, Daisy, aliens built the pyramids."

"We lived among you, for a time, and we suffered. All the wonderful knowledge we shared with you, all the growth we provided you, the peace we offered, was returned only with disease and ruin. Your planet is one of the only planets in the universe like ours, and your people, so similar to us in starmatter... It should have been a second home, especially when we shared our very language with you. Our blood." He shakes his head. "Think of it! Some of your ancestors are our kind, but your people chose to forget us." Taug snorts. "No wonder Griffin likes it here so much. He fits right in with all of you—ungrateful, weak."

I filter this through my mind quickly, thinking of Griffin's weakened state and the missing necklace. "You never found another planet, did you?" I demand. "That's why you're fighting over the one you have, instead of going somewhere else. You can't go anywhere else."

Taug looks at me with new curiosity. "Don't think, girl, that just because we can't live for an extended period on your planet means that you're safe. If you interfere with our plans, I might find special use for your planet... harvesting or labor. Who knows?"

Devon arrives then, escorted by just one bodyguard. "Griffin!" he says, and Griffin takes a step toward him before hesitating.

"Are you alright, Dev?" Griffin asks, twisting his hands together in front of himself.

They exchange a look across the room at each other that seems like a full conversation in a few silent seconds, and then Griffin takes several steps backward.

"Your friend's here now, Griffin. It's time for you to do the right thing," Taug says, flicking a switch on the camera and turning a knob. "Sit down, and we can begin."

"What's he trying to make you do?" Devon asks, his normally perfect blond hair flopped down over his eyes. He looks incredibly disheveled, which is jarring at best, but the worst thing is probably the worried expression on his face. Dev's supposed to be unflappable British—err— alien calm. "Griff, talk to me. What's he want you to do?"

"He's going to send a message home," Taug says. "Now that his father's dead, we're almost finished with this mess once and for all."

Any remaining color in Devon's face drains away. "You're a disgrace," he says, and I'm glad he's not talking to me. His voice, filled to the brim with burning disgust, is enough to make someone spontaneously combust. "The Emperor President might not be a soft man, but he's always wanted the best for all of us!"

"Anterys is dead now. Thank you for your speech, Dev, but I'm not as easily swayed by you as everyone else seems to be."

"Griffin, don't cooperate with him."

"Stop, Dev," Griffin says in a very quiet voice.

"If you think holding me as captive will make Griffin bow to your wishes, you're wrong," Devon says. "Neither of us will have any part in your plot. Griffin's your Emperor President now. He knows what he has to do."

Taug lets out an exasperated sigh. "Shut him up, will you?" he says to the bodyguard holding Dev. Kammie attempts to claw her way out of the strangle-hold her two guards have on her, but they stop her from making much progress.

The air around Griffin crackles, and the floor under my feet shakes. A window rattles and then shatters, sending glass everywhere, including raining down over Griffin's head. His eyes remain fixed in Dev's direction, even as he raises his hand high and snaps his fingers.

Another window breaks, and then another; I squeeze my eyes closed in an attempt to protect my eyes as glass falls around me.

The smelly alien releases me, and I open my eyes to find Taug and three of the bodyguards rushing Griffin, but they all freeze before they can reach him. A sickly, gurgling sound emits from the bodyguard behind Devon, and he collapses to the floor with a loud gasp.

"Griffin, stop it!" Devon shouts, but he, too, seems to be frozen in place.

One of the bodyguards rises into the air, his arms stiff at his sides, until he's levitating with his back against the roof. All at once, he falls to the ground, like a toy that's been dropped, and lands close enough to me that I hear the crunch of his bones as they break.

A shriek escapes me before I can stop it, and I jump back, away from the body.

Breaking through the hold, one of the bodyguards makes a rush for Griffin, but he doesn't make it very far before his whole body lights up. He screams and falls into a writhing, glowing jumble on the floor.

The last of them, and arguably the biggest, slowly claps his hands together as if he's dragging them through water. A glowing, red shape forms between his hands. He pulls his arm back to throw it at Griffin, but then he hesitates and throws it at Taug instead, who barely bats it away.

Behind me, the displaced furniture shakes and bursts apart, as if someone's blown it up. I fall instinctively to the ground and cover my head, praying the giant, flying shards of wood won't land on me.

When I dare to sit up again, I find that the last of the bodyguards has fallen, leaving only Taug and Griffin, both of whom are floating several inches off the ground.

I know, without needing to be told, that Griffin's used up most everything he has left in him, not just his magic. His whole body shakes with rage, and I can feel an overwhelming sense of exhaustion rolling off him in waves, reaching me by way of our weird mind-connection thing.

"Griffin." My voice sounds too weak, so I clear my throat and try again, though not much louder. "Griffin, you're hurting yourself."

"She's right, Griffin," Taug says, and the room shakes with the violence of an earthquake. "But you're not who you pretend to be, are you? You're stronger than I thought, stronger than any of us thought. And you're ruthless! Look, look at all of this devastation you caused. Griffin Tamanoc Anterysli, you... you are one of us."

"No, I'm not!" Griffin screams, sending Taug flying across the room and into a pile of broken furniture rubble. "I will never let you destroy our home. Never! They may hate me all they want, but I will not let them fall into your evil hands."

Taug climbs back to his feet, but with difficulty, and he disappears from sight, only to reappear in front of Griffin. He sends his elbow crashing into Griffin, doubling him over, and hits him on the back of his neck. The room shakes again, sending a crack racing across the floor and several pieces of the roof crashing down around us.

A sound, a horrible sound like thunder, cracks overhead,

deafening me. I cover my ears, but it doesn't block out the noise.

The room shakes again as Griffin charges Taug, throwing all of his weight into him and hitting somewhat blindly. They grapple for what feels like forever, inflicting damage to each other but never quite breaking the dangerous cycle of energy they've built. When Taug finally catches hold of Griffin, the crack in the floor widens and the rest of the windows in the room shatter.

"You're going to kill your pretty little human, Griffin, and your best friend, if you're not more careful. Wouldn't that be a shame?" Taug asks, sinking his fingers into Griffin's dark hair and yanking, forcing his head up. "Would it be like when you killed your own mother?"

Griffin snarls and his whole body flames with glowing blue light as he shoves Taug away. "Your organization killed her!"

"Are you sure? Or were you so afraid of us that you lost control and accidentally killed her yourself?"

Griffin's hands fall to his sides and his glow dims. "No. No, I didn't. I remember what happened!"

Memory flashes of red-uniformed intruders dance across my vision, shared from Griffin's mind, and I see one of the intruders sink a knife deep into the chest of a tall, graceful woman…

"He's lying to you, Griffin. You do remember what happened!" I say, but then Taug rushes Griffin, slamming into him and setting off a massive blue explosion that shakes the room again. "Griffin!" I shout, even though my voice is drowned out by the deafening hiss of the energy that surrounds and shields the aliens from my eyes. One glance at Kammie and Devon tells me they can't move at all, but they also seem to be shielded from everything flying around them, so I take a few deep breaths and run toward the crackling, blue energy.

Halfway there, I realize what a stupid idea this is, but there's no stopping it. I leap into the snapping, popping, blue-tinged airwaves and find Griffin and Taug locked into something that looks altogether too much like a sorcerer battle. I throw myself against Taug, clawing at his neck for the home stone necklace that I know must be there. Sure enough, I grab hold of a thin strip of metal and yank as hard as I possibly can, using every bit of that first-place-in-a-tug-of-war-contest strength to break the necklace, and throw it toward Griffin.

Griffin catches the necklace and locks eyes with me for a brief second. His gaze is terrifying, electric blue, and deadly, so much that I'm glad when he looks away from me again.

"What will you do?" Taug demands, though there's fear in his voice now. "Go home, kill Mali? Kill everyone in our organization?"

"If I can, I will," Griffin says, quietly, and Taug's body lights up from within, exploding into too many pieces to count.

After a few breaths, a few seconds of barely suppressed shock, I look at Griffin. "You did it," I say. "You can stop now."

I don't think he can hear me, however, because he just stares at the space where Taug had been and quakes with rage and rippling energy.

"Griffin. Griffin, listen, Dev and I are waiting for you, right here! It's okay now; you can stop!" I say, but I receive no response. "Griffin! You're not the bad alien; you're not like the alien in that stupid movie!" Anger, hurt, and the strength of dying energy fight for control in my head, washing over from Griffin, but I force them all aside and take a step toward him. When he doesn't respond, I take another step, and then another, until I'm standing directly in front of him. His voice whispers in my mind that he's dangerous, that he's lost, but I shake my head and dare to loop my arms around him.

"No. You're mine," I whisper, and every sound in the room falls silent, all the light dying out. And Griffin crumbles to the floor, despite my best attempt to hold onto him.

DEVON AND KAMMIE ARE STILL FROZEN IN PLACE WITH THEIR protection spells or whatever, so I find myself alone to help Griffin in the empty, destroyed room. His pale face is even whiter than usual, and his chest barely rises and falls with his weak breaths. It's as if he's empty, missing, right in front of my eyes.

How do you fix a broken alien? My mom definitely never prepared me for this situation.

"Griffin," I whisper, but I wince at the sound of my voice in the silence of the room. "You're tired, I know you're really tired, but you have to wake up. I promise you can rest soon, but you need to free Devon and Kammie, so they can help me fix you. Griffin?"

Not even the flutter of an eyelash.

After a few seconds of frantically looking around and searching my brain for any answer, I notice the chain I'd yanked off Taug's neck, and the small, gold stone attached to a pendant. The home stone!

I snatch the necklace up. "Please help," I whisper to it, and then look down at Griffin again as I straddle him. His tuxedo has survived the day's events without much damage, other than a popped button, a slightly frayed sleeve, and a rip in one knee. With shaking hands, I unbutton his fancy white dress shirt and slip the home stone over his heart, pressing it against his skin.

He'd said something about self-healing, hadn't he? He'd said it was more difficult than healing someone else. And it was harder without being on his planet, because he didn't have as much power as usual.

"Come on, home stone," I say. "Come on, come on. Come on!"

Griffin's face remains slack and empty, his limbs splayed out haphazardly without so much as a twitch.

"You can't do this to me," I say, but this time to Griffin. "You can't just show up on my planet and kidnap me and drag me around and drive me crazy and run around wearing that ugly sweater and—and—and..." Tears choke my voice, which is kind of beyond annoying at a moment like this. "You're a pop star, remember? Everyone loves you here. Think about all the people on Twitter. Think about the people at the concert!"

No response.

"And what about Dev? He's your best friend. What's he going to do? I mean, he's stuck over there, for one thing."

No response. This damned home stone isn't doing anything at all!

With a creeping sensation of hopelessness, I lean down and place my hands on either side of Griffin's face, like every prince ever does to the sleeping princesses in fairy tales.

"You promised me, Griffin Valentino. You promised you wouldn't leave without saying goodbye."

I press a kiss to his cold lips, fully expecting him to wake up. When I pull away, he's still deathly pale and motionless.

This isn't how it's supposed to be.

My whole body aches from everything we've been through today—the early start, the plane, getting knocked out and waking up on the floor, and everything that just happened in this room. With a deep sigh of resignation, I shift my weight so I can lay down with my head on Griffin's chest.

Crying won't do any good, of course, but I feel like crying, so I don't even resist when a few fat, warm teardrops roll down my cheeks and land on Griffin.

"You made me cry," I mutter, through wet, noisy sniffles. "Why don't you just wake up and apologize? We could go... we could go shopping for some new Michael Kors shoes."

A quiet wheeze rustles from Griffin's mouth, so I sit up straight.

"Michael Kors," I say again, in case he can only hear in designer labels. Somehow, I wouldn't put it past him. "Dior. Errr... Gucci."

Nothing.

I'm about to stand up and go look for help when Griffin splutters just a little and his eyes flutter open, halfway. The eerie, blue glow of his eyes is dimmed considerably from what it should be, and I have to lean down over him before he seems to register I'm there.

"Griffin! Griffin, you have to free Devon. He'll know how to help you," I say, but I can't resist kissing him quickly, just because. "Griffin, can you hear me?"

I think I can hear his voice in my head, but I can't be sure, so I lock gazes with him. Without really knowing what I'm doing, I tell myself to connect with him, to look *into* him.

This time, Griffin's memories are dull and painted like watercolors, dripping at the edges.

I search through his mind frantically, running into pain and emptiness at almost every turn. There has to be *something* here that can help—some clue of what I can do to help. How did Griffin recover last time he burned out?

Instead of answers, I find only one core truth standing out above all else, tightly protected at the center of Griffin's mind. *Dev, Daisy, safe. Loved ones, safe.*

Heal yourself! You have the home stone! I shout at him. *You have a wager to win, and fans and a planet to go back to, and great clothes to wear. And you have me, and Dev. We're okay. Heal yourself!*

A powerful, intimidating presence fills Griffin's memory, spilling over into my mind. His father, a man of cold strength and menace, barreling unasked into our mental hideout.

I yell at Griffin again and again, though my thoughts wander and I slip into some of my own memories, because they're stronger than his blurry recollections. There's the time I stood up to my teacher for the sake of my friend in third grade, which got me sent directly to the principal's office. Mostly, I just remember feeling proud of myself for being a little kid and still winning against an adult, even when the principal called my mom and she freaked out over the phone so loud that I could hear her from my seat across the room.

We're pretty good at fighting back, I think, both for Griffin and for my own affirmation. *We can do this.*

There's another part of his mind that glows a little brighter than the rest, and I nudge it, finding a warm and comforting shell around it. Wait—is that the healing part? Yes, yes, that must be the healing part. Wow, I'm inside of an alien's brain!

Kammie is going to be so—no, no, stop it, stop, this is important, back to the task at hand...

I concentrate on his healing ability and will it to expand.

Something disrupts our connection, and I find myself blinking and staring down at Griffin. He's blinking, which is a hopeful sign.

"Griffin?"

"Wanda..."

"Griffin, you have to free Devon! You don't need to protect him anymore; he's safe now. He'll know what to do."

Griffin squeezes his eyes closed and winces. "My father..."

"I know, I'm so sorry about your dad, Griffin, but you have to concentrate right now. You have to free Devon and heal yourself. I sort of tapped into your brain or something, so, I hope that helped."

"No, he's... he's... He's here..."

Oh no. "Griffin, look, don't you dare walk into the light or something, even if you see your dad waiting for you. You are not going to die!"

"Step back, human."

Instinctively, I jump up and turn around, prepared to fight if I have to. I've only taken half a self-defense class, once upon a time, but they always say that in the moment of need, most people gain a bunch of adrenaline and can pick up cars and stuff.

"Leave us alone!" I say, and then realize that the grim, blue-eyed creature in front of me is Griffin's dad. "Oh. I thought you were...?" It's never polite to tell someone they're supposed to be dead, so I just stand up straighter and raise my chin. "Can you help Griffin?"

Two, three, four, five more aliens appear in the room, creating swirling, hissing entrances with their arrival.

Griffin's dad brushes me aside and crouches beside his son. He mutters something that sounds scolding, but then he looks back at me. "You saved him."

"Well, we all sort of helped each other through this," I say. "Will he be okay?"

"He needs to go home." Griffin's dad turns and motions his hand at Dev and Kammie, which effectively releases them from their protective shield. Dev darts for Griffin so fast that he trips on his way; he jumps back up and then falls on his knees beside his friend.

Dev speaks to Griffin frantically in their native language, as if they are the only beings in the room, and hugs him with reckless abandon. The other new aliens close in, pushing me farther and farther away from Griffin.

I turn to look for Kammie, who's tearing her fingers through her hair and slapping her own cheeks, as if to wake herself up after a long sleep. "Oh my God, Kammie. Are you okay?"

"Me? Not the best, but then, I've never been attacked by aliens before, so that's to be expected, I suppose," Kammie says, walking on unsteady legs toward me. "You were like an action hero! Indiana Jones would be so proud."

I pull my friend into a tight hug, clinging to her. "I'm so glad you're okay."

"Wait until everyone on my conspiracy message board hears about this," she says. "Hey, are they leaving?"

It all seems to happen at once. Griffin's levitating above the ground, suspended by seemingly nothing, with Devon standing by his side, and then both of them have vanished from sight, along with all the other aliens except for Griffin's father.

"No!" I shout, before I can stop myself. "No, you can't

leave us!"

Griffin's father turns slightly and looks at me, his bright blue eyes frightening in their intensity. Though he's not much taller than Griffin, he seems to fill the room, fill even my insides. "You belong here," he says in a voice that invites no question or argument.

"Yeah, I do, but you can't leave us behind after everything we've just been through." My voice is shaking way more than I'd like it to, so I prop my hands on my hips in the most faux-authoritative gesture maybe ever. "I saved his life, so in return, I want you to—to take me back to your planet. At least for a couple of days."

Kammie steps up so she's standing by my side. "I want to come, too."

"Every other being in this building will sleep for hours, providing you with adequate time to escape and return to your homes. Thank you for services to my son." He turns away, so I leap forward, closing the distance between us rather easily, and grab hold of his arm.

"Griffin and I have a mind-connection thing, because of our star matter," I say in a rush. "Please, please just let me at least see him one more time, and then you can send me back here if you want." It's only then, as I can see that he's about to relent, that I hesitate. "Well, I'm not going to be torn to pieces in space or something, am I?"

The Emperor President peers at me with narrowed eyes, but finally, he shakes his head. "Not if you're traveling with me."

I'm about to ask him some questions about the whole space travel thing when I'm hurtled full-throttle into a kaleidoscope of colors and lights and painful stretching and a crushing, buzzing noise that takes over my whole head...

Chapter 27

"Daisy?"

It's Griffin's voice, I know that, but I'm not really sure where it's coming from at first. I'm comfortably dreaming about living in the woods surrounded by a bunch of cuddly animals when Griffin's voice breaks through.

"Hmm?"

I open my eyes and Griffin's leaned over me, still pale as a ghost, but smiling.

"Are you alright, Daisy?"

"Please don't tell me that my legs are on backward or something," I say, noting that my arms and legs hurt and my back seems ready to join in the fun. "Hey, are we on... your planet?"

Griffin nods and unbuttons my—wait, why am I wearing a uniform? I wasn't wearing this before! I was wearing that useless, paper-thin designer dress.

"Uhh, is it a good time for that?" I ask as he rushes to unbutton it clear down the front and slip his hands inside, over my bare, warm skin. "I'm a little confused about a lot of things, and as happy as I am to see you, maybe we shouldn't have sex just now?"

"Don't be daft, Daisy; I'm just healing you!" he says with a scowl. "Hold still, would you?"

Oh.

"Well, should you be doing that, either?" I ask. "I mean, since you kind of sapped your energy back there with the bad alien and friends?"

"I'm getting my energy back."

Griffin's dark hair sticks up at a lot of odd angles, setting off the serious pallor of his face. I can't help wondering if he's even supposed to be out of bed, never mind healing people, but I hold still while he dances his cold fingertips over my skin.

"There now," he says at last, in a whisper. "How's that?"

"I'd still like some confirmation that nothing on my body has moved to a location where it shouldn't be, but otherwise, I think I'm alright!" I pull on the collar of the uniform shirt. "So what's with this?"

"Oh. Standard uniform for relaxation or leisure," Griffin says with a little grimace. "Wait until you see the standard uniforms for work and public appearance. Bloody awful. So boring you'll want to claw your eyes out."

"That sounds pretty bad."

"I miss my purple jumper. I wanted to bring it home when we returned."

Even though the purple sweater is one of the most godawful articles of clothing ever created on Earth, I suddenly wish I could hand it over to Griffin. I'd even let him wear it, if I could. Well, maybe just for a little while.

"Your planet feels remarkably similar to mine," I say, hoping to distract him from the deep funk that missing an ugly, purple jumper might put him in.

"Well, of course, that's why we chose your planet for experimentation and research, ages ago, when we first discovered you. Your planet's heavier, though. Or, I felt heavier, anyway."

"Oh! So I'll feel lighter here? I think I could get used to that." I sit up, fighting a wave of nausea. "Is it normal that my stomach feels queasy?"

"Most people puke their guts up—real big mess."

"Not their... literal guts, right? You're just using an expression for dramatic effect."

Griffin stares at me as if I've lost my mind. "When have I ever not been dramatic? But anyway, I settled your stomach just now."

Devon bursts into the room with Kammie on his heels. "Griffin! What are you doing out of bed?" he demands, balancing a plate on one hand. The plate seems to be piled high with gray goop, and I desperately hope it's not something that is supposed to be consumed.

"I had to check on Daisy," Griffin says, laying down beside me and stretching out on his back. "I'm staying right here with her, too, so don't even think of sending me back to that horrible room. It's cold and boring in there."

"You're supposed to be resting."

"Don't frown at me like that; you can't change my mind." Griffin moves closer, bumping his hip into mine and reaching up to place his hand on my middle, which reminds me all at once that my shirt is hanging open. I hurriedly button it, all the while fighting a monster blush. "See? Daisy needs me here with her while she adjusts to our world."

246

Kammie steps around Dev and leans over me, inspecting my face. "You look quite healthy and whole to me," she announces. "Darling, wait until you get to look around! Dev took me for a quick walk, because we were so hungry..."

I look again at the gray goop. "Hmmm."

"Oh, it's not nearly as bad as it looks. And Dev shared some local fruit with me, too. It's delicious!" She lowers her voice to a whisper in my ear, "They lived on our planet a long time ago and changed some things about our atmosphere to improve it. We're partly descended from their kind. I told you!" Kammie's glowing with smug satisfaction and something that looks remarkably like... happiness. Real happiness.

"Alright, but that doesn't mean there are alligators in the sewers," I say.

"Yes, there are. My friend saw one."

I laugh so hard that I feel like I'm going to throw up, but I go on laughing anyway.

"She's delirious, see?" Griffin says, pointing at me. "I need to stay with her."

"Daisy, you wouldn't mind if Griffin got some rest, would you?" Devon asks, in his most reasonable voice.

"No, of course not."

Griffin huffs and puffs a few times for good measure. "If you want me to go back to that room, you'll have to drag me. And you and I both know you can't do that for more than five steps." He snickers and laces his fingers together behind his head, crossing his legs at the ankle.

"If you weren't in a weakened state, I'd do exactly that," Dev says, shaking his head. "And give you a few good bumps on the head while I was at it." He looks at me then. "Daisy, you must be hungry. Feel free to eat however much you want."

I'm not quite hungry enough yet to stick the gray goop

in my mouth, no matter how good Kammie says it is, so I just smile and shake my head.

"Oy! Dev. Where's the Emperor President?" Griffin interjects, as if he hasn't been allowed to speak in forever and can barely hold it in anymore.

"Looking into what happened with our... our..." Devon hesitates. "Our security team."

"Traitors," Kammie say. "How awful, all of it. You boys never deserved anything like that! Never mind those horrid old men with the Origin or whatever it's called, turning you over. I'd like to get my hands on them. Making them fall asleep was not at all punishment enough, in my opinion."

Devon sighs. "Well, it wasn't all of our security team. Several of them tried to keep us safe, but they were... Well, anyway, your father's working to sort it out and set a trial for Mali. He discovered her plan, arrested her, and reached us just in time."

"Not in time," Griffin says. "If it'd been him alone, he'd have been too late. Daisy's the real hero."

Kammie gives a hearty nod. "Well, of course she is. Daisy might not have told you this, but she used to always slay me at *Fantasy Gem Miners*. And she won a tug-of-war contest at the state level, before I knew her."

Oh, God. The last thing I need anyone to know is that my greatest achievements in life up until this week have been an embarrassing video game you can legally download for free and a tug-of-war contest. "Never mind all that," I say. "We were talking about the Origin Collective and the scary bodyguards and stuff."

"They really were quite scary, always popping up when you least expected them," Kammie says.

"Well, their purpose was to keep Griff safe during our

journey, but according to the Emperor President, Mali placed the terrorists into our group at the last minute." Devon lets out another sigh, staring at the floor. "They hid their thoughts well. Griff and I had no idea about their intentions. I should have... I should have gone through their files, myself, before we left."

I shrug, noting the downward slope of his shoulders. "You can't blame yourself, Dev."

Kammie taps my shoulder and places her finger over her lips. When I cast a confused look, she points at Griffin, who is... fast asleep.

"I knew he was tired," Dev mutters, picking up the plate of uneaten food. "You sure you're not hungry?"

I carefully extract myself from Griffin and slide off the bed. After a few seconds of adjusting to standing again and a quick glance back at my sleeping alien, I accept Kammie's offered hand and shuffle out of the room with her, Dev following right behind.

"He needs as much rest as possible," Dev says. "If you hadn't... well, done whatever you did, we would have lost him." He pulls me into a one-armed hug, since he's still holding the plate, but it's as warm and strong a hug as I've ever had. "Thank you, Daisy. Thank you for saving my friend."

I give him a gentle squeeze and pat his back. "No problem. I'm relatively attached to the little weirdo, myself."

"The doctors said he used up all of his energy, with what he did," Devon says, pulling away. "He'll need time to rest and recover, though knowing him, he'll want to bounce right back into action."

"Don't worry; I'll help you make him rest. We can always threaten to send someone back to Earth to burn his purple sweater. That seems to be a supremely motivating factor in his life."

Dev laughs, a relieved sort of laugh that echoes all around us, and then he stares down at the plate of mysterious food stuff. "I wonder if we should have made Griffin eat something while he was awake..."

"Dev likes to make sure people eat," Kammie says. "He's already fed me twice since I woke up."

"Well, I just want to make sure everyone's alright!"

I put my hand on his shoulder. "Dev, it's okay. I know you're worried about Griffin, and you're feeling like a mother hen right now, but it's alright. Promise."

"He's my... my dearest friend."

"I know, Dev. He'll be alright. Between you and me, he's got all the care he needs." Still, I can't help the uneasy silent questions circling in my head. If he was betrayed by his security guards, who else might try to betray him?

Dev glances at Kammie. "I know you probably want to look around more, don't you, my love?"

The red that sprouts in Kammie's face tells me that this 'my love' thing is very, very welcome. "Oh, well, of course. But we don't have to just yet, if you want to stay with Griffin for a while."

"Just for a bit, maybe?" Dev asks, taking Kammie's hand and bringing it to his lips. He stares at her so tenderly that I nearly melt on the spot for her sake. *Geez.* "Would you join me, Kammie?"

"Good idea," a voice says from behind me, effectively making me jump several inches off the ground. I slowly turn around to find Griffin's father standing behind us, his head held high and his hands behind his back. He seems even more intimidating now, up close, though he's certainly less angry. "Devon, you and your friend will take a turn watching over my son. See that he rests." He hesitates. "He won't want to, but he must regain his strength."

"Alright," Dev says. "But Daisy—"

"Daisy will come with me. I'd like to speak with her privately."

I try to control the trembling that seems to have taken over my body. "Privately?"

The Emperor President doesn't allow for much argument between the hard line of his mouth and the stern expression in his eyes. "Will you follow me, Daisy?"

I hug Kammie goodbye, offer Dev a quick smile, and then follow Griffin's dad down a hallway and up a huge set of stairs. From there, he leads me to another corridor, only stopping once he reaches the end of it. Inside, I find an office, minimalist to my eyes. I can't quite spot a source of light in the room, but I realize after a few seconds of staring that the walls set off a gentle glow.

"Is this like your Oval Office?" I ask, before I can stop myself.

"Oval Office?"

"Well, I mean, is it your office?"

The Emperor President nods. "Please, sit down." He waits as I struggle with one of the pod-like chairs and then sits in his own, a high-backed one that looks incredibly uncomfortable and leaves him sitting up straight and stiff.

I feel a bit like I'm in the principal's office again. "Uh, you wanted to talk to me?" Should I call him Your Highness? President? Pops? *Hmmm.*

"I cleared my schedule for the next two days," he says, but it doesn't sound like a response to my question. He stares in my direction, but sort of over my head, as if he's thinking. "We were all foolishly vulnerable to Mali and her cohorts. Mali was my son's betrothed."

"Evil fiancée, yeah." I clear my throat.

"Had you not acted when you did, my son would be lost," he says, and his eyes flick down to mine. I feel like he's looking into my childhood memories and deepest secrets. It's not nearly as comforting as when Griffin does it. "Why? Why did you save him, Daisy Elena Kirkwood?"

As much as I want to look away from him, I know I can't give in to fear. I squirm a bit in my seat, but then I suck in a deep breath and raise my head high. "He was willing to save all of us, even if it meant he died. I couldn't let him fail, especially when he had a wager to win, with you."

The Emperor President considers this. "You love him."

The last time I told a male who wasn't a blood relative that I loved him was when I had a bit too much to drink last year and expressed undying devotion to Jagger, my teddy bear. The idea of saying it to a real person has always been foreign, right up there with having enough money to spend a month floating around the world on a party yacht. "Um…" I say, but there's no use lying to this creature. He'd see through me, anyway. "Yes, I think I do."

"And what good will that do for you? You don't belong here, with us."

Maybe he's trying to scare me away. "Griffin made me feel stronger and braver," I say, leaning forward in my pod-chair. "He's good at that. He can inspire people to believe in themselves. And he's good at a lot of other stuff, too, that you don't need to hear about!" I give him a stern look in return, waiting for him to be embarrassed by my weak attempt at suggesting his son is a sex god.

Instead, he remains expressionless. "And?"

"Even if I have to go home, I got something from knowing him," I say, but as I'm saying it, I can feel angry tears forming around the corners of my eyes. "I don't want to say goodbye to him."

"You'd stay here, with my son?"

"Yes. But we'd have to visit my family sometimes."

"You know what you're asking for? You'd marry him in our ceremony, under the seal of our officials, and you would be Queen President. You'd be expected to learn our ways and take part in them."

"Griffin hasn't asked me to marry him."

The Emperor President peers back at me with those unnerving eyes, and the air around us crackles with static tension. "Taug didn't mean to send home a transmission of everything that took place, but without Mali in place to stop it, it broadcasted. Widely, I'll add. It's clear to any sentient being that my son returns your affection. I may not understand him, but I do understand that his actions stemmed from something far stronger than adoration. If I allow you to stay here, he will want to marry you."

"Wait, it broadcasted?" Griffin's heroics, played out for everyone to see? This could be a miracle in disguise. "Maybe everyone will finally stop treating him like crap all the time and making up fake rumors about him. Griffin's a better person than they think. He's a better person than even you think."

"Perhaps they've underestimated him," he says in a cold tone. Just as I'm about to blurt something I probably shouldn't, he adds, "I know that I have underestimated him."

Wow. WOW! I wish Griffin could hear this right now, but I just store it away for later, to tell him. For now, I struggle to keep my face passive.

"He said we're made from the same stuff. I think he's right. If I stay here with Griffin, I'll bring what I know, and what I feel, to your people, the same as he will."

Griffin's dad stands up, sending a shiver of energy through the room. "It's important that the Emperor President has an heir, to keep useless chaos and jostling for power from taking place. I fully intend my bloodline to continue. I've been informed that the females of your world are incredibly fertile. Are you fertile, Daisy?"

Up until this point, I've been able to remain mostly intimidated and careful under his stern voice and hard eyes, but this is just too much. I stand up, frowning at him.

"You know, I'm not exactly sure of my reproductive state, but if you're expecting a blow by blow of my menstrual history, I guess you're just going to have to keep waiting."

Surprise flashes through his eyes, though he catches it relatively quickly. "Very few speak to me with that tone of voice."

"Very few besides my mother, my nosy aunt, and my doctor have asked me about my fertility."

He nods to me, just once, and then walks around me, to the doorway. "You've shown courage and intelligence, even when other citizens of your planet turned against us and behaved traitorously. And you saved my son's life, when I could not," he says after a long pause. "If you decide that you'd like to remain here, then you have my approval."

I have a feeling this is a *huge* deal, especially given everything Griffin's told me. "Thank you." I walk to him, wanting to slip by and run away, but instead, I tip my head up to meet his gaze again. "Griffin won the wager, you know. He has so many good ideas, if you'd just give him a chance to prove himself." I take a deep breath. "Oh, and Kammie's staying here, too, if she wants."

With that, I walk away, retracing my steps back to Griffin, Devon, and Kammie. After all, you can only face off with an alien king for so long. I'll have to remember to tell my mom that for her 'worst-case scenario' journal, later.

Chapter 28

IT'S NOT SO BAD, REALLY, WAKING UP ON A WEIRD PLANET, CLIMBING out of bed, walking across the cold, hard floor to the window, and looking out at an unfamiliar landscape. It's really not that different from following your favorite band on tour all over America, actually. You just never know what new sight you'll see from your window.

What's really great about the whole situation is returning to bed and climbing back under the covers for a while, cuddled up close to the warm, sleeping form of your alien pop star prince boyfriend.

And can I say? I like it. I like cuddling with my alien pop star boyfriend, even when his hair is a complete mess, his mouth is hanging partly open, and he's violently tossed and turned in his sleep for the last handful of hours.

"Daisy," Griffin mutters, without opening his eyes. He hooks a leg over my hip and hugs himself closer to me, our faces almost touching. "How long have I been asleep?"

"Since yesterday. Your days are weird, you know? They're shorter than ours."

Griffin yawns, a wide-mouthed yawn, but still doesn't open his eyes. "Mmmm. Has my father visited or asked after me or anything?"

I consider what I should tell him, and settle on the truth. "He wanted to talk to me yesterday and I… well, I sort of bossed him around a little."

"You did what?" Griffin opens one eye and peers at me.

"Well, he was talking about my fertility, and I lost it on him. I'm sorry. But he did say I could stay for a while, if I want."

Griffin sits up, dragging his pale hands across his face and rubbing his eyes vigorously with his palms. "No one talks back to my father, you know."

"I guess I'm no one?"

"Well, he'll either hate you or love you for it. He respects when someone's decisive, but he really, really loathes it when anyone argues with him." He peeks at me between splayed fingers. "Did I really sleep that long?"

"You did."

"They must have transported me over here at some point," he says with a heavy sigh. "I hate these medical rooms."

"It's not as bad as the hospitals back on Earth," I say. "Less watercolor paintings of fences, for one thing. And you have a window!" I point at the window. "Speaking of windows, when do I get a tour of your planet?"

Griffin narrows his eyes and closes the distance between us, pushing me down and straddling my hips. "My planet is very, very big, Daisy," he says. "You make it sound like I could just show you the whole thing in a day…"

Is he making some kind of suggestive joke? Well, I can

keep up with that kind of banter. *Really!* "You sound very defensive about the size of your planet," I say, in as sexy and sultry of a voice as I can manage with an alien leaned over me. "Maybe I just need another look at it, to decide how big it is for myself..."

Griffin frowns down at me like I'm a complete idiot. "Another look? You've never been here before, Daisy."

Oh. So he *was* talking about his planet. *Oops.*

"I wonder where Devon is," Griffin says then, climbing off the bed and stalking to the door. "Think he's busy with Kammie?"

"They've been pretty much joined at the hip since we arrived, yeah, but he stayed with you for several hours while you slept."

Griffin throws open the door to our room and disappears from view before I've even had a chance to climb off the bed. I hurry after him, determined not to get lost. Most of the aliens can speak English if I try to communicate with them, which Dev says is because they gave us a lot of the building blocks for English when they visited Earth back in the medieval times. Plus, they have vastly superior communication skills that allow them to pick up languages almost instantly.

You'd think Griffin has a built-in homing device where Dev is concerned, because he finds him in under a minute, launching himself into his best friend's arms for an enthusiastic hug. They speak quietly in their language, and Griffin kisses the side of Devon's head before hugging him again, even tighter this time.

Kammie, who'd been standing with Dev before Griffin pounced, waves at me with a heavy-lidded satisfaction of someone who has already had a very good morning. Her red hair hangs loose around her face for once, and it's dotted here and there by little white flowers.

She pulls me into a hug. "Have you been outside yet? Dev and I took a walk this morning, talked for ages. I like it here. Once I've got my record player and books, I think I'll stay. And you know? Dev and I talked about coffee grounds. They might really help the soil…"

Leave it to Kammie to settle right in and find a home for herself wherever she goes. Judging by the color in her cheeks, her chemistry with Dev has only gotten better and better, which just makes me feel incredibly proud of myself for accidentally introducing them, and also incredibly happy for my friend. She's kissed her fair share of frogs, leading up to Devon.

"Griffin's dad wants the boys to give a speech," she says. "I tried to give Devon some tips about speech-making, but then I remembered I'm not very good at it."

"Um, no. You're horrible at it, judging by what happened the night after I moved to New York." We both laugh at that and I close my eyes, laying my head against her shoulder. "I'm glad you're here with me."

"Oh, come now, you know I belong in outer space! Besides, I promised that if you moved to the big city, I'd keep an eye on you, remember? That wasn't limited to staying in the city."

Griffin clears his throat quite dramatically to signal that we need to stop hugging and go back to paying attention to him. "I have to speak in front of everyone," he says, raising his chin. "And Daisy, you're going to join me."

"Am I?"

"Yes. You're as much responsible for things turning out alright as I am." He casts me one of his famous imperious glances. "And I don't like speaking in front of people alone."

"Dev's joining you, I thought."

"Yes, and so are you."

Of course.

"Well, I'd really like some clothes," I say, motioning at the uniform I woke up in the day before. "And I'd still like to know how I got in this outfit."

"The medical team changed you out of your dress." He looks apologetic suddenly. "I'm sorry you don't have any of your nice clothes."

I shrug. "I'd just like something that fits…"

"Of course." Griffin twirls on one heel, somehow still quite impressive even in his light gray hospital clothes, which resemble pajamas. He leaves us for all of thirty seconds, and then reappears with a purple-eyed alien woman. "Daisy, Sor will help you find some clothes. I'll meet you in the room we spent the night in, and we'll go up for the speech."

"Now? You're not going to practice or something first?"

"He said he wanted us to speak to everyone as soon as Griffin woke up," Dev says, and I can hear some tension in his voice as he slips his arm around Griffin's shoulders and leans in close to say something to him. They walk away together, and I'm escorted off by Sor for fresh clothes.

Okay, so it's not exactly what I imagined myself wearing to a speech in front of aliens, but it's better than the weird, unflattering uniform someone had helpfully dressed me in while I was unconscious after traveling across the known and unknown universe.

I'm wearing a black, button-down shirt and snug, black pants, which miraculously fit my butt in a flattering manner. It's boring, yes, but it's actually a little bit rock and roll when you unbutton the top three buttons and rough your hair up a little—okay, a lot. And perhaps, most importantly, it's what everyone else seems to be wearing, which drops the amount of stares I receive by maybe… I don't know—two percent. In the case of a human on an alien planet, even that two percent makes a remarkable difference.

Kammie somehow managed to find herself a loose gray skirt to match with her black shirt. The only clue she'll give me of its origin is that Dev knows someone who knows someone.

I hear a lot of scuffling outside the door of my room before I actually see Griffin. He walks into the room with a rather sheepish expression on his face, followed closely by Dev. Both of them are wearing black, military-style jackets and slim-legged pants, looking ridiculously attractive, so much so that I let out a little sigh of appreciation, echoed by Kammie.

Griffin's gaze bounces from me to Kammie and then back again, and he tugs at his collar with one hand, his other hand trailing down the row of shiny, gold buttons on his jacket. His hair has finally been tamed, and the boots he's wearing make him look just a little taller.

I'd really like to tackle him to the floor.

"Our uniforms," he says, "I know they're boring—"

"Boring?"

Griffin casts me another nervous look. "Well, they're not like what you wear on your planet."

"No, no, you've got that right. But right now, I want to plaster you to the wall because of that outfit, so you don't have anything to worry about. You look incredible."

Kammie pipes up behind me. "Yes, you boys look delicious."

Dev's smile is contrasted by Griffin's confused look, but then we're all ushered away by a few broad-chested aliens who look to be soldiers, and before I know what's happening, I'm finally stepping outside into this place that might be my new home.

Kalesstria, Griffin's planet, feels colder than Earth, in a strange, tingling way that I sense more inside than outside, and the planet's light source seems further away and smaller in the distance than our good old sun back home.

And the air tastes disgusting in my mouth, heavy in my lungs, even before I start coughing.

"Are you alright?" Griffin whispers to me, slipping his arm around my back and leaning in close.

"Is the air always like this?"

Griffin stares at me. "Well, it's cleaner today than usual, if that's what you mean."

"Oh. Great." After a few seconds more of wild coughing, my lungs seem to adjust, at least a little.

We're joined by more soldiers as we walk, heading down a path, away from the massive capital building where we've spent all our time since arriving. I peer left and right, trying to catch glimpses at the world around me, but it's hard with how fast our entourage moves. The ground seems to be covered in patches of ugly, gray vegetation that vaguely resembles grass. In the distance, I can see grand, minimalist buildings stretching into the sky, and pedestrians moving about their day.

Around the back of the capital building, a crowd has gathered, and an empty stage waits for us, dotted only with something that appears to be a mic stand.

"Big crowd," Griffin says.

"It'll be just like when you talk on TV or have a concert," I say and shrug, though my stomach twists with the very idea of having to stand in front of a crowd of aliens, even if Griffin's the one doing all the talking.

"My father's given a hundred speeches up there." Griffin

lets out a few quiet breaths. "Sometimes, he has me stand on the stage, behind him, but I'm never the one speaking."

"You performed in front of a venue full of New Yorkers, Griffin. You'll be just fine."

Someone calls out an exclamation that sounds urgent, and I turn my head just in time to see Griffin's father marching toward us, dressed spectacularly in a uniform quite similar to what the boys are wearing. The older alien's gray-brown hair is slicked back from his face, and several small pins and medals adorn his jacket. In the weak sunlight, he seems older than he did before, but certainly no less intimidating.

"Begin," he says to Griffin once he's reached us.

Griffin squeezes my hand just once before raising his chin and stepping up onto the stage. Dev follows close behind him, taking his place on Griffin's left side. I follow somewhat slower and hesitantly step up to Griffin's right side, with Kammie beside me.

With more than a little surprise, I realize Griffin's dad is standing behind us. *Behind!*

Griffin clears his throat and steps up to the mic stand. He speaks in his native language, and though I can't understand what he's saying, I note the way his jaw seems too tight and his hands keep curling into loose fists.

I just wish I had some idea what he's saying.

"Listen," Griffin says, or I think he does, but he's still speaking to the crowd, his words unintelligible to my ears. "Listen closely. Remember…"

Wait, is he talking in my head again?

I'm confused, but I attempt to 'listen closely.' At first, I have no idea what Griffin wants me to do, but the more I meditate on the rise and fall of his voice and the unfamiliar words falling from his mouth, the more it all molds into a somewhat recognizable shape.

"…You have only my humblest promise to become worthy of the title I will one day take, the role my father has held for countless years with strength and honor. As for what took place on Earth… anything I did that might have been seen as courageous was matched or exceeded by the bravery of Daisy Kirkwood," he says, turning his head in my direction. I feel dizzy, maybe from nerves or maybe from translating his words with our mental connection, but I manage somehow to glance out at the silent audience.

Am I supposed to say something?

Before I can react, someone raises her hands over her head and claps twice. Another person does the same thing, and then another and another, and soon, everyone in the crowd has followed suit.

"Is… is that good or bad?" I whisper to Griffin, unable to tear my eyes away from the alien audience.

Griffin doesn't say anything, but a smile lifts his lips and his eyes shine a bit brighter than usual when he looks at me. Must be good, then.

"Say something," he whispers, nudging me.

My life sort of flashes before my eyes, all the worst stuff jumping out in batches, especially the embarrassing high school memories, but I force myself to step closer to the mic. Griffin slips his arm around my waist, as if he knows how unsteady and nervous I am.

"Uh, hello," I say, and then look at Griffin. "Will they understand me?"

He nods and motions toward the audience. "We're a vastly superior race, Daisy. We understand almost all languages, unlike your people, who struggle with only one at a time."

I want to punch him, but it might not be a good time to

do so.

"Thank you for allowing me to visit," I say, my voice shaking. "I'm not sure how long I'll be here, but it's an honor to see your planet." I glance at Griffin and take a deep breath. "Griffin cares about all of you more than you know. I've seen how annoying he can be, but I've also seen how loyal and loving he is. He talked about all of you in a generous and respectful manner while he was far away and none of you could hear. I offered to let him stay with me on my planet and continue to be pampered, spoiled, loved, and adored by... well, by me and by all the people on my planet who fell in love with him. But he turned me down, because he knew he couldn't abandon his responsibility to you."

Griffin's arm tightens around my waist. "You could talk about yourself, you know," he whispers. "They want to hear about you."

About me? Now I feel like I'm at a job interview and some suit is smiling across a desk at me, asking for three adjectives to describe myself. What should I even say?

"I... I love music," I say. "I love it so much that I quit my job and followed a band around the country for a while. My country, back home, I mean. And my mom thought I was insane, and she actually told my aunt that I had a psychotic break. But I loved it. I loved ending up in some really scary hotel rooms with sinks that barely worked. I loved waking up in new cities. I loved eating at all these places I'd never eaten before and always trying not to run out of money before the next tour stop."

Everyone's staring at me, and I'm pretty sure none of them have any idea what I'm talking about, but I go on anyway.

"I'd never felt more let down or disappointed than when the tour ended and I had to go home again. A return flight is just the most depressing thing ever. And then when Griffin visited my planet, I experienced that all over again. I've been putting off saying goodbye to him since the beginning, I think, and... I'd like to put it off a little longer. I don't want the return flight yet." I take another deep breath. "I don't just mean from him. I mean, I'd like to stay for a little while, if you'll let me."

At first, there's no response, which is probably the most nerve-wracking thing that could ever happen to someone who's visiting an alien planet, but then a few of them clap for me.

Somehow, I don't really feel like I need them to. I'm proud of myself.

Dev kisses my cheek, Kammie hugs me, and Griffin nudges me toward the steps so we can leave the stage, but Griffin's father catches my arm in one of his hands. His grip is both insistent and a little scary, so I halt immediately and turn my eyes up to his to find out what he wants.

"Thank you," he says to me, and then releases my arm.

Before I can say anything else, he's pulled Griffin into an awkward, stiff hug that looks incredibly uncomfortable for both of them, arms looped around his son at a strange angle. Griffin's arms hang limp at his sides for most of the hug, but finally, he raises them just enough to pat his dad on the back once.

Griffin's dad quietly says something, something I can't understand, but it sounds almost... encouraging?

And with that, he steps away from Griffin and turns back into the big, bad Emperor President, his lips pressed into a hard line and his eyes emotionless. He walks away from us without another word, leaving Griffin to stand with his mouth hanging partly open.

"Well done," Dev says, breaking the silence that falls over

us. "Come on; let's get back inside, Griff. You haven't had enough rest yet. The medic said you need more sleep before you'll be back to your usual antics."

Griff allows us to coax him inside, never saying a word. He seems to have gone into some kind of post-hug shock, and I can't help wondering if his dad's ever hugged him before. Of course, you don't want to ask something like that out loud, as it's a little insensitive, so I just determine to ask Dev about it later.

"You were wonderful out there, Daisy," Dev says, flashing me one of his toothy smiles as we make our way through the royal home. A few members of the staff descend upon us and sequester Griffin for questions and a bit of fussing, so Dev, Kammie, and I follow a few paces behind.

"Oh. Thanks. It seemed to work out a little better than my project in sixth grade, at least. Red-eyed tree frogs didn't turn out to be a compelling subject for a ten-minute presentation, no matter how many cute pictures I included."

Dev raises an eyebrow. "Red-eyed tree frogs?"

"Never mind, long story." I glance ahead at Griffin, who has both hands in the air, motioning animatedly while he speaks. He seems to have recovered from his shock. "Anyway, how long do you think Griffin's dad will let me stay?"

Please say at least a couple of days. Just a couple of days.

"I'm not sure, but I know you're not allowed to leave for at least a few weeks of your time," Dev says. "The paths aren't safe to travel right now."

"Paths…?"

"We travel through doors, a bit like your flight patterns, I suppose," Dev says with the patient tone of a teacher. "Sometimes, the paths are closed, or they're too narrow to travel through safely, due to natural causes. Sometimes, they're occupied by others traveling in the same direction."

I think about this for a few seconds. "Are other aliens going to my planet...?"

"Oh, I don't believe so, because Griffin's father shut down any paths to your planet a long time ago, in case we needed to go back. He didn't want anyone else to beat us there and try to colonize you or something, and most everyone forgot about you after a while. Nothing to worry about, Daisy!" Dev looks between Kammie and me. "But you won't be able to go home for a few weeks. Will that be alright, ladies?"

Most of me thinks, *Yeah, of course that'll be fine!* After all, I want some more time with Griffin, want to explore this weird world he's from, and want to learn about aliens and the universe. But a small part of me can't help feeling anxious now that I know returning home isn't a possibility.

"So, not even if I wanted to?" I ask.

"No, I'm afraid not. It's quite dangerous at the moment, but it'll be open for travel again in no time."

Kammie reaches for my hand, briefly entwining our fingers. "Will you be alright, Daisy?" She must sense my hesitation, because she pulls me into a hug.

"Well, I just... I guess it would have been nice to tell my parents where I was going, and maybe to have gotten a few of my things." For some reason, I think of my teddy bear, Jagger. My roommates, at this point, might be ready to rent the room out to someone else. Ugh, that would mean all of my clothes would probably end up in some weird secondhand shop in Queens.

"Do you think your mom will freak out?" Kammie asks, still hugging me.

"Of course. The level of freaking out will be in proportion with how long it's been since I answered one of her texts. By now, she might not have called the cops, but give it a few days…"

Griffin calls for Dev and our little group spins back into action, leaving me to push worries about my mom into a little box in the back of my head. For now.

Chapter 29

THAT NIGHT, I SETTLE AS BEST I CAN INTO THE LITTLE ROOM THAT I'VE been assigned. Five different aliens have knocked at the door in just the last hour or so, checking on me and asking if I need anything. One of them was kind enough to drop off some fresh fruit to me, though I haven't been able to find my appetite enough to actually sample any of it.

Griffin's been gone since just after his speech; according to Devon, he had a lot of important meetings to attend with his father, catching up on what had happened while the boys were gone. A near uprising by way of alien terrorists and an evil fiancée leads to a lot of extra security precautions and such.

For the first time since arriving, I wonder and worry if maybe I've made a mistake. I don't regret telling Griffin's dad to bring me here, and I look forward to spending more time with Griffin, but knowing that I'm cut off from home is a little scary.

Dating an Alien Popstar

What if I have a bad reaction to the food here? What if I'm allergic to something in the atmosphere? What if the aliens start to hate me for some reason? What if I really, really, *really* want to listen to Arcade Fire, or the Twilight Sad?

A knock at the door stirs me from troubled thoughts, but I don't bother getting up to answer it. "I'm fine!" I say. "Everything's fine; thank you!"

"May I come in?"

Oh, it's Griffin.

I leap off the bed without hesitation, crossing the small room in a fraction of a second and yanking the door open. My alien's still wearing his spiffy, black uniform from earlier, but now, his hair's all messy on one side and flat on the other, as if he's spent a lot of time in a windy climate.

"Hello," he says, and I throw my arms around his neck, dragging him into the room and kicking the door shut behind him. "Did you miss me, Wanda?"

"No. But I've been dying for a closer look at this sexy uniform for most of the day." I plant a firm and claiming kiss on his lips, and then let my hands drop to the black, double-breasted military-style jacket he's wearing. "This is very rock 'n' roll. I like it."

"I always thought it was terribly boring, but I'm glad you like it."

"I like it enough to want to take it off you immediately. Or, rather, to take off a few necessary pieces and leave the rest. I'm not too picky." I lean in and kiss him again. This time, it's the kind of kiss where you both tilt your heads into it and forget what planet you're on. He responds with a happy, buzzy noise from deep within his throat. It'll probably take more than my few weeks of alien exile to get used to all the weird things he can do and sounds he can make.

Griffin breaks our kiss long enough to trace his lips up my jawline to my ear. "You're worried about not being able to go home, aren't you?" he whispers.

"Well, my mom. And my stuff. And... I dunno. Yeah."

"I think I know something that would make you feel more at home."

For a second, I think he's acting all sultry with me again, maybe planning to shove me on the bed and do unspeakable things, but instead, Griffin lets me go, opens the door, and disappears from sight.

Wow, okay. *Nice.* I've been abandoned by my alien pop star boyfriend.

Griffin reappears in the doorway, dragging a huge bag behind him. He hauls it into my room and closes the door once again, turning around to grin at me.

"Hmm, look what I found in here," he says, opening the bag and fishing around a bit. He withdraws something that looks both familiar and out of place all at the same time. It takes me a few blinks to process what I'm looking at.

"Jagger?"

"You seemed rather disappointed to leave him behind," Griffin says, handing my teddy bear to me.

It's never really been a point of pride to admit to being almost thirty years old and still owning a teddy bear, but I'd certainly never pictured revealing the existence of Jagger to a... well, a guy.

Griffin's face is open and bright-eyed, however, and no hint of derision shadows his features.

"How...?" I ask finally, hugging Jagger close to my chest. "I thought we couldn't go back right now because of the doors or whatever."

"Well," Griffin says, holding a finger up to his lips, "Don't tell anyone, and I won't. How about that?"

"Did you go back?"

"Only a quick trip—no one has to know. I thought you might like to have a few of your belongings while you're here. Brought some of your clothes while I was at it. Wanted to bring your music, but hauling a record player through a half-shut dimension door on a secret mission was a bit too much even for me."

Tears spring to my eyes, leaving me both embarrassed and pleased beyond all belief. "Thank you, Griff. Thank you so much..."

"Still couldn't find David Bowie," Griffin says.

"That's fine," I say, and I proceed to smother him in kisses. "We'll just go back soon and track him down. How about that?" The room tints gray, with glittering, silver flashes falling around us. "I have some bad news for you, though."

"Bad news?"

"David Bowie's not really an alien, no matter how weird and cool he is. He doesn't walk through space for his girlfriend or change the color of the room when he's happy. He's just a boring old human like me."

"Then he must be quite extraordinary, if he's anything like you." Griffin loops his arms around me, letting one of his hands drape shamelessly over my butt. "But I think even the great David Bowie can't compare to my Wanda Kirkwood."

"That was stupid and cheesy, but you look so good in this jacket that I don't mind too much. Plus, you brought me Jagger. And some clothes."

"Well, I couldn't very well leave all of my clothes behind, either," Griffin says, crouching down to rummage through the bag until he retrieves that horrid, fuzzy, purple sweater. Of course.

Somehow, I've never been happier to see it.

Acknowledgements

THIS BOOK COULD NOT HAVE BEEN PROPERLY WRITTEN WITHOUT THE love and support of many, many people. Just a few of those people are: Karmen Viitanen, Aya Felling, Tamar Elmensdorp-Lijzenga, Katie Sharp, Crystal Johnson, Trisha Wooldridge, Kym Detato, and everyone who makes up the #AlienSquad

I wouldn't be sane enough to write without Dusty Alexander and Sarah Hamilton. There's no way to list all of the things you have done to make my life better, all the personal jokes, all the beautiful moments. We've left some glittery, crazy trails of awesome everywhere we've been together. You girls are the Dev to my Griffin.

Thank you to my amazing publisher Crimson Tree, for making this happen!

Thank you to the amazing ladies I've met at concerts, before concerts, after concerts, while waiting for concerts, or just online talking about concerts. You inspire me more than you will ever know, and I hope Daisy is a heroine you can truly love and relate to.

Thank you to the Concord Starbucks crew, The Fabulous Miss Charlotte Raines, and Michael (that pep talk, though!), Jennifer AP, Kate Kaynak, and Sophie. Thank you Gonia, Nic, David, Josh, and Cecile for London. Thank you to my fashion and Project Runway/BPR crew. Thank you Brittany Foster and Anthony Villalta for being so kind. Thank you sooooo much Dante/Slake, for the artwork. All of my Tumblr, Twitter, Facebook, and Instagram followers, thank you.

Thank you to my family for believing in me about the important stuff.

About the Author

KENDRA L. SAUNDERS IS A TIME-AND-SPACE TRAVELING FASHIONISTA author who writes books about magical, dark-haired men, interviews famous people, and suggests way too many bands to you via whatever social media platform she can get her hands on. She writes with good humor because humor is the best weapon for a girl who can't learn karate or ballroom dancing.

CPSIA information can be obtained
at www.ICGtesting.com
Printed in the USA
LVOW12s2042240716

497224LV00002B/12/P

9 781634 221757